Game Theory

Thomas Jones

JM ORIGINALS

First published in Great Britain in 2018 by JM Originals
An imprint of John Murray (Publishers)
An Hachette UK Company

1

A CIP catalogue record for this title is available from the British Library

ISBN 978-1-47367-961-0
Ebook ISBN 978-1-47367-962-7

Typeset in Minion Pro 11.5/14.5 pt by Palimpsest Book Production Limited,
Falkirk, Stirlingshire

Printed and bound by CPI Group (UK) Ltd, Croydon, CRO 4YY

John Murray policy is to use papers that are natural, renewable and
recyclable products and made from wood grown in sustainable forests.
The logging and manufacturing processes are expected to conform
to the environmental regulations of the country of origin.

John Murray (Publishers)
Carmelite House
50 Victoria Embankment
London EC4Y ODZ

www.johnmurray.co.uk

ⓂORIGINALS

NEW WRITING FROM
BRITAIN'S OLDEST PUBLISHER

This is the fourth year of JM Originals,
a list from John Murray.
It is a home for fresh and distinctive new writing;
for books that provoke and entertain.

To Emma

Order of Play

1. How to Cheat at Croquet   1
2. Frisbee   11
3. Crosswords   24
4. Backgammon   38
5. Five Hundred   53
6. Twister   79
7. Chess   99
8. Ping   108
9. Tennis   124
10. Village Cricket   141
11. Pool   161
12. Snap   175
13. Swimming   195
14. Hide-and-Seek   218
15. Not-Boggle   246
16. Scrabble   263
17. Croquet   288

'They have chosen to be boxed up in games.'
H.G. Wells, *The Croquet Player* (1936)

'The actions of the players are up to a certain point
personal moves – i.e. dependent upon their free decision –
and beyond this point chance moves, the probabilities
being characteristics of the player in question.'
John von Neumann and Oskar Morgenstern,
Theory of Games and Economic Behaviour (1953)

'Live in the game, and die in it!'
Herman Melville, *Moby-Dick* (1851)

1

How to Cheat at Croquet

August 2006, the last days of summer

A lex looked down at the blue ball between his feet, wishing he didn't have to go first. He shuffled backwards, wriggled his toes, adjusted his balance so his weight was evenly distributed across his heels and the balls of his feet. He let the mallet swing in his left hand, like a pendulum or metronome, the ribs rubbing against his palm. The Kentish sun was warm on the back of his neck; the wood was warm in his fingers. His prescription sunglasses had slipped down his nose. He pushed them back into place then seized the mallet halfway down, arresting its movement. He lined its head up behind the ball, glanced at the hoop six yards away, looked back down at the blue ball between his feet.

'Everything all right, Alex?' Clare asked.

'Yes,' he said. 'Sorry.'

'No rush,' Victoria said. 'Take all the time you need.'

'Within reason,' Henry said.

Alex tilted the mallet back between his legs, and swung. The blue ball barrelled across the lawn and into a hosta in the flower-bed at the far end. It had missed the first hoop by six inches.

'Bugger,' Alex said.

'Didn't it go through?' Vic asked.

'No,' said Henry.

Clare stifled a laugh.

'You didn't have to do that, Alex, you know,' Henry said. 'House rules. We're playing no roquets before you've been through the first hoop. Or had you forgotten? Would you like to take the shot again?'

'No,' Alex said. 'Thanks.' Henry's house rules were the only rules he'd ever played by. He had once, ten years ago, come across a copy of the official croquet rules in a secondhand bookshop; the game it described, as far as he could make sense of it, bore little resemblance to the game Henry made his friends play when they stayed at his parents' house in the university holidays – they might as well have been hitting hedgehogs with flamingos. Alex had thought those days were long behind them. If he'd known there was going to be compulsory croquet at Henry and Vic's this weekend, he'd have worn a different pair of shoes. And a looser pair of trousers (Henry, showing off his calves, was in knee-length red denim shorts). He wouldn't have drunk so much at lunchtime, either. Saturday afternoon croquet was all very well in theory, but in practice had too much in common with the ritual humiliations of sports day at primary school.

Henry positioned the red ball on the baulk line, looked up once towards the hoop, then down towards the ball, and gave it a firm tap. It stopped a foot short of its target. Henry smiled. Alex smiled too. 'Never mind,' he said. 'You should get through next go.'

'Hope so,' Henry said.

'What do you think I should do, partner?' Vic asked.

Alex looked thoughtful. 'Play it safe probably,' he said. 'Hit it gently, leave it a foot or so behind Henry. That way you'll be sure of getting through next time. And you'll be blocking Clare.'

'There's no need to be vindictive,' Clare said.

'Just playing the game,' Alex said.

'Are you now.'

'I think I'll just try to go through,' Vic said, dropping the black ball on the grass. She pulled her dark blonde hair back into a ponytail, snapping it in place with an electric-blue elastic she took out of her pocket.

'Maybe you want to position it a bit more carefully?' Alex said.

Vic shrugged. 'It's okay there, I think,' she said, picking up her mallet.

Alex was about to tell her she was holding it too close to the top to control her swing properly, but as she leaned down to take her shot he got an accidental eyeful of tanned cleavage, and was left speechless by the way her breasts framed her obscene grip on the ribbed mallet handle. She hit the black ball hard, striking down into the grass. The ball bounced into the air, hopped over Henry's ball, dropped through the hoop, and rolled halfway to the next one. Her mallet had left a deep divot in the lawn.

'Nice shot,' Clare said.

'Did it go through?' Vic asked.

'Yes,' said Henry.

Vic laughed. 'That was lucky,' she said.

Alex said nothing as he went to retrieve his ball from the

clutches of the hosta. As he placed it on the lawn, one assiduous mallet's length in, Vic's ball rolled through the second hoop. With her next shot she nudged it towards Alex's. The black kissed the blue with a gratifying snap. Alex stood back in admiration as Vic bent over the balls. Her dark blue jeans, like her white T-shirt, were tight, but not too tight. A perfect fit. She adjusted her stance, shifting her weight from one wedge sandal to the other with a sway of the hips. The blue ball rocketed back to the start of the course; the black went off at a right angle towards the third hoop.

'Which way do I go through this one?' Vic asked.

'Uphill,' Henry called, indicating the direction with a sweep of his arm. 'Away from the flowerbed.'

Vic set herself up on the flowerbed side of the hoop. Alex walked after his ball, hoping no one had noticed him re-arranging himself inside his trousers. He looked up at the climbing rose sprawled across the back of the house, dozens of dead heads lolling in the late August heat. Clare and Henry were discussing tactics in a conspiratorial murmur.

'How was your dirty weekend in Prague?' Henry asked as Alex joined them.

'Birthday weekend, you mean,' Clare said.

'That's what I said.'

'And we went to Berlin.'

'Of course. Nice?'

'Yes, very nice. Surprisingly clean.'

'Berlin?'

'The weekend.'

Alex blushed, because Clare was telling the disappointing truth. He supposed that Henry and Vic, who had been together for only five years compared to Alex and Clare's ten, had more and more various sex on an average Wednesday than he and Clare managed in six months in their cramped bedroom in Tufnell Park. He'd hoped that a holiday, a change of scene, might rekindle their sex life – though his inability to articulate what he wanted without resorting to the clichés of the agony column wasn't a promising sign – but nothing had happened. The weekend in Berlin, to celebrate their second wedding anniversary as well as Clare's thirtieth birthday, had been nice enough in many respects; but sex-wise it had been, as Clare hadn't quite said, all too predictably clean. So perhaps it shouldn't have been very surprising, however embarrassing it was, that he was getting turned on by something so innocent, so staid, so sexlessly middle-aged, as a session of mixed-doubles croquet.

It was Clare's turn. She brushed aside the lock of dark brown hair falling across her face and tucked it behind her ear. She made sure the balls were in line, and struck the yellow firmly. It smacked into the red, knocking it through the hoop and coming to rest itself just on the near side.

Henry looked up from his phone. 'Nice,' he murmured.

'Got any messages?' Alex called.

'What?' Henry said. He looked at his phone again. 'Oh, I see. No.'

Alex was in a tricky position. Not having been through the first hoop, he couldn't roquet either Henry's or Clare's ball. Since Clare had nudged Henry through, however, Henry would be able to attack Alex next go. Ideally, he would go through the hoop now, roquet red, come back round and smash Clare into the furthest flowerbed. But the yellow was blocking his way.

'Why don't you just come over here?' Vic called.

But Alex had a better idea: to replicate her daring opener. He would leapfrog yellow, go through the hoop and wreak havoc, dispatching Henry into the flowerbed and sending Clare to the far side of the lawn, where Vic could make merciless use of her.

His mallet gouged a healthy chunk of turf out of the lawn. The blue ball dribbled forward a few inches, stopping well short of the yellow.

'Bugger,' Alex said.

'Didn't it go through?' Vic asked.

'No,' said Henry.

Clare stifled a laugh.

'Shall I?' Henry asked, raising an eyebrow at Clare.

'There's no need to be vindictive,' Alex said.

'Just playing the game,' said Clare.

Henry retraced the path his ball had taken through the hoop to roquet Clare, put her through, send Alex off once more among the hostas, and leave his own ball near Clare's, setting them both up for the second hoop.

Alex left his ball in the flowerbed and went to discuss tactics with his teammate. Having gone through the third hoop, she was squatting on her heels, estimating the velocity required to reach and disrupt her opponents. A tanned strip of skin was visible between her jeans and the pink lace band of her knickers. Alex glanced over to see if Clare or Henry had spotted him staring down the back of Vic's trousers. Perhaps his sunglasses didn't obscure his eyes as well as he imagined. But they were talking and laughing together, and paying no attention to him. Vic stood up and hit her ball across the lawn. Black struck yellow with a resounding crack.

'Why don't you fish your ball out of the flowerbed?' she said over her shoulder as she walked away, hips swaying, diamond studs flashing in her ears, to lay waste to her opponents.

Clare and Henry stepped aside as Vic casually reversed, once again, the dynamic of the game. By the time she'd finished, yellow was on the wrong side of the second hoop, red was in the furthest flowerbed, blue was almost in a position to go through the first hoop, and black was standing by to lend him a hand.

'What do you think I should do?' Clare called to Henry as he was bringing his ball back onto the lawn.

He shrugged. 'It's up to you really. You could either set yourself up, or come over here. Whatever you want.'

She sent her ball scudding over the grass to join his.

'Who's been through what again?' Vic asked.

'You've been through three hoops,' Henry said, 'Clare and I have both been through one, and Alex has yet to go through any.'

'What shall I do?' Alex asked Vic's breasts. A few millimetres of pink lace were visible inside the neckline of her T-shirt. Clare never wore matching underwear.

'Set yourself up, maybe?' Vic suggested.

He obeyed.

Henry roqueted Clare, and sent them both back across the lawn to the second hoop.

Vic roqueted Alex, and put him, at last, through the first hoop.

Clare manoeuvred first the red ball and then the yellow through the second hoop, and sent them on to the third.

Alex, finding himself in the game all of a sudden, decided he ought to try a little harder – and, miraculously, managed to roquet Vic's ball. 'Just you wait, you fuckers,' he said to

Clare and Henry as he nestled the blue ball against the black, their snug curves reminding him of Vic's jeans. He set himself up for the second hoop, but then failed to go through, clunking instead into one of its legs. 'Bugger.'

Henry steered first yellow then red through the third hoop, before sending them both smartly up the lawn towards the fourth. He and Clare sauntered along behind, in step.

Vic had given up pretending not to know what was going on. She put Alex through the second hoop with a powerful shot, ricocheting the blue ball off the leg of the hoop and blasting the black diagonally across the lawn towards red and yellow. She used yellow to split the hoop, went through, sent yellow into a flowerbed, knocked red most of the way towards blue, and then positioned herself near the third hoop. 'You can use me to put yourself through,' she explained to Alex.

'Great,' he said. 'Thanks.'

'I think I'll just keep out of harm's way,' Clare said.

'Good thinking,' said Henry.

Working closely together, Clare and Henry got through the fourth and fifth hoops without too much difficulty, though Vic was able to slow them down for long enough to bring Alex up level – he helped a little, going through the fourth hoop unassisted – while finding time to nip through the fifth herself, too.

It was when everyone was on the sixth and final hoop that Vic made her first and only error of the game.

'How many circuits are we doing?' Alex asked.

Henry opened his mouth to reply.

'One,' said Vic, through gritted teeth.

She had disposed of red and yellow, banishing them to opposite corners of the lawn, and roqueted blue. A straight line ran from Alex's ball through the final hoop to the post. Vic placed the black behind the blue. The other dimensions of the universe fell away, everything narrowing to that single line. In two strokes, Vic – and, nominally, Alex – would have won the game. She exhaled, and swung.

The blue ball whanged into the leg of the hoop and bounced back a few inches. Black still had a clear run through.

'Shit,' Vic said.

'Just go through and peg out,' Alex said, sensing an opportunity for heroism, a last-minute chance to earn his place on the winners' podium beside Vic. He imagined hugging her in celebration. 'I don't think even I'd be able to miss that one.'

'Okay,' she said. She tapped her ball through the hoop and on to the post. Alex watched as she bent down to pick up her ball before walking away. If he stared hard enough, perhaps the shape of her would sear itself onto his retinas for ever, like sunspots. 'I'll make a start on supper,' she said over her shoulder as she disappeared into the house.

'Good thinking,' said Henry.

Clare dug her ball from the flowerbed and positioned it on the lawn. She cast a predatory eye towards the final hoop, and Alex's ball beside it – exposed, alone, vulnerable. The setting sun was behind her. Her shadow stretched out across the grass. If she lifted her arm above her head, Alex thought, it would reach the blue ball.

With Vic's disappearance into the house, it was as if a spell had been lifted from the garden. Alex blinked, shook his head, wondered at his foolishness. The sun, low in the sky behind his wife, lit her heroically as, slender and dignified, she prepared for her shot. He couldn't see clearly – but didn't need to, could imagine without seeing – the arch of her eyebrows as she frowned with concentration, the strong lines of her nose and cheekbones, the muscles around her mouth, the glint in her grey eyes. She tucked her hair behind her ear. The gesture was as familiar to him as the feel of his front teeth against his tongue. He willed her ball to go wherever she wanted. He didn't notice the way Henry was looking at her too.

Clare swung her mallet. The yellow ball flew hard and fast along the path of her shadow.

2

Frisbee

The muffled sound of stately ragtime seeped through the gaps between the warped Victorian windows and their frames. Henry paused on the doorstep. Through the pale wooden slats of the Venetian blind he could see Clare sitting at the piano. Overhead, pigeons wheezed in the gutters. It was one of those warm afternoons in late September that he liked better than any other time of year. Fine weather in the spring and summer he felt was his due; but a stolen moment like this, when summer had spilled over into autumn, as wrong as rain in July, was a surprise gift, an illicit pleasure. He shifted the weight of his overnight bag – or *baise-en-ville*, as a French girlfriend had once called it – across to his other shoulder and rang the bell.

Clare improvised a rest of half a beat.

'I'll get it,' Alex called, hurrying through from the kitchen, undoing his apron as he skidded down the hall in his socks.

'Henry!' he said, throwing the door open. 'Good to see you.'

'Thanks for having me.'

'Any time.'

Clare watched from the doorway of the front room as the men hugged awkwardly, slapping each other on the back and pretending to make a joke out of it. Henry's bag slid round and knocked against Alex's waist.

'Thanks for bringing the rocks,' Alex said, detaching himself.

Henry laughed politely. 'Laptop,' he said, patting the case as he shrugged the strap higher on his shoulder. 'I need it for the presentation tomorrow.'

'Of course. Well, come on in.'

'Smells good.'

'Roast pork. Hope that's okay.'

'Delicious. Hello, Clare.'

She walked calmly over to him. 'Hello, Henry,' she said.

They kissed each other on both cheeks, like the old friends they were.

'It's good to see you,' Henry said, his hands lingering comfortably on her shoulders.

'You too. You're very brown. How was Greece?'

'As you'd expect: sunny, sandy, sea-y.'

'Why don't you show Henry to his room and I'll put some drinks together,' Alex said. 'Gin and tonic all right for you?'

'Sounds good.'

'Here you go,' Clare said, opening the bedroom door. 'There's a clean towel there for you.'

12

'Thanks,' Henry said, going in, pausing for a heartbeat as he brushed past her, not quite touching, but close enough for the thin aura of warm air that surrounded him to mingle with hers.

She watched as he swung his bag from his shoulder onto a chair, turned to her and smiled.

'This is great,' he said. 'Thanks.'

They stood like that for a few moments, not moving, looking at each other across the room, the bed silent and pristine between them.

'How's work?' he asked.

'Fine, thanks.' She folded her arms. 'You?'

'I'll let you know tomorrow.'

She laughed politely. 'How's Victoria?'

'Fine,' he said, scratching the back of his neck. 'Fine. Very well. Thanks. Sends her love.'

Clare doubted that. But this was anyway a conversation that neither of them wanted to have. 'I should go and see if Alex needs any help with anything,' she said. 'I'll leave you to unpack.'

They both looked at his minimal luggage.

'Sure thing,' he said. 'See you in a minute.'

She returned to the front room and sat back down at the piano. Not sure what she wanted, rather wishing that Henry hadn't come, she thumped through the opening bars of Chopin's unduly cheerful Polonaise in A major.

In the bathroom to piss and wash his hands before going down to lunch, Henry looked at Alex and Clare's toothbrushes kissing in the mug on the shelf beside the basin, and wished that he hadn't come.

*

Opening the oven to the fizz of boiling pork fat and a great gust of steam that fogged his glasses, Alex stepped back smiling to let the heat and mist clear. 'Lunch in ten minutes,' he called out happily. He couldn't remember the last time the three of them, and only the three of them, had spent time together. He still missed the days, or rather nights, at university, when they'd known each other only a matter of months, but felt as if they'd been friends all their lives, when they would spend countless hours in each other's company, staying up till sunrise because whatever time it was, it was always early – days that seemed now as if they belonged to a different lifetime. He tried to say as much when they were sitting down to lunch, sunlight streaming through the window, XFM playing quietly on the stereo.

'I don't think things really have changed,' Clare said. 'It's just that the people who used to ask you where you went to school now ask you what you do, and complain about their work and mortgages rather than essay crises and overdrafts. Nice wine, Henry.'

'Thanks,' Henry said. 'I get it from a wholesaler who lives locally. If you buy it that way it's half the price.'

'Twice the fun,' Alex said.

'Fifty per cent cheaper than 0891,' Henry said.

'Gay cruise!' in unison.

'I can't believe you still remember that,' Clare said.

'Don't tell me you don't,' Alex said. 'All those half-naked men lifting weights. I don't suppose you get those ads anymore, do you? Though maybe it's just that I watch a lot less TV at three in the morning than I used to.'

'It's all online now I think,' Henry said. 'Gaydar and all that.'

'Where straight people never see it,' Clare said. 'Which is a pity.'

'Is it Gaydar you're meeting with tomorrow?' Alex asked.

'No one so exciting, unfortunately. How's your work going?'

Alex shrugged. 'Long hours, tedious contracts, the usual.'

'Big paycheques.'

Alex laughed. 'Big enough.'

'More than,' Clare said.

'Though once we've paid the mortgage on this place,' Alex began.

'What did I tell you?' Clare interrupted. 'Two for two.'

'What do you mean?'

'Nothing, sorry. Go on.'

'Clare's work is much more interesting than mine,' Alex said. 'She's got some great books coming out this autumn.'

'Such as?' Henry asked him.

Alex half opened his mouth. Henry and Clare both looked at him expectantly. 'She'll be able to tell you better than me. I'll just get it wrong.'

'There's nothing that special,' she said. 'The list is fine. I'll give you a catalogue if you want.'

'I'd like that. Thanks.'

The conversation paused. Pulp's 'Common People' came on the radio.

'Oh god, turn it off,' Clare said.

'You always hated this song,' Henry said.

'Because it's so hypocritical: he's attacking the rich girl for simultaneously romanticising and denigrating English working-class life, when that's exactly what he's doing, too.'

'Catchy tune though.'

Alex turned the radio off. 'How's Vic?' he asked.

'She's fine, thank you. Sends her love.'

Clare looked at Henry. He was still handsome, had the same openness about him he'd always had, the same curl of friendly amusement in his mouth, the same reassuring strength to his body, even if he was a bit on the heavy side now, and his sandy hair was thinner than it once had been.

'If you want I can order a few cases for you,' he was saying. 'You can pick them up next time you come and stay.'

He looked at her.

She smiled reflexively. Gin and tonic, conversation about wine, Sunday lunch: *we're turning into our parents*, she thought. No, worse, they were turning into Alex's parents. No, worst of all, they'd already turned into them. And they didn't even have children to make them boring. What was their excuse? And what would they have thought when they were nineteen if they could have seen themselves now?

After lunch, Henry and Clare fumbled laughing through a Schubert duet on the piano. 'That has to be the most horrible noise I've ever heard,' Alex said. 'Why don't we go for a walk on the Heath? It's a beautiful day.'

And so it was. A few translucent clouds drifted across a clear sky above Hampstead Heath, propelled by a gentle wind that now and then ruffled the leaves, which were just beginning to turn. The autumn afternoon light threw precise shadows, distinguishing everything with pleasingly sharp outlines, as if the trees and houses were wearing eyeliner. On Parliament

Hill, a pair of optimistic kite flyers were struggling against the calm weather. Their kites – one striped like a wasp, the other like a Union Jack – fluttered into the air, twitched and flapped, then drifted back to earth. A squadron of crows wheeled overhead. The three friends strolled below them in companionable silence.

Clare's mind strayed back once again to that weekend in August at Henry's house. Perhaps nothing would have happened if they hadn't played croquet on the Saturday afternoon. Fucking *croquet*. Before she met Henry she'd only come across the game in *Little Women* and *Heathers*. A group of them had once played, in a collectively ironic frame of mind, at Henry's parents' house as part of a decadent weekend ten years earlier. But in 1996 Clare had also protested against the Newbury bypass; worked nights stretching polyester covers, in several shades of grey, onto carseat headrests; taken ecstasy and stayed up past dawn dancing to techno. It had all been playacting of one kind or another, as she had half-realised at the time. Much of what she did now – going to work, owning half a mortgage, being married – still felt like playacting, but her repertoire had been sadly reduced, and here she was, barely thirty years old, indulging in gin and croquet without a road protest, factory floor or nightclub in sight. With every stroke of the mallet that afternoon, a small part of her soul had died. But that was no reason not to try to win. Nor was it an excuse for what had happened next, though it might have been among the reasons for it.

Her thoughts were interrupted by a low-flying frisbee, which tapped against her knee and clattered to the ground. She looked across to see a slim-built man in his early forties running apologetically towards them. A boy with his arms folded was

17

scowling at him. Clare bent down to pick up the frisbee, took a few steps forward and sent the fluorescent yellow disk skimming along the air towards the angry infant. The man stopped running, leaned forward and put his hands on his thighs to catch his breath. 'Thanks,' he said, turning to admire the frisbee's line of flight – clean, horizontal and unwavering – giving for a few seconds the impression that it could continue on that course for ever, like a surfer catching a wave that would never break, as if it had found a magical tangent along which it was able to evade the earth's gravitational pull.

'No problem,' said Clare, watching the grumpy little boy fumble the frisbee to the ground, pick it up and launch it wobbling towards a slightly larger, more serene-looking boy a few feet away.

'Kids,' said the man, whether as announcement or apology she didn't know, but it was superfluous either way.

'They yours?' Clare asked.

The man pointed at the cross child. 'That one is. The other boy's his friend. You have any?'

'No,' Clare said, perhaps rather too emphatically. 'I mean, not yet.'

The man nodded. 'It's a beautiful day, isn't it?'

'Yes, it's lovely,' she said.

The frisbee was arcing through the air towards them. Henry ran up to intercept it, flicked it nimbly back towards one of the boys. 'Hello,' he said.

'Hello,' the man said. 'Your, er' – he glanced down at Clare's hand, her wedding ring glinting in the sunlight – 'wife has been showing up my lack of frisbee skills.' The frisbee dropped at his feet. 'See what I mean?' He picked it up, chucked it to his son's friend, who threw it back towards the adults.

18

Henry laughed, pinching the frisbee effortlessly out of the air and throwing it behind his back to the other boy.

'Show off,' Clare said.

'Nice catch!' Henry called.

The boy tried to copy Henry. The frisbee flew off in the wrong direction. It landed on the path, spun round a few times, nearly fell flat to the ground, but caught itself, or was caught by a gust of wind, flipped onto its edge, and rolled off down the hill.

'I'll get it,' called Alex, who'd been hovering at the edge of the group, waiting hopefully, in his usual passive way, for someone to pass the frisbee to him.

'Oh, we're not married,' Henry said to the father. 'That's to say, we are married – only not to each other. My wife's not in town. I mean, I – we – don't live in town. Got a place down in Kent, in the country. I'm up on business, staying with Clare – and Alex, obviously.' He gestured towards Alex, still in pursuit of the frisbee, which was accelerating away down the hill like the runaway pancake. 'They're old friends. I mean, it's not as if my wife doesn't know what I'm up to. Not that I – we're – "up to" anything, so to speak.' He coughed.

Clare had backed away, and was looking at him from beneath raised eyebrows. The man nodded and lifted his hands. 'Thanks again,' he said.

'What the fuck was all that about?' Clare asked, in semi-amusement, as they turned away. 'Hello, stranger. We're not adulterers, if that's what you're thinking.'

'Aren't we?' Henry said, looking out across London, as if trying to focus on the Crystal Palace radio mast far away to the south-east.

'I don't think so,' Clare said. 'I mean, I'm glad we did – I wouldn't want to have lived my whole life without knowing, without ever once having – but there's Alex, and I love Alex, and there's Victoria – and you – and the way things are now, we're all still friends – aren't we? – and I'd like to keep it that way. Not that it wasn't, I mean – it was kind of wonderful, a wonderful – indiscretion – but let's keep it that way, let's not turn it into something complicated and sordid and – and full of deceit. I don't want – I don't want anyone to get hurt.' She fell silent, and looked out across the city, waiting for him – only inches away from her, but the distance seemed to expand with every moment that he didn't speak – to say something. Her mind reached irresistibly back to that Sunday afternoon five weeks ago, Victoria and Alex watching the football, and she had gone down to the converted outhouse where Henry worked, the look of happy surprise on his face as he turned to see her closing the door behind her, the combined sense of purpose and vertigo as she crossed the room, took his face in her hands and kissed him. The vertigo came back as she stood looking across London, waiting for him to tell her she was wrong.

Clare was right, Henry knew. For fifteen years he'd had a policy of no romantic entanglements – which is to say, no fucking – with girls who were already his friends. It kept things simple, and separate, and clear. What had happened with Clare – or rather the fallout from it, i.e. what was happening now – was complicated, and confused, and opaque. It was like swimming in mud, while having to pretend he was in crystal waters. Twelve years ago, Clare had tried to argue, theoretically, that sex could be thought of as 'an extrapolation of friendship'.

Alex, all too obviously hoping to get in her pants, had nodded in vigorous agreement. Henry had conceded that it could, of course, in theory, but was better if it wasn't. He was more sure now than ever that he'd been right. But that didn't stop him wanting her. He remembered the look on her face, full of resolve and desire, when she had come to him that afternoon in August. It gave him a hard-on just thinking about it. He put his hand in his pocket and discreetly shifted his cock to a less uncomfortable angle. 'You're right,' he said. 'Don't let's spoil things.'

She shivered. 'What's happened to Alex?'

Alex was toiling back up the hill, recovered frisbee in hand, feeling like a disgruntled Labrador, if that wasn't an oxymoron. He paused for breath, considered throwing the frisbee ahead of him, either to one of the children or to Henry – whichever would be less likely to humiliate him. He didn't trust himself to throw it straight. If it went wide of one of the small boys, it might look like their fault rather than his. But Henry would probably be able to compensate for any error on his part, running to snatch the frisbee from the air if it veered off course, perhaps making them both look good in the process. He opened his mouth to shout to his friend, looked up to see where he was and prepared to visualise the trajectory he wanted the frisbee to take, hoping his motor neurons and muscle fibres would be able to perform the necessary uncon-scious calculations, the vectors and parabolas.

Up on the ridge line, Clare and Henry came into focus. For an instant he didn't recognise them, their posture so unfamiliar they looked like strangers: standing close, leaning in but not touching, an intimacy between them that Alex had never seen before. Anyone who didn't know them would assume they were a couple. They had the air – if they were figures in a painting or a sculpture, he'd have said they had the composition – of two people who were sleeping with each other. Clare put a casual hand on Henry's sleeve. He took his hands from his pockets, turned to look where she was looking. Arms synchronised, they waved to Alex.

Alex clamped his mouth shut, walked on, handed the frisbee back to the father, who thanked him: 'That was above and beyond.'

'My pleasure,' Alex smiled and nodded. He continued towards Clare and Henry, who had stepped apart from each other and were standing in silence as they watched his approach. He was still undecided as to what, if anything, he would say when he reached them. Perhaps something nicely ambiguous to sound them out, like: 'What's going on?' Which they would respond to guiltily if they had something to feel guilty about.

The waspish kite and the Union Jack crashed into each other and plummeted towards the ground. Alex stumbled backwards, out of their way. At the last minute a small gust of wind caught the waspish one and sent it scudding sideways at head height towards Henry and Clare. Clare flicked her head to look at it, leaned back, watched as it zipped past in front of her, smack into Henry's face.

Alex couldn't help smiling. It seemed, just for a moment, as if the universe were bending itself to his unconscious will. There was no need to say anything. The wind and gravity had said it for him. He toiled on.

'Oh shit,' the kite flyer was shouting, running towards Henry and Clare. 'Oh shit. I'm so sorry. You all right, mate?'

Henry took his hand away from his eye. Blood pooled in his left nostril and trickled down his upper lip. He tried to lick it away. It dripped from his chin onto the toe of his white trainer. 'I will be,' he said. 'I can still see, anyway. You should be more careful.'

'I will, sorry. Can I . . . ?'

'I think it's better if you do nothing,' Henry said, pinching his nose and wiping his shoe on the grass.

Clare burst out laughing.

3

Crosswords

'Before lent car crashes into van, mangling it, I'm inside, a learner (8)'. 'Ludicrous notion (4,6)'. Henry sighed, put down the paper and looked out the window. The train was just pulling into Sevenoaks. He could see the faint reflection of his bruised and swollen face superimposed on a grimy brick wall. He didn't really enjoy crosswords; he certainly wasn't any good at them. But he couldn't concentrate on anything else, and needed distracting from the confrontation ahead. He knew it was a foolish thing to do. No good would come of the confession. But it wasn't fair for Vic not to know. It would possibly mean the end of their marriage, at least for a while, and would certainly mean the end of his friendship with Clare and Alex. But that was surely over already, had disintegrated, in fact, the moment Clare kissed him, even if the dust from its collapse had only settled yesterday. He looked again at the crossword. 'Rubbish outfit time (7)'.

*

'Garbage'. Vic filled in the final clue. Today's crossword was even easier than usual. She sighed, put the paper down and looked out the window at the garden. It was a beautiful autumn day. She wished Henry was there. It had been her idea that he stay with Alex and Clare before his meeting in London. She had tried over the years, she really had, but she couldn't find it in herself to like any of Henry's university friends, with their tedious stories of generic student exploits, and the way they all assumed that since they had known Henry first, they must therefore know him better than she did. And Clare was the worst of them, the most unreasonably possessive of the lot, the way she literally looked down her big nose at Vic as bad as Alex's gawping at her boobs. Something had happened between the three of them on the weekend that Alex and Clare came to stay. Henry denied it when she asked him, and she wasn't really interested in the details – they'd stayed up drinking whisky and dredging their shared past long after she'd gone to bed, happy to leave them to it – but the atmosphere had been strained when they said goodbye and Henry had made no effort to communicate with them since. So Vic had suggested he invite himself to stay with them, and she hoped they'd worked out whatever it was that needed working out. It was an arrangement that ought to suit everyone: Henry got to see his friends, and she didn't have to.

But now she wished he was home, that she hadn't come back from the GP to an empty house. She hadn't really been expecting the test to be positive. She'd always had a vague sense that only teenagers got pregnant by mistake, whereas women in their thirties could have babies only if they 'tried for' them – though 'accidents' sometimes happened two or three kids down the line, and she'd been twenty-five the only time she'd thought she might be pregnant before. At least this time she could be sure it was Henry's.

A few years ago, long before they moved in together, when they still lived in separate one-bedroom flats in different parts of north London, when they'd only been going out for a few months, when neither of them knew how serious it was, or was going to be, Henry and Vic had made a kind of pact, or bet, or strange agreement.

They were drunk and naked, slumped on the sofa in the living room of Vic's flat, sticky from sex, watching TV. Henry went to the fridge for another bottle of wine. Vic browsed through the channels. 'Oh look!' she said. 'John Cusack.'

'John Cusack?' Henry said, refilling her wine glass and spilling some on her breasts. It trickled down across her tan line. He knelt to kiss it from her nipple, settled back against the cushions and refilled his glass.

Vic leaned back into the corner of the sofa, extending her legs, resting her calves across his thighs. The action reminded Henry of a cat stretching. He ran a finger along her shinbone. 'You need to shave your legs,' he said.

'No I don't,' she said. 'I'm growing them.'

'Longer legs? I'll drink to that.' He topped up their glasses. She took the blanket from the back of the sofa and wrapped it round her shoulders.

'He looks a bit like Tim, doesn't he,' Henry said.

'Who?'

'Tim, your ex. Remember him?'

'Yes. I mean, who looks like him?'

'John Cusack.'

'Oh. No,' Vic said too quickly. Tim didn't look much like John Cusack. But the person who really didn't look like John Cusack – the person who, if you were trying to think of famous people they looked like, you'd never in a million years say John Cusack – was Henry. *Oops.*

'If you say so,' Henry said. 'I mean, you should know. But to me, he looks a bit like Tim.'

'Well, maybe. But so what if he does? Tim and I broke up months ago.'

'There's no need to be so defensive: I'm only joking. But you've got to wonder, when someone who looks like your ex comes on TV and you get all excited about it. It's a bit – suggestive, that's all.'

'Well I'd still say Tim was good-looking, objectively speaking. But I don't fancy him anymore.'

Henry drained his glass, and said nothing.

'Oh come on,' Vic said. 'Like you never look at another girl and think she's good-looking. I saw the way you were looking at that waitress tonight. Are you seriously trying to tell me you didn't fancy her?'

'Oh, sure. Of course I did. You know, objectively speaking.'

'So if you weren't going out with me, and you met her at a party, you wouldn't try it on? If you weren't going out with me?'

'Maybe, sure, if we weren't going out. But we are, so it doesn't really apply.'

'You feel inhibited by our relationship.'

'Yes, of course.'

'So you do want to sleep with other women.'

'No I don't. You're turning this all upside-down. This is crazy talk.'

'No it's not. I'm not sure I don't want to sleep with other men. I mean, I certainly don't feel ready to say I'll never sleep with another man again in my whole life.'

'That's okay. I'm not asking you to marry me.'

'I know. But I worry. I worry I should be sure I don't want to sleep with anyone else, and I'm not.'

'Are you breaking up with me?'

'No. No: absolutely not. I just think maybe, maybe – to be certain, I mean – maybe we should have a, what do you call it, a time out, a get-out-of-jail-free moment.'

'I don't understand.'

'Like this weekend: maybe, on Saturday night, we should go out separately, and each sleep with someone else. Or not, if we find we don't want to. But maybe we should be allowed to. So we can know, for certain, that we only want each other.'

'Are you being serious?'

'I think so.'

'I'll think about it,' he said. 'Shall we go to bed?'

'So,' Henry said the next morning, pouring the coffee. 'Are you still serious, about what you suggested last night?'

'What?'

'You know, about making this Saturday night a kind of, what did you call it? Like a private carnival.'

'Oh, that,' Vic said, rubbing her temple. 'I've got a killer hangover. No, not really. I was drunk. Forget about it. Oh, crap. I'm going to be late for work again. I really must stop drinking on Wednesday nights. See you tonight?'

*

Vic sat at her desk, not working. Apart from the hangover, she was worried about what she might have set in motion with her unguarded remarks the night before. She'd been telling the truth, meant everything she'd said, but the trouble – or part of the trouble – was that saying it out loud had made it cease to be true: voicing the concern had been enough to dispel it. She was now sure, for the moment at least, that she didn't want to sleep with anyone apart from Henry. Though she didn't much want to sleep with him just at the minute, partly because of the hangover, and partly because of his reaction to her expressing her doubts. Henry had not treated it as a thought experiment. When he'd brought it up again at breakfast she'd been repelled, but she had to admit that it had been her idea. Was it possible she unconsciously wanted Henry to sleep with someone else to give her an excuse to dump him?

She pressed her fingers against her temples. There was an email from the office manager canvassing staff opinions on 'the advisability of installing automated and frequency-adjustable fragrance dispensers in the rest rooms'. She deleted it, then retrieved it from the recycle bin. It was the best email she'd received all week. She read it again, thought about forwarding it to Henry, deleted it again. This direct-marketing mail-shot wasn't going to write itself. She made a mental note to kill the next person who suggested that advertising copywriting was a glamorous profession. Though who did, really, apart from her parents? And what did they know? Her mother hadn't worked since Vic was born; her father was a phone engineer. 'Oh, how interesting,' Henry's mother had said, the one, excruciating time their parents had met. 'So we both work in communication.' Madeleine ran a PR firm. They were in a bar at the National Theatre. By appalling coincidence, both sets of parents had tickets to see *My Fair Lady* on the same evening. Henry had thought it would be nice if the six of them had a drink beforehand; Vic had acquiesced.

'I suppose so,' Trevor said, laughing politely. If he'd had a hat, Vic thought, he'd have doffed it. She wanted him to disagree, to point out that his work actually enabled communication, whereas Madeleine's deliberately distorted it – as, admittedly, did Vic's. Her parents had nothing to be ashamed of, but she was ashamed of their deference. It wasn't as if they really felt deferential – she was sure her father privately despised Henry's parents – so why behave like it? It didn't help that, when she was alone with Henry's mother, they got on pretty well. Madeleine could be funny, at least. Henry's father, however, was an overbearing bore. 'Can I get you another one of those, Linda?' he asked. Vic's mother simpered into her tonic water. 'No, thank you.'

Idiot, Vic thought. She shook her head, got down to work.

'All right,' she said that evening, after half a bottle of wine. 'Let's do this thing. Saturday night. We're both free to sleep with whoever we want to, no repercussions. To clear the air.' She focused on the middle distance beyond Henry's shoulder, to avoid seeing whatever expression might have formed on his face.

Vic's plan for Saturday was to go out with her friend Amy somewhere on Upper Street, somewhere that did good, strong cocktails, get really drunk, and try not to think about Henry.

She arrived at the bar on the stroke of half past seven. At 7.45 she was most of the way through a mojito, failing to concentrate on her book, and there was no sign of Amy. She checked her phone for messages, though there hadn't been any when she'd checked a minute earlier, and the bar was still empty and quiet enough that she couldn't have failed to hear if Amy had rung or texted her: her ears were primed for the sound of her phone like a mother's to her baby's crying. She called Amy, got her answerphone. She must have still been on the Tube. There was no point leaving a message. She hung up, downed the rest of her drink, went to the bar for another.

At five to eight, Amy rang. 'Vic, hi, I'm really, really sorry about this, but I'm not going to be able to make it tonight.'

'What do you mean?'

'Something's come up at work. I'm on my way into the office.'

'It's eight o'clock on a Saturday night.'

'You're telling me. It's this proposed merger – someone's got wind of a rival bid and so all of a sudden they need all the paperwork finished by Monday morning.'

'What merger?'

Amy was always making mysterious references to her mysterious job as if Vic ought to know what she was talking about.

'I can't really tell you. Sorry. Top secret. Listen, I have to go. We'll talk on Tuesday, yeah? You guys have a great time tonight. Don't think I'm not wildly jealous. Bye!'

'Bye.'

Vic wondered who else she could call. It had been foolish to rely on Amy: her stamina at the bottle and lack of interest in Henry's whereabouts were guaranteed, but her turning up wasn't. Vic scrolled through her phone's address book, rejecting her friends one by one – would definitely be busy; would want to talk about Henry; wouldn't drink enough; definitely busy; on holiday; would want to talk about Henry – before giving up somewhere in the Gs. She would finish her drink and read her book, as if that had always been her intention, then go home, open a bottle of wine and watch a DVD: *The Princess Bride*, perhaps, or *Ferris Bueller's Day Off*.

Henry, meanwhile, had gone back to Soho, to the Italian restaurant where he and Vic had been on Wednesday night, when their relationship had still seemed straightforward and fresh and delightful. He peered through the doorway, hoping to catch a glimpse of the waitress. And there she was, rounding the corner at speed and striding towards him. Her legs were shorter than he remembered.

'Table for one, sir?' She smiled, a smile full of professional friendliness. 'Or are you waiting for someone?'

'No, thank you. Sorry. I was looking for someone, but they're not here. Sorry.' He hurried away into the night.

Stalking the streets of the West End, passing the sex shops and prostitutes' doorways, hands plunged furiously in pockets, Henry felt surrounded, besieged by sexual opportunity: everywhere he turned, groups of sparsely clad women in their twenties charged laughing past him into bars. It was simply a matter of following them in, buying two of them a drink, and working out which would be more likely to sleep with him. But none of them was Vic.

*

'*Adam Bede* by George Eliot.'

Vic glanced up. The man was contorting his neck to read the cover of her book. He wasn't especially good-looking, but he had twinkling grey eyes and excellent skin, and a loose, rangey ease about him. 'Or is it *George Eliot* by Adam Bede?'

'How long did it take you to think that one up?' she said, putting the book down.

'About as long as you've been sitting there pretending to read it. Who's stood you up?'

'No one.' She folded her arms.

'I'm sorry. None of my business. And I shouldn't jump to conclusions. It's just, you're the first person I've met who gets their kicks by going out to a bar on a Saturday night with a book they don't want to read and a phone they get angry at every five minutes.'

She raised her eyebrows.

'The thing is,' he went on, 'I *have* been stood up, and before going home to watch *Ferris Bueller's Day Off* with only a four-pack of cheap Dutch lager for company and then falling asleep on the sofa, I wondered if I might buy you another mojito?'

'Okay, okay,' she said, smiling despite herself. 'I give in. Another mojito would be lovely, thank you.'

'My pleasure,' he said. 'I'm James, by the way.'

'Victoria,' she said.

Three hours later, she said: 'So do you want to come back to mine and watch *Ferris Bueller*?'

She was woken by the phone ringing. It hurt her head. She flailed at it. The noise stopped. Her head still hurt. She reached for a cooler pillow from the other side of the bed. The pillowcase felt brittle, as if made of paper, and came away in her hands. Someone had sent her a letter, which had been delivered to her bed. That wasn't normal. She pulled herself up into a sitting position and fumbled for her glasses, relieved that she hadn't been too drunk to throw away her contact lenses before falling asleep.

'Dear Victoria,' the note said. 'Sorry I've had to disappear – had to catch a train to see my family for lunch in Dorset. I've programmed my number into your phone – hope you don't mind – give me a ring next time you're not in the mood for George Eliot (soon, I hope). James xxx.'

She put the note down and picked up her phone. It beeped aggressively at her. There was a new message from Henry: 'We need to see each other. Call me?' She scrolled rapidly through her address book to J, deleted James's number before giving herself time to change her mind, screwed his note up and threw it in the waste paper basket with her contact lenses and the condom. Then she stripped the bed, put the sheets in the washing machine with all her clothes from the night before, and took a shower. She dressed quickly, then took the rubbish out in a tightly knotted plastic bag and dumped it in the neighbours' bin, trying not to think about how nice the sex had been.

Once all physical traces of James were erased, she put some coffee on and called Henry.

'Hi.'

'Hi.'

'How are you?'

'Hungover. You?'

'Hungover.'

'Shall I come round to yours or do you want to come here?'

'I could do with some breakfast. That cafe in Camden?'

'Sure. See you there in, what, half an hour?'

'Okay.'

'Do we want to know? Ought we to say?'

'I don't know. I think so, probably. I mean, not knowing, suspecting, would be worse, don't you think?'

'I suppose so.'

'Shall I go first?'

'I don't mind.'

'Okay. Did you?'

'Did you?'

They spoke simultaneously, each giving the answer they thought the other would expect to hear; or the answer that each secretly hoped or feared to hear from the other.

'No,' Vic said.

'Yes,' Henry said.

The coffee cooled in their cups. The oil congealed around their fried eggs.

'I don't think this is going to work,' Vic said.

But they saw each other again a few months later, at the New Year's Eve party of a friend neither of them had realised the other knew. And the moment they locked eyes across the room, both were certain they would end up in bed together before sunrise.

'So has there been anyone else?' Vic asked a few days later.

'No,' Henry said. 'I've been busy. Besides, you're a hard act to follow. You?'

'There was this one guy,' she said, suppressing the surge of recalled panic that rose in her throat at the memory of sleeping with James, breaking up with Henry, and waiting an anxious week longer than usual for her period. 'But it wasn't anything serious.'

Eighteen months later they were married. Two years after that, they moved out of London to the Kent countryside to be nearer to her parents, to have a bigger house, to have a garden, because it was the next item on his unwritten list of things to do. And a year after that, Henry came home after a night away in London, determined to stop lying to his wife. His iron resolve didn't waver as he got off the train at Tunbridge Wells and went through the ticket barrier to the car park, or as he paused to buy an overpriced bunch of tired roses from the florist he'd always ignored in the past, or as he drove impatiently home, ten per cent faster than the speed limit (someone, his father probably, had once told him that that was a speed camera's margin of error). He didn't falter, not once, until the moment Vic opened the front door to him, anticipating his juggling of keys and flowers and *baise-en-ville*. And then he looked up at his wife, radiant in the doorway, and his mind flooded with doubt.

'I have something to tell you,' he said quickly, before the last rusty traces of his intent dissolved away.

'What happened to your face?' she asked.

'Nothing. Silly accident. I'm fine. That isn't what I have to tell you.'

'I have something to tell you too,' she said.

'Good news?' he asked.

'You first,' she said.

'No, no,' he said. 'You first.'

'I'm pregnant,' she said.

He dumped everything he was carrying on the doorstep and put his arms round her, instinctively holding his pelvis away, for fear of damaging something.

'Come here, silly,' she said, pulling him close. 'What did you want to tell me?'

Her news had changed everything, made the stakes too high. Besides, he calculated, he had admitted to infidelity once, and been unfaithful once. His trangression with Clare could be construed as the fulfilment of that old dishonest confession. The previous lie and the more recent betrayal cancelled each other out, in a way.

'Just that I missed you,' he said, bending down to pick the roses up from the doorstep.

4

Backgammon

Every night, for an hour or so, Alex would sit quite still in his armchair in the dark and listen to the woman downstairs taking a bath. He had never met the woman downstairs, or even seen her, though he knew her name from sorting through the post in the hall: letters arrived for Miranda Barrowby, First Floor, three or four times a week. He'd passed her boyfriend – Edward something-or-other – a couple of times on the front steps on a Sunday morning, and they'd nodded hello. Edward was around Alex's age, perhaps a year or two younger, and not bad-looking, so Alex assumed Miranda would be the same.

The ritual generally began at around half past eleven. Alex was often already sitting in the armchair in the dark; but if he wasn't, it didn't take him long to turn off the TV, shut down the computer or close his book, switch off the lamp and settle down to listen. The creak of the bathroom door, the click of the light, the sputtering of the taps, and he was ready.

The sounds that reached Alex's ears were indeterminate – sloshing, splashing, scrubbing, squelching, sighing – but if he concentrated, he could use them to reconstruct what might be happening in the room below. He had never been in his neighbours' bathroom, but he had a fixed mental image of it: the pale blue tiles, the bath against the wall to the left of the door, the fern on the windowsill, the bright (but not harsh) lighting, the potion bottles in the wire basket at the end of the bath, the chrome taps, the hook on the back of the door where Miranda hung her green towelling dressing gown.

Alex knew that his behaviour was creepy. But eavesdropping wasn't the same as spying on a woman taking a bath. Overhearing such noises was to some extent unavoidable. And the thrill wasn't sexual: he didn't masturbate, or take his clothes off, or anything like that. It wasn't even a thrill, really. He found the experience calming, even companionable, a break from the pressure of work and the loneliness of life since he and Clare had separated – which is to say, since Clare had left him. Listening to the woman downstairs take a bath for an hour or so every night was a form of therapy, like meditation.

Because he had never seen her, he was able to imagine her naked body unconstrained by any known facts: in Schrödinger's bathtub, as he thought of it, her skin tone, height, weight, hair, all changed nightly, sometimes morphing from one form to another or through several variations in the course of an evening. It didn't really matter to Alex what she looked like. She was relaxing in the sanctuary of her bath, and he was unobtrusively sharing her experience. The less he knew of her, the better.

He sometimes thought about going out for the evening but could never summon the energy. His friends and colleagues had been solicitous in the first few weeks after Clare left, but the invitations had long since dried up. He had thought about online dating, and about internet pornography, but didn't much like the idea of either. Sex held little appeal for him these days, whether with someone else or by himself. The only faint sense of arousal he'd felt in weeks had crept up on him one morning while he was rinsing his cereal bowl in the kitchen sink: looking out the window, across the back gardens, he had caught sight, through another window, of a woman pulling on a pair of washing-up gloves.

He preferred to sit quietly in the dark, listening to the woman downstairs have her bath. The first time it happened, he had been sitting at his computer in the semi-darkness, enveloped in the bubble of half-light projected by the screen, playing backgammon with an anonymous stranger. He had hooked himself into the internet using an unknown neighbour's unsecured wireless network. This was illegal, in contravention of Section 125 of the 2003 Communications Act ('dishonestly obtaining electronic communications services'), but Alex didn't suppose he was any more likely to be prosecuted under it than he was to be arrested for driving at 75 miles an hour on the motorway, or having smoked dope as a teenager. His opponent had been comfortably on top for most of the game, but a risky move, exposing three of his pieces, followed by a couple of lucky throws, turned it in Alex's favour. So his opponent quit. There ought to be some way of stigmatising people who did that, Alex thought, so that you could avoid playing them, and to discourage them from doing it. He clicked 'new opponent'. Then he lost the wireless connection. He was just about to begin a game of solitaire, when he heard from downstairs the creak of a door, the click of a light, the sputtering of taps. A new period in his life had begun.

When Clare had told him she 'needed a break', he hadn't been especially surprised. Would it have helped if he'd challenged her about sleeping with Henry? But if so, when? When she told him she was leaving? Or when he first suspected something? Would that have cleared the air? Or forced the crisis sooner? At what point had their marriage been doomed? Since it had failed, it had surely, in retrospect, been doomed from the start. And yet there must have been a moment, which one or the other or both of them had missed, when their relationship could have been salvaged.

After moving out and going to stay with a colleague in Camberwell, Clare had suggested Alex buy her share of the capital they'd already sunk into the house – his salary was more than enough to cover the mortgage – but the prospect of living there alone was intolerable. So they put the house on the market, and as soon as the sale came through Clare quit her job and bought herself a round-the-world plane ticket. The last Alex had heard, from a comment a mutual friend had made on one of Clare's Facebook status updates, she was in Guatemala. He hoped she was enjoying herself.

The only things Alex really missed about the house in Tufnell Park were the bookshelves in the sitting room, built by a carpenter at exorbitant cost. They, more than anything – more certainly than being a 'homeowner' – made him feel as if he'd arrived at adulthood. He'd populated them with the texts he'd accumulated over his three years at Oxford, from *Beowulf* to Virginia Woolf. The books now were still in the cardboard boxes they'd been packed in when he moved out. He supposed he should unpack them, though it wasn't as if he'd ever taken any of them down to read during the years they were arrayed chronologically on the expensive shelves.

It had been Henry's idea that Alex rent Vic's flat. 'Just while you're sorting yourself out,' he'd said. 'The current tenant's moving out, and it'll save on agent's fees if nothing else. Nicer to have someone we know in there anyway. And after last month, I feel we both owe you one.' Alex couldn't think of a reason to refuse.

Sometimes, at the weekend, the woman downstairs would take her bath in the morning. Alex didn't find it so soothing to listen to her in the light of day. In fact, hearing her splashing around at 10 a.m. on a Saturday detracted from the solemnity of the night-time ritual. He put the radio on and turned up the volume. A strident woman was talking in a mock-humorous tone about her holidays. While he was searching for a more neutral frequency, the doorbell rang. Reminding himself yet again to get the intercom fixed, he went downstairs to talk to the deliveryman. He wasn't expecting anything: the package would probably be for the woman downstairs, or her boyfriend, but she was in the bath, and he was probably out, so the least Alex could do, as a good neighbour, was sign for her parcel for her.

The man on the doorstep wasn't dressed as a deliveryman. He wasn't carrying any parcels, either. Alex peered down the street for his van.

'Hello?' he said.

'Er, hello,' the man said. His eyes were the same colour as Clare's. 'This may sound like a weird question, but does Victoria still live here?'

'No,' Alex said. 'Sorry. She still owns the flat, but I'm renting it from her. Can I, er, take a message?'

'No, that's fine. I used to know her, years ago, and I happened to be passing so thought I'd drop by. Silly of me, really. Should have expected her to have moved.'

'Well, she still owns the flat,' said Alex. 'So not that silly. I'm Alex, by the way.'

'James.'

They shook hands.

'So you're a friend of Vic's from college, or something?' Alex said, trying not to admit to himself how pleasant it was to be having a conversation with a friend of a friend he'd just met.

'Something like that. Is she a friend of yours, as well as your landlady?'

'Yes, she is. Though I suppose I'm more a friend of Henry's really. At least, I knew him first.'

'Henry?'

'Vic's husband.'

'Ah.'

'You didn't know?'

'Like I said, it was years ago that I knew her. It was silly of me to stop by.'

Alex was on the point of inviting James in for a drink, but decided it would be too weird, and anyway didn't feel up to enduring yet another rejection, however small. 'I'll tell Vic you stopped by,' he said, then retreated into the house and shut the door.

Later that afternoon, Henry rang to ask Alex to lunch the next day. Alex felt vaguely insulted that Henry not only assumed he would be free, but didn't see any need to pretend otherwise. He could, surely, have called a few days earlier, and said, 'You're probably busy, but on the off chance . . .' or, 'I'm sure it's too late to ask you, but . . .' Alex considered refusing the invitation on principle. But the prospect of yet another day spent alone at home was unbearable, so he decided to accept. He wondered if he should pretend to have had plans that had just this minute been cancelled, but thought that might seem sadder than having had nothing to do in the first place. 'That would be lovely,' he said. 'What sort of time train should I catch?'

'This Northern Rock business doesn't look good, does it,' Henry said. 'I'd say you got out of the housing market just in time.'

'Me and Tony Blair both,' Alex said.

'Do you think he knew?'

'He couldn't have done, could he? You know, that's a terrible euphemism,' Alex said.

'What?'

'Getting out of the housing market.'

'Oh. Yes. Sorry.'

Alex knew that Henry was only trying to look on the bright side – of both the recent collapse of Alex's personal life and the imminent collapse of global capitalism – in order to be kind. But Alex didn't respond well to kindness just at the moment. Especially not from Henry. Then again, he didn't respond well to anything just at the moment. Especially not from Henry. They were drinking gin in the kitchen, Henry with half an eye on the oven.

'It's just a beef stew and baked potatoes. It's hard for either of us to find the time to cook anything more elaborate with Jessica.'

'Beef stew and baked potatoes is pretty elaborate by my standards.'

'What do you mean? You're a great cook.'

'Maybe I was once. I don't really bother with it much these days.'

They sat in awkward silence. Alex had enjoyed cooking when he lived with Clare, on the evenings he wasn't too late home, stopping off at the Tesco Metro next to the Tube station in the City or at one of the small grocers in Tufnell Park for ingredients, frying a couple of tuna steaks with a chilli and lime sauce, or making a risotto with the stock from the chicken he'd roasted for Sunday lunch. He tried to keep up the habit after Clare left, but soon lapsed, subsisting instead on sandwiches and takeaways. He had once gone to a good restaurant by himself, but spent the evening fighting the urge to get up from the table and walk out, not tasting the food as he forced himself to eat it, all three courses, able to keep going only by telling himself that he would never do this again.

Other bachelor habits, too, proved more trouble than they were worth. 'At least you don't have to worry about putting the toilet seat down,' one of his colleagues had consoled him. But the gesture of flushing and closing the lid was too ingrained in his motor memory. He had once turned back at the bathroom door to lift the seat. He looked at it. Then he put it back down. So much for that. He stopped shaving. After a few days he wondered when not shaving translated into growing a beard. He had once not taken a razor on holiday and Clare had told him, in the nicest possible way, that his chin looked like the pale end of a spring onion. He'd bought a disposable razor the next morning. One evening the spring onions in Tesco caught his eye. When he got home he looked in the bathroom mirror as he washed his hands after closing the toilet seat. He started shaving again.

'Top you up?' Henry said, lunging for the refuge of the gin bottle.

'Thanks. You doing okay?'

'Fine. Yes. Well, even. Thank you. You really talked some sense into me. Cheers.'

'To family life,' Alex said.

Henry lifted his glass to his face and held it there like a mask.

'What have I missed?' Vic said from the doorway.

'Gin, mostly, but I suppose you'd have missed that if you'd been here, too. Is she asleep? Drink?'

'For now. Make me a weak one, would you?' She turned on the baby monitor and slumped into a chair.

Henry went to the fridge for the tonic water. Alex looked at the row of small bottles full of Vic's expressed milk.

'How's the flat, Alex?' Vic asked. 'Everything okay?'

'Everything's great, thanks. Oh, an old friend of yours stopped by yesterday, looking for you.'

Vic frowned, tucked in her chin. 'Really? That's weird. I can't think of anyone who knew I lived there who doesn't know I live here now. Who was it?'

'Some guy called James. From before you met Henry, if that helps place him.'

Vic still looked puzzled. 'What did he look like?'

'About my height, skinny, grey eyes.'

'Oh, *him*,' Vic said.

'Him who?' said Henry.

'This guy – what did you say his name was? James? – I went out with once when you and I weren't going out. And when I say once, I mean like one time only. He didn't seem the creepy stalker type.'

'You mean the "there was this one guy but it wasn't anything serious" guy?'

'If that's what I said.'

Alex thought about the woman downstairs, wondered if Vic would consider him the creepy stalker type.

The gurgles and rustlings on the baby monitor erupted into distorted wails.

'Shit,' Vic said. 'We shouldn't have let her sleep so long this morning. The perils of a lie-in. It'll come back and bite you on the arse at lunchtime.'

'Shall I?' Henry said.

'No, it's fine. Do you mind if I feed her in here, Alex?'

'Of course not.'

Time was, not so long ago, that the prospect of seeing one of Vic's nipples, even stuffed in the mouth of a guzzling infant, would have sent Alex into a frenzy of lust. But now he looked on with equanimity – if you could describe his persistent state of flattened affect as equanimity – as Vic flipped open her maternity bra. Alex thought of his mother's response, when he'd told her that he and Clare were separating: 'At least you don't have any children.' She'd still somehow managed to make it sound like a reproach. Vic and Henry were talking about sleeplessness. Alex had plenty to say on the subject, but kept quiet since his brand of insomnia could hardly compete with theirs, morally speaking.

Henry watched Alex watching Vic feeding Jessica. It was odd, he thought, how unfussed he now was by another man staring at his wife's breasts. The idea of Alex and Vic spending any time alone together, however, filled him with morbid anxiety. He had a reputation – not undeserved, he'd always thought – for being a fairly frank and open kind of guy. Yet over the last year or so Henry had been accumulating secrets like toxic debt. And Alex knew them all (or nearly all: he didn't know the truth about Henry's work). Henry didn't, rationally, believe that Alex would mention to Vic his brief, abortive attempt to leave her, or that he and Clare had had sex, which Alex surely knew – why else had he and Clare separated? – but had his own reasons for pretending not to. Part of that pretence involved staying friendly with Henry, and Henry both pitied and despised Alex for that, which made it easier to carry on his side of the pretence, to look Alex in the eye without flinching. And yet Henry couldn't bear the thought of leaving Alex and Vic alone together even for a moment, because it would mean that he couldn't know for sure that he hadn't told her.

Vic scooped her breast back into her bra, turned Jessica round and unscooped the other breast. 'The potatoes are probably done, aren't they? Why don't you dish up? Don't wait for me.'

Alex, Henry and Jessica ate.

After lunch, Alex helped Henry with the washing-up while Vic went for a nap. Both men looked at her bum as she left the kitchen.

'You know what Vic said when Jessica was born?' Henry said, passing Alex a wineglass, too fragile for the dishwasher, in a glistening cocoon of soap suds. 'She didn't know she had it in her to love anyone so completely.'

'And you?' Alex said, drying the glass.

48

Henry shrugged. 'When I take her to the supermarket, I don't look at other women anymore. I only look at her.'

'What about Vic?'

'Vic only looks at her too.'

'Very funny.'

'No, seriously. We're too tired for sex anyway.'

The awkward silence descended again. Both men did their best to pretend it hadn't. Alex considered dropping the wineglass he was drying. He imagined the splinters exploding from the floor tiles in high-definition slow-motion close-up. He gave it a last wipe and put it on the table with the others.

Lying in bed, exhausted but unable to sleep, Vic listened to the noises drifting up from the kitchen: baritone murmuring, the clink of cutlery and crockery, the light thud of cupboard doors. She was glad Henry was so happy to take on all the kitchen chores, and glad he was such a good and generous cook. But she wished he thought more about puddings. What she really wanted, more than anything, was a large slice of chocolate cake. She'd once helped her father make a chocolate cake for her mother's birthday. But something had gone wrong – perhaps they'd used plain instead of self-raising flour – and it came out of the oven a sad, slumped, misshapen thing. Her father had put a brave face on it, but Vic found his failure heartbreaking, as well as being disappointed that the cake she'd been so looking forward to eating, and surprising her mother with, was inedible. But her mother had been strangely un-bothered, even pleased by the failure, perhaps because she felt it confirmed her role as the supreme – the only – baker in the family. Vic tried to believe it had been deliberate, a cunning ploy on her father's part, because otherwise she felt too sorry for him, and she hated feeling that. She hoped Jessica would never have reason to feel sorry for Henry.

After he'd gone, Vic said: 'Why don't we ask Alex?'

'Are you serious? Why?'

'He's one of your best friends?'

'You've never liked him though.'

'That's not fair.'

'You said he stared at your boobs the whole time. That hasn't changed.'

'He was looking at Jessica. He's interested in her.'

'You mean like the scene in *Grosse Pointe Blank* where John Cusack stares into the baby's eyes and understands the wrongness of his life as a hitman?'

'Yes, that's exactly what I mean. However did you guess? Alex reminds me of John Cusack, which means I secretly fancy him. I thought it would be nice because I thought he was your fucking friend. Fuck you, Henry.'

'What are you talking about?'

'Your apparent obsession with my non-existent obsession with John Cusack. And don't tell me I'm imagining it.'

'I'd completely forgotten about that. Honestly. I just like that movie. It's a good scene. I promise never to mention it again though.'

'Sorry. I'm just so tired.'

'No, I'm sorry. You're right. It's a nice idea. Let's ask him.'

*

When he got home that evening, Alex had just put his key in the lock and started to turn it when the door was opened from the inside. He stumbled forwards, into the arms of the man downstairs. The man downstairs laughed. Alex blushed. 'I'm not actually drunk,' he said, straightening himself up. 'I'm just behaving that way.'

The man downstairs laughed again. 'Alex, isn't it?' he said.

'That's right. Edward?'

'Ednan. Ed. Nice to meet you.'

They shook hands, and continued to stand in each other's way, Alex on the doorstep, Ed inside the house, holding the door open. Alex pointed at the lock. 'Any chance I could have my keys back?'

'Sure. Sorry. There you go. Er, would you like to be?'

'To be what?'

'You know, drunk. To give you an excuse for behaving that way. I'm just nipping out to the Trough for a cheeky Sunday evening pint. Numb myself for work tomorrow.'

'Okay,' Alex said, surprising himself. 'Why not? That would be nice.'

Alex had almost forgotten how easy it was to make polite conversation with a stranger. Settled at a corner table in the Plough, they asked each other about their jobs (Ed worked for a small charity Alex had never heard of), how long they'd lived in their respective flats, where they'd lived before, whether they knew any of the same people (they didn't, not even Vic), none of it in any way memorable, but all very agreeable, both of them making sure to laugh when the other one said something that could pass for a joke.

'Where's your girlfriend this evening?' Alex said, bringing their third pair of pints to the table and letting fall the packet of crisps he'd been holding pressed against one of the glasses with his little finger, an old habit – perhaps you could even call it a skill – he'd forgotten he had.

'Girlfriend?' Ed said, lifting his beer to his lips.

'Sorry,' Alex said. 'I wasn't sure what to call her. Wife? Partner? Flatmate?'

'None of the above,' Ed said with an easy laugh. 'I live alone. Hey, is that a backgammon board over there?'

'Looks like it.'

'You know how to play?'

'Sure.'

5

Five Hundred

Clare was feeling seriously unwell by the time she got off the bus from Potosí. She didn't know if it was the altitude, or the cold empanadas she'd bought at the bus station, or the hot springs at Tarapaya that she'd bathed in the previous evening. She could worry about causes later. For now, she had to concentrate on dealing with consequences, on keeping her guts in till she could find somewhere private to unload them with a minimum of fuss and mess. She dragged her rucksack down the steps of the bus and heaved it onto her back, took a slow deep breath of cold desert air, and looked for signs of a lavatory.

'Are you looking for a tour of the Salar?' The boy was English, probably on his gap year fresh out of public school, though with his thicket of dirty blond hair and round pink cheeks he didn't look much older than fourteen.

'Where's the nearest hotel?' she replied.

'I'm staying just round the corner but . . .' His eyes drifted to the other disembarking passengers.

'I'll sign up to your tour, but first you need to show me the way to your hotel.'

He hesitated.

'Please?' she smiled, and reached out to take his arm.

The hotel was arranged on two floors around a three-sided courtyard. There were no internal corridors; as in a motel, the rooms opened directly onto the outside. An external wooden walkway provided access to the rooms on the upper storey. Clare's room was upstairs, at the far end of one of the wings. The bathroom was at the other end, a dozen rooms away. The hotel had running water, but it was switched off during the night, when the temperature dropped below zero, to prevent the pipes from bursting. For flushing the toilet after dark there was a fifty-gallon plastic barrel full of water and a bucket to dunk in it.

It was three o'clock in the morning. Clare shivered on the lavatory, recovering from her latest bout of diarrhoea. The flush-bucket was at her feet, awash with bile and the rehydrating fluid she'd failed to keep down. She'd lost count of the number of times she'd trekked along the wooden walkway from her room to the bathroom, through the desert night, beneath the moon's cold lamp. It had been every twenty minutes or so at first, when she still had the energy to look at her watch, and didn't feel as if it had let up.

The longer she waited to return to her room, the less time she would have to rest and try to warm up in her sleeping-bag before her rebellious bowels drove her back to the bathroom. But her sleeping-bag was such a long way off. She rested her elbows on her knees and closed her eyes. Her head rang over and over with a soprano voice singing a line from a song she didn't even realise she knew, dredged up from some useless recess of her memory – *on a cold frosty morning, past three o'clock*. She didn't know the next line, what happened on that cold frosty morning, past three o'clock. The song was stuck on that line, stuck in her head, and she was stuck on a toilet four thousand metres above sea level, four thousand miles from home, four degrees below zero, without the strength or the will even to stand up. *On a cold frosty morning, past three o'clock*. She stood up, pulled up her knickers and jeans, wrapped her poncho around her – she was sleeping fully clothed, hat and boots and all – tipped the liquid from the bucket into the toilet, plunged the bucket into the barrel through the film of ice that had begun to form since the last time she'd done this, twenty minutes and several eons ago, and poured the freezing water into the toilet.

Shivering in her sleeping bag, toes numb in her boots, eyes closed, drifting towards unconsciousness, she told herself she would rather die than be woken yet again by a wave of nausea and swept staggering out of her room along the walkway to the bathroom, the toilet and the bucket. *On a cold frosty morning, past three o'clock*. She would happily die. Her stomach clenched, her bowels jolted, the room spun her awake. She unzipped the sleeping bag, swung her shaking legs to the floor, lurched for the door.

She woke at last in daylight, still cold, still shivering, but no longer feeling sick. She lay for a while on her back, breathing the cold air. She unzipped her sleeping bag and lowered a foot to the floor. Then the other foot. One hand on the hard mattress, the other on her stomach, she raised herself to a sitting position. Her head span. She waited. The dizziness passed. Her stomach clenched. She needed to eat something. Her hand still on her stomach, as if holding her guts in, she stood, and shuffled to the door.

'Hello.'

She was sitting in a pocket of sunlight against the wall of her room, out of the wind and with the wooden boards of the walkway almost warm under her jeans, reading *Vile Bodies*, which she'd brought with her in case of just such an emergency as this. She'd eaten a yoghurt and drunk a small carton of orange juice, and begun to feel as if life was probably worth carrying on with after all. She wondered how close she'd come to succumbing last night. Not very, in all probability, but it had certainly felt like it at times. It would have been a lonely way to die, in a Spartan hotel room in south-west Bolivia, but there were worse things than loneliness, and she'd seen people – Alex, her parents – do the most degrading things to try to avoid it. She was happy by herself, and above all she was happy now, sitting in the sunlight, with her book and her pot of yoghurt. That there should be fresh yoghurt for sale in this frontier town, with its grid of dusty roads and nondescript low-rise buildings, not many more blocks than there are squares on a chessboard, seemed almost miraculous.

'Hello?'

She looked up. The boy who'd accosted her as she was getting off the bus was standing by the railing a polite distance away.

'Hello,' she replied.

'I was down there, my room's down there, and I saw you up here, and so I thought I'd come and say, um, hello.'

'Hello,' she said again.

His pink cheeks glowed even pinker. His hair shook like a gorse bush in a sudden gust of wind.

'Why don't you sit down,' she said. 'It's fairly sheltered here.'

'I don't want to disturb you. I just thought I should let you know we're going to the travel agent at twelve.'

'Okay, thanks. Well, good luck with that.'

'Right. The thing is, you have to come too.'

'I do?'

'Yeah. You, um, said last night that you'd sign up to the tour if I showed you where this place was, and if you don't come we'll have to find someone else which probably means waiting for tonight's bus from Potosí and waiting here another day, or all paying extra, and I don't think the Australians will be prepared to do that.'

'The Australians?'

'They got the train.'

'You've lost me.'

'Sorry. But the thing is you said last night . . .'

'You're right, I did. But as you may have noticed, I wasn't entirely well. The travel agent at twelve?'

'That's right.'

'I don't know where the travel agent is.'

'I'll see you at 11.45 here then.'

'It's a date.'

He blushed again.

'You're sure you won't stay for a yoghurt?'

He shook his head. 'Thanks, though.'

*

57

The Australians, Ollie and Sophie, were already at the travel agent when Clare and Sam – she'd got round to asking him his name on the walk from the hotel; he'd had to tell her twice, shouting over the wind – arrived, along with Axel, who was from Sweden, and an Italian couple, Marco and Daniela. Everyone introduced themselves and shook hands with everyone else. Clare, who in the three months since leaving England had until now successfully avoided signing up for any kind of guided tour, felt as if she'd mistakenly been included in a delegation from a minor United Nations agency. She wondered if delegates from minor UN agencies felt like tourists. Sophie – athletic, tanned, dark blonde hair scraped back in a ponytail, evidently accustomed since her school days to leading teams – led the group over to a desk where a young woman was waiting for them with a severe smile on her face. Spanish was spoken; sheets of paper were passed around, signed and exchanged; cash was pooled; other sheets of paper were distributed.

'Right then,' Sophie said. 'We're meeting our driver here tomorrow morning. We'll need to get provisions this afternoon but otherwise everything's sorted. We can either decide now how much we all want to spend on food and stuff or we can go shopping first and divvy up afterwards.'

Clare looked from face to face, waiting for someone else to make a decision.

'Lunch?' Axel said.

'So what happened to your face?' Ollie asked.

They were sitting over the remains of lunch: burnt crusts, congealed cheese, the detritus you'd find in pizza restaurants the

58

world over. Sam had asked why they didn't go somewhere that served *pique macho* but he'd been overruled, or ignored. Clare wasn't bothered where they went, since she still didn't feel up to anything more complicated than yoghurt, and had resolved to let other people make her decisions for her for the duration. That was, after all, pretty much the whole point of guided tours.

Axel's face was covered with scabs and scratches, but everyone so far had been too polite to mention it. 'A skiing accident,' he said.

'Skiing?' Sophie said. 'Seriously? Where?'

'Here. That is, Chacaltaya. The glacier is melting, they say it will be gone completely in three years. But it is still the world's highest ski resort, so how could I not go? There isn't any snow, and I had to bribe this guy to open the lift – officially it is closed – but seriously. It was fucking awesome.'

'But you fell?'

'All the way down the mountain. There was no snow, just ice and rocks. It was fucking awesome.' He took out a pouch of tobacco and rolled himself a cigarette, pausing halfway through to offer the papers and tobacco to the others. Everyone declined. Marco brought out a pack of American filter tips. Sophie asked for the bill.

Clare and Sam were again the last to arrive at the travel agent the next morning. The others were variously lounging or waiting impatiently beside a dirty, beaten-up Toyota 4x4, its roofrack loaded with a fifty-gallon steel drum and baggage wrapped in tarpaulin. The only person Clare didn't know was a man she assumed must be the driver. '*Buenos días señor*,' she said. '*Yo me llamo Clare*.'

He nodded despondently, gestured for her rucksack, clambered up onto the roof and secured it under the tarpaulin, then gestured for Sam to pass his pack up too. Back on the ground he looked at Clare and said: 'Enrique.' Then he climbed into the driver's seat and started the engine. The six passengers exchanged glances and got in too: Axel in the front beside Enrique, the Australians and Clare in the middle, Sam and the Italians in the back.

The windows immediately steamed up. But Enrique didn't seem to need to be able to see out the windscreen, and with the heater going full blast, its roar competing with the Andean pop jiving out of the stereo, the mist gradually cleared. Clare caught a glimpse of the statue of the railway mechanic outside the station. After a brief stop to admire the rusting hulks of old steam engines in the Cementerio de Trenes on the outskirts of town, they were soon heading out into the open desert.

Clare rubbed the last of the condensation off the window and looked out – sky, mountains, sand, the familiar bleak, majestic landscape of the Altiplano, no sign as yet of the famous salt flats – feeling the chill of her damp glove along the edge of her hand, trying to ignore Ollie's muscular thigh pressing against hers. Hard to tell if that was deliberate or not. He obviously considered himself handsome – broad shoulders, broad smile, probably a hefty dick, too – and, annoyingly, wasn't completely wrong to think so.

'What's up with him do you think?' Ollie asked.

Clare turned her attention back into the jeep.

'He's paid, no doubt very badly, to drive us around, not to be cheerful,' Sam said from the backseat.

'You think this is his way of earning a tip?'

'Ollie,' Sophie said.

60

He shrugged.

Axel spoke to Enrique in Spanish. Enrique unleashed a volley of complaint. Axel turned the stereo down. Enrique turned it up again and shouted louder. They were picking up speed. A small dust cloud ahead of them became a bigger dust cloud and the bigger dust cloud became another jeep. Enrique overtook it, yelled '¡Cabrones!' and fell silent.

'That's one word I do understand,' Ollie said. 'Who's he talking about? Us or the guys in the other car? And where did you learn to speak Spanish?'

'At school, and I had a Spanish girlfriend once,' Axel said. 'The motherfuckers are either the Bolivian football team or the Peruvian football team. Or possibly both. And the referee. Bolivia lost two-nil in yesterday's friendly.'

'What did you say to set him off?'

'I asked him if he'd seen the game.'

Enrique asked Axel a question. Axel said something about los australianos. Enrique laughed.

'What was that?' Ollie asked.

'It doesn't matter,' Axel said. 'Look.'

Enrique swung the jeep off the road. The gleaming white blank of the Salar de Uyuni was spread out in front of them, like a vast frozen lake covered with a thin layer of snow.

'It's beautiful,' Sophie said.

'It is as if, when God was creating the world, there was a little piece he forgot to finish,' Daniela said.

Clare was beginning to feel seriously ashamed of her monoglotism.

Sam turned to Daniela. 'You don't think,' he began.

'No,' she said. 'Don't worry. My parents are Catholic but I know about the Big Bang and evolution and all those things.'

'I didn't mean,' Sam said.

'It's beautiful,' Sophie said again.

'Half of the world's known lithium reserves under there,' Ollie said. 'Ten thousand square kilometres. Just think how many cellphone batteries you could make with all that.'

They drove out onto the salt.

'Did anyone else feel as if we were about to plunge in just then?' Ollie asked.

'Yeah,' Clare said. 'A bit like stepping onto a stopped escalator.'

He gave her a quizzical look, as if he couldn't tell whether she was being sarcastic or not. As it happened, she wasn't sure either.

Out in the middle of the Salar, Enrique stopped the jeep and said something to Axel. 'Photo stop,' Axel translated. They all piled out onto the salt. The Australians rummaged in their daypacks and, with the glee of amateur magicians, produced a series of incongruous objects: two small bottles of whisky, one empty, one full, a corkscrew, a pack of playing cards, a toy kangaroo, a camera. Sophie gave the corkscrew to Axel and asked him to hold it as if uncorking a bottle. Ollie went running off across the salt until Sophie, watching him through the screen of the camera, shouted at him to stop. Ollie put his hands to the side of his head and opened his mouth in a silent scream. Sophie shuffled sideways and asked Axel to lower the corkscrew. 'Stop! There. Perfect. That's hilarious,' she said.

'May I?' Clare asked.

Sophie showed her the picture. Ollie appeared to be about

to have his head removed by a giant corkscrew, the bright blankness of the Salar wiping out any sense of perspective.

'Clever,' Clare said.

'Haven't you seen all the ones people have put online? We planned ours before leaving home.'

'I wasn't even sure I was going to come here before last week.'

'No way. Well, you don't want to miss out. Let's do one of you with the kangaroo. We bought it at Brisbane airport specially.'

'Okay,' Clare said, not wanting to make an enemy of Sophie so early on in the tour, and sensing that she was the kind of person who took a dim view of people who didn't join in.

Twenty minutes later, Sophie's camera loaded with trick photographs of them all – apart from Sam, who'd gone off by himself to reflect on the sublime – variously opening, drinking and having been knocked out by a giant bottle of whisky, sitting in a house of cards, or perched in a giant kangaroo's pouch, Enrique herded them all back into the jeep.

'Just wait till I get these on Facebook,' Sophie said. 'We mustn't forget to all friend each other.'

'I don't have a Facebook account,' Sam said.

'How do you keep up with all your student buddies?' Sophie asked.

'Maybe he doesn't have any,' Ollie said.

'I haven't started university yet,' Sam said.

'Schoolfriends?' Sophie asked.

'Like I said,' Ollie said.

'We're not on Facebook,' Sam said.

'What, are you ideologically opposed to it or something?'

Sam blushed. 'Actually, yes.'

'Don't like computers?'

'Don't have a problem with computers,' Sam said. 'It's the, um, the commodification of social relations that we object to.'

'Oh right,' Ollie said. 'Zuckerberg must be quaking in his boots. Enrique!' He slapped the back of Axel's seat. 'What are we waiting for? ¡*Vamos!*'

After lunch on the Isla del Pescado, a rocky outcrop in the middle of the Salar covered in twenty-foot cactuses, back in the jeep again, Ollie asked: 'Is everyone happy with this?'

'What, the seating arrangements?' Clare said. Axel was still in the front seat.

'No, the music. If I have to listen to *amor* rhyming with *por favor* one more time I'll go insane.'

'It's a tape deck,' Axel said. 'Unless you have brought some tapes with you, I think you're out of luck. Though I could maybe ask him to turn it down.'

'Ask him to change the tape. It can't all be like this.'

After a brief consultation with Enrique, Axel opened the glove box and took out a handful of cassettes. Seeing them gave Clare a jolt of nostalgia. She could have been nine years old again, venturing into the music section of WHSmith to spend her pocket money on *Like a Virgin*, wondering what her mother would say when she saw it. Axel passed the tapes back to Ollie. 'Take your pick,' he said.

'This'll have to do,' Ollie said, passing one of them back to Axel. '*Fijación Oral*. At least everyone's heard of Shakira.'

'Her hips don't lie,' Clare said.

Enrique glanced at her in the rear view mirror, briefly smiled

– in complicity or reproach, she couldn't tell, unless he was just checking for traffic – and changed the tape.

'Maybe we should settle up for the provisions now?' Sophie said.

It was cold in the refuge. They were huddled round a thicket of candles that had overflown their foil holders and stuck to the formica table beside the ramshackle stack of plastic plates glued together by the congealed half-eaten remains of their unappetising dinner, now dusted with cigarette ash and butts among the pasta, which even with extra salt and extra time in the pot to compensate for the lower boiling temperature of water at altitude – everyone had had a theory and a turn at stirring the pot – had been unpleasantly chewy. Ollie's jokes about it being *al dente* had been met with polite smiles by the Italians. It was not, perhaps, the best time for Sophie to ask everyone to pay for the food.

'Maybe in the morning,' Marco said. 'I need to go to bed.'

'You don't want to stay for a game of cards?' Ollie said. 'Open another round of beers?'

'No, thank you. Goodnight everyone,' Daniela said.

Axel went outside for a smoke under the stars.

'I wouldn't mind a game of cards,' Sam said.

'Sure, why not,' Clare said.

'Great,' Sophie said. 'Do you guys know how to play Five Hundred?'

'No,' they both said.

It turned out to be a bit like whist, and so brought back more childhood memories for Clare, of rainy summer holidays in Devon. But it also wasn't like whist – there were fiddly rules to do with the jacks – and so the others had to keep reminding Clare that the 'left bower' was in fact a trump if, say, she threw the jack of diamonds on a diamond trick when hearts were trumps. Sam, who was partnering Sophie, picked the rules up all too easily. Clare suspected him of having played before.

'So how long have you guys been travelling?' Sophie asked.

'About three months now,' Clare said.

'Five weeks,' Sam said.

'So you didn't set out at the same time?'

'No,' Sam blushed in the candlelight.

'We only met in Uyuni,' Clare said.

'Fast work,' Ollie said.

Sam glanced at Clare then looked at the floor. 'We're not, um, together,' he said.

'How about you two?' Clare asked.

'Just a couple of weeks actually,' Sophie said.

'And you did leave Australia together.'

'Yeah, we've been together a few years now.'

'Married?'

'Funny you should ask, actually. We talked about it, but decided, instead of spending all that money on a wedding, to take six months off and buy round-the-world plane tickets.'

'What a good idea.'

'Well, it may be our last chance. We're planning to start a family when we get home. I'm going to be thirty next year.'

'Come on, Soph,' Ollie said. 'It's your bid.'

'He doesn't like talking about it. Six diamonds.'

'I don't mind talking about it. I just think other people maybe don't like hearing about it. Six hearts.'

Sam supported Sophie's bid with seven diamonds. Clare passed. Sam picked up the kitty.

66

Clare wondered why everyone felt obliged to tell the truth about themselves to the other people they met travelling. You would never see them again and they had no way of knowing whether or not you were lying. Or perhaps that was the reason everyone was so frank. There was nothing to be lost by telling the truth.

'Good call,' Clare said.

'Seven diamonds, you mean?' Sam said.

'No, I mean not getting married.'

'Why, are you ideologically opposed to that too?' Ollie asked.

'No, nothing ideological. Something personal though.' She held up her left hand, the fading tan mark on her ring finger still just about visible.

'How old were you?' Sophie asked. 'Sixteen?'

'I'm flattered, but no. It was three years ago, and I was twenty-eight. I'm spending my half of the recovered house deposit on this trip.'

'Trying to escape the cliché of a stifling bourgeois existence?'

'Partly. Though I'm also trying to escape the cliché of trying to escape the cliché of a stifling bourgeois existence.'

'Bourgeois in what sense?' Sam asked.

'In the sense of having a Facebook account,' Ollie said.

'That's not . . .'

'I know.'

'Yes,' Clare said. 'I have a Facebook account. And I also have the joker.' She took the trick.

'Nice,' Ollie said. 'It's not enough though. They've made their seven, and that pushes them over five hundred. Well done, guys. Time to call it a night?'

*

Despite the cold, Clare went to take a look at the stars before turning in. The newish moon was low in the west, a thin gold ring thickening along the ninety degrees of arc closest to the horizon. It looked like a hole punched in the sky, or one of those optical illusions that oscillates as you stare at it between relief and counter-relief, lump and dent. She thought of that line quoted by Coleridge about the new moon holding the old moon in its arms, though it was a long time till midnight and too dry for frost. If that was even the right poem. Here there was nowhere for her to look it up.

Victoria's pregnancy had been one of the reasons she split up with Alex. Not out of jealousy, either for Henry or the baby's sake, but because of the sense it gave her of time passing. Having sex with Henry had been a throwback to a previous life, which made being married to Alex seem like a throwback too. Clare and Alex had talked about having a baby. She didn't particularly want one, but it was the next item on the unwritten list – job, cohabitation, mortgage, marriage – and people seemed to expect it of them. Given the irregularity of her cycle, purposeful procreative sex was difficult to schedule, but they'd given up using contraception, to give chance a chance, though since they'd more or less given up having sex, too, chance would have been a fine thing. She felt as if she was living a hangover of an old life that wasn't hers anymore. And Henry and Victoria were having a baby. He'd phoned her at work the day after leaving her in London. 'We're not officially telling anyone yet,' he said. 'But I thought you should know.'

'Your secret's safe with me,' she said. 'Congratulations.'

'Thank you.'

A few months later, in the cold dark days of the new year, she said to Alex: 'I need to get away.'

'Okay. Good idea. Where shall we go?'

'I don't mean us. I mean me.'

'Okay. You get more holiday than me so it makes sense.'

'I don't mean a holiday. I mean everything.'

'You want to quit your job?'

'My job, London, everything. I'm not saying this well. There's no good way to say it. I think our marriage isn't working.' She didn't know now if she'd been hoping he'd put up more of a fight. She didn't tell him about Henry, though she knew he suspected something. She told herself she wanted them to be able to stay friends.

She'd never been so far from home; she'd never seen so many stars. The air was so thin up here. She shivered, smiled, and went back inside.

It was both comforting and dispiriting, how quickly they settled into a routine. The second day passed in much the same way as the first: an early and very cold start, though less cold for the Australians and the Italians, as each couple had zipped their sleeping bags together; an indigestible breakfast of stale bread rolls and bitter coffee; and into the jeep. Without talking or even thinking about it, they all climbed into the same seats as the day before, the seats they'd already come to think of as theirs, Shakira looping on the stereo like the narrow playlist of a very local radio station.

It felt to Clare more like a trip on a school minibus than a journey into the desert. Deserts were supposed to be places of solitude, rich with the infinite possibilities of emptiness in which to find yourself by losing yourself – so long as you didn't die of thirst – but Clare saw no opportunities for enlightenment here. They looked at inactive volcanos, and lakes of many colours, and stands of flamingos, and rocks, carved by the wind, which looked like trees – a mirage of sorts. Everyone took photographs of the same things and huddled against the cold and laughed at each other's jokes which they couldn't hear over the wind and climbed back into the jeep and listened to Shakira and gazed out the window at the landscape underscored by the tyre tracks of countless jeeps filled with tourists that had passed this way before them.

The second evening, in a different but functionally identical refuge, followed the same pattern as the evening before. The stodgy plates of rice were pushed aside; the Italians went to bed; Axel went outside for a smoke under the stars before settling down in a chair in the corner with his book; the English-speakers played cards, the Australians against the English this time.

'I'm sorry about the rice,' Sophie said.

'It's hardly your fault,' Clare said. She hadn't eaten anything since the yoghurt she'd had for breakfast two days earlier. And she was feeling fine. She was feeling good, even, in a very particular way that she hadn't felt for nearly fifteen years. Its familiarity was both frightening and exhilarating. She would have to be careful. She promised herself she'd eat a decent breakfast.

'Was it easy getting time off work for your trip?' Sophie asked.

'Very easy,' Clare said. 'I quit.'

Ollie laughed. 'Me too,' he said.

'What did you do?' Sophie asked.

'Publishing. What about you?'

'I was a trader on the ABX,' Ollie said.

'Australian bullion exchange,' Sophie explained. 'I'm a schoolteacher. What are you going to be studying, Sam?' Sophie asked.

'English,' he said, looking at Clare as if he wanted to say something to her but couldn't quite bring himself to.

'I studied English literature,' Ollie said. 'Six diamonds. For a couple of years. Then I dropped out. Got a job as a waiter, thought I'd write short stories. You're all passing? Seriously? Oh well. I should have said seven straight off. And I was working at these events, being paid minimum wage and fuck-all in tips to serve drinks to guys I'd been at school with, who weren't even that smart but were making a killing as bankers or traders. And I thought, anything they can do' – he took Clare's king of diamonds with the ace, then laid the rest of his cards, a run of low trumps and the three highest remaining spades, on the table – 'I can do better. We took all ten so that's two hundred and fifty points and the game.'

Sam tried to smile. 'Well played,' he said.

Clare pushed her chair back. 'I need a break.'

Sam looked at her with the same expression as before.

'What do you think?' Clare said, taking pity on him. 'Shall we go outside, look at the stars, talk tactics?'

'Um, okay,' he said.

'I might call it a night,' Sophie said. 'Ollie?'

Ollie poured himself another half-beaker of whisky. 'I'll be there in a minute.'

Clare put her hat and gloves on, opened a beer and went outside. Sam followed her. She took a swig and passed him the bottle. 'If you've got a manuscript of a novel in your ruck-sack, there's no point giving it to me.'

He drank, spluttered, passed the bottle back. 'Some stories, actually, and a one-act play. But I don't have them with me. And I wouldn't expect you to read them. I just thought you might be able to give me some advice. The play's about an imaginary meeting between Karl Marx and Robert Browning in the British Museum Reading Room in 1863.'

'Save it for the first-year drama festival.'

'But it's about *Capital* and *The Ring and the Book* . . .'

'Save it for the PhD.'

'Oh right. Well, the other thing is I worked in this warehouse to earn the money to come out here, and wrote a collection of intersecting stories about the lives of the men who work in a warehouse.'

His earnestness, as well as the pink softness of his skin, lit unflatteringly but in dramatic chiaroscuro by the fluorescent light spilling out of the windows of the refuge – he can't have shaved more often than once a fortnight – reminded her of Alex when they'd first met, teenagers in love who couldn't keep their hands off each other, who had sex as often as they could manage; more often, sometimes.

'I love you,' he'd said one post-coital afternoon.

'Do you?'

'Eyebrows to ankles,' he'd said, kissing them.

'What about my forehead and feet?'

'Oh, I hate those,' he'd said, biting her toes.

She'd laughed. But she couldn't remember if she'd said then that she'd loved him too, though of course she'd said it plenty of times since. But that time, the first time, when she didn't know if she had or not, seemed to her now to be the only time when it would really have mattered.

Sam was looking expectantly at her.

'Give me your email address and I'll send you a list of agents who may be looking for new clients. But don't get your hopes up.' She drained the beer. 'I'm freezing. Let's go back in.'

Ollie pointed at the book Sam had left on the table. 'What are you reading that for?' he asked. 'It won't help you win at cards.'

Sam blushed. 'Let us finally imagine, for a change,' he said, reciting from memory with less ease than he'd clearly have liked, 'an association of free men, working with the means of production held in common, and expending their many different forms of labour-power in full self-awareness as one single social labour force.'

'It says that on the back,' Ollie said.

'It says it in the text too.'

'Have you been to the Cerro Rico yet?' Ollie asked. 'Those miners all work in co-ops now: I think that means that the means of production are held in common. And they all still die of lung disease in their forties.'

'But there are centuries of colonial exploitation behind that.'

'I'm not saying there aren't. But I'd still rather work in McDonald's in Brisbane or London or New York. Jesus, I'd rather work in McDonald's in La Paz than down that mine.'

'That's not . . .'

'Didn't you find those low tunnels really hard to walk through?' Clare asked, not because she wanted to shut Sam down but because the argument wasn't going anywhere; neither of the men was going to change the other's mind. 'I scraped my back really badly at one point.'

'Yeah, it was a fucking nightmare. I'm surprised the mountain hasn't collapsed, it's so full of tunnels. It's like an old table with really bad woodworm. As I said, I'd rather work in McDonald's. Or on a coca farm.'

Axel closed his book and stood up. 'Goodnight everyone,' he said.

'Goodnight, mate,' Ollie said. 'You seemed lost in your book there. You're not reading Marx too, are you? What sort of work do you do? Translator or something?'

Axel smiled. 'No, I'm a carpenter. And I'm reading Kafka. In Swedish. Good night.'

On the third and final morning of the tour they set out before dawn to watch the sunrise from the Sol de Mañana geothermal field: pits of boiling mud, the stink of sulphur and an inverted spire of steam jetting fifty metres into the air. Axel called it a geyser but Ollie said it wasn't.

At two in the afternoon they watched the waters of Laguna Verde change from blue to green. No one knew whether it was a biological or a chemical phenomenon. A general lassitude had descended on the group, now ready to disperse. Marco and Daniela were the first to break free. Going on to Chile, they transferred their packs to a minivan heading for the border and made their goodbyes.

'*Buon proseguimento*,' Marco said.

'Cheers,' Ollie said.

Everyone waved. Enrique herded them back into the jeep, crunched it into gear and began the long drive back to Uyuni. Clare, Sam, Ollie and Sophie had more room to spread out without the Italians and drifted into sleep as Enrique gunned for home.

*

'So here we are,' Ollie said. 'Back in civilisation.'

'What are everyone's plans now?' Sophie asked.

'I have had enough of this fucking cold,' Axel said. 'I am going surfing in Venezuela.'

'Can you surf in Venezuela?'

'Of course. It's even better than the skiing in Bolivia.'

'We're going to Peru,' Sophie said. 'Cusco, Inca Trail, Machu Picchu.'

'I haven't really thought about it,' Clare said. 'Maybe head to Argentina.'

'Well if no one's leaving town tonight, how about we all meet up here for pizza in an hour?'

Clare looked at the others, caught Sam's expectant eye. He looked away.

She'd showered and started to get dressed when the knock came at the door. It couldn't be Sam – he wouldn't be so bold – but it couldn't be anyone else either and she realised then she didn't want it to be anyone else. She finished buttoning up her shirt and pulled a jumper over her wet hair. Maybe he wanted to talk about his ridiculous play. And he was only a child, really. But there would be no harm in kissing him.

'Oh, hello,' she said.

'Hi,' said Ollie. 'Can I come in?'

The wrap of cocaine lay on the bedside table. Marco had given it to Axel at Laguna Verde because he didn't want to cross the Chilean border with it. Axel had given it to Ollie because he'd been clean for three years. Clare and Ollie sat side by side on the bed looking at it.

'What about Sophie?'

'She's in the shower. I said I'd meet her downstairs with everyone else. And she's not really into this kind of stuff, to be honest.'

'How do you know I am?'

He shrugged. 'If you're not, you're not. But if you are, well . . . And we are in Bolivia. No Mexicans or Jamaicans have died, et cetera. This is as clean as you'll ever taste it.'

She turned to look at him more closely. 'You've already had some, haven't you.'

A huge smile spread across his face.

The way Ollie had talked it up, Clare expected the cocaine to give her a hit she'd never felt before, as new as a first orgasm or coming up on ecstasy for the first time, but it didn't. She took it the way Henry had explained she should the first time she did it at Oxford, in a short hard sniff to get it into her nose but not down the back of her throat. It numbed her nostrils on its way into her bloodstream. But it didn't blow her mind. She gave Ollie a triumphant smile. She had survived a fatal illness, endured three days in the desert without food, and was immune to pure cocaine. She was invincible. She'd never felt so clean. This rarefied air. She was also, she noticed, talking. Without having to think about what she was saying. Now this was style. This was skill. This was multitasking. She could do anything.

She rubbed her nose with the back of her hand. 'You know why I had to quit my job?' she was saying. 'What I suddenly saw that meant I couldn't keep going? I wasn't doing anything. None of us were. I don't mean the books. Well, maybe I do mean the books. Maybe one book a year, if we were lucky, was really worth publishing. One a year. At the outside. The rest of them, why bother? When all those so-called readers out there haven't read, I don't know, Marx or Browning, why not just stop? Why not just stop publishing books so people have to read what's already there? And everyone else I know, my so-called friends, it's even worse. Lawyers, copywriters, journalists, bankers, management consultants, web designers – they don't do anything, they don't make anything.'

'Give me your eyes,' Ollie said, taking her wrist in one of his hands and pointing to his eyes with the index and middle fingers of the other. 'Give me your eyes.'

She looked into his eyes. His pupils were huge.

'You're high on the strongest coke you'll ever sample in your life, and you're fighting it,' he said. 'Don't. It's like a wave. You've got to ride it.'

She breathed in. She thought of the statue outside the railway station, the giant chrome mechanic striding forwards on top of a giant concrete anvil, spanner in one hand, wheel in the other, a socialist-realist silver surfer, huge and invulnerable. She felt her heart pound. She imagined a train thundering at full speed through the desert. She smiled. 'I am riding it,' she said.

There was a noise at the door. It was ajar. Hadn't Ollie closed it when he came in? There was movement. A smear of dirty blond hair against the dark blue sky. Sam had come to her room to be kissed but gone away again when he'd seen Ollie. Clare had resolved to kiss him, and wasn't going to let anything put her off. She leaned over, put her arms round Ollie's neck, kissed him. He put his arm around her waist and kissed her in return. But she didn't really notice what he was doing, because she was so impressed by what she was doing, by what an exceptionally good kisser she was. Sam had come and gone. She'd never see him again. Ollie would soon be gone. He was here now. She was kissing him. She was really very good at kissing. Perhaps she'd have sex with him. She was really very good at sex too. Or perhaps she wouldn't. It made no difference to anything – the force of the epiphany overwhelmed her – whether she slept with him or not. Her heart pounded. The mechanic strode on his anvil. The train roared across the desert. Time for another line.

6

Twister

E d opened his door one Friday morning in the spring as
Alex was rushing downstairs on the way to work to say
that he was having a party that evening.

'That's all right,' Alex said, recovering his footing and
fumbling with the strap of his bicycle helmet.

'Huh?'

'Don't worry about the noise. It's not a problem. Be as loud
as you like.'

'Oh. Are you going away for the weekend?'

'No, I'll be here. But I don't mind about the noise. Be as
loud as you like, as late as you like.'

'Er, okay. Thanks . . . But actually I was going to ask you if
you wanted to come.'

'Oh right.' Alex felt himself blushing. 'Thank you. Maybe
I'll drop in if I'm not busy. If it's that kind of party?'

Ed smiled. 'Yes, it's that kind of party. See you tonight I hope.'

*

Cycling home that evening, watching his shadow sneak smoothly up on him and overtake before fading in the glow of the next street lamp, Alex decided he would go to Ed's party. He'd been feeling better about himself since he'd started cycling to work. Or possibly he'd started cycling to work because he was feeling better about himself. All day, part of him was looking forward to the journey home, and it was a while since he'd looked forward to anything. There'd been a few alarming moments in the early days: he'd knocked the near-side wing mirror off a car trying to slither past it in the run up to a red light, and been nearly squashed between two buses, but he'd grown more cautious with experience, or at least had a better sense of his own limits. He was surprised to find himself looking forward to the party. He freewheeled round the corner into his street, lime berries popping under his tyres. Every time he turned into his street from this direction, he was reminded of the time he'd been shouted at by three eleven-year-old girls on the other side of the road. 'Oy!' they'd called in unison. He glanced round. 'What the fuck are you looking at, you PERVERT?' He hurried away, wondering if this was how mistaken-identity paedophile witch-hunts got started.

He chained his bike to the railings by the bins outside the house, unclipped his helmet and ran up the steps to the front door. It was after nine o'clock; music was pulsing out from Ed's flat, an indie guitar band that Alex didn't recognise. Anxious not to be caught on the stairs in his work clothes and cycling gear, feeling the pinch of his cycle clips through his suit trousers, he kept on running till he was safely on the top landing and unlocking the door of his flat.

In the shower, he began to have doubts about going to the

party: what would he wear, how much should he drink, who would he talk to, who would talk to him? He imagined himself as the melancholy drunk alone in the corner in a pair of dad-jeans and an unfashionable shirt, the sad upstairs neighbour who had to be invited and came because he had nothing better to do. How much worse, though, to be the sad upstairs neighbour stomping around by himself at home, invited yet absent with nothing better to do. He dug a pair of not too terrible jeans and a not too ostentatious shirt out of his wardrobe, ruffled his hair with his towel then patted it down with his hands, and went through to the kitchen. Hungry now, he made himself a quick sandwich from the remains of the previous weekend's roast chicken for one, and washed it down with a bottle of beer. Trying to fix his hair in the mirror in the sitting room he caught a whiff of garlic on his breath and went to clean his teeth. By the time he'd finished gargling with mouthwash his hair had subsided again into a centre parting. He found some old wax in the bathroom cupboard. A few minutes' tweaking made it look as if he'd gone to a lot of effort to make his hair look crap. He washed the wax off his hands, dried them and rubbed his head vigorously with the towel. He looked as if he'd just got out of the shower: that would have to do. Fingering the spots growing along his jawline, he tried to remember how long it was since he'd changed the bedsheets and pillow cases: one of Clare's old chores, and something for him to do when he got home after the party. He went back to the kitchen, grabbed four bottles of beer from the fridge, snatched up his wallet and keys from the counter and hurried downstairs, avoiding the mirror, before he could change his mind about going.

The door was opened by someone who wasn't Ed, but who

seemed inexplicably familiar. Perhaps it was just that his eyes were a similar colour to Clare's. But there was as much recognition as welcome in his smile. 'Hello,' he said. 'You live upstairs in Victoria's flat. Alex, isn't it?'

'Yes,' Alex said.

'James. I rang your doorbell in September on the off chance Victoria still lived there.'

'Of course you did. Sorry. I'm terrible with names. And faces. Terrible with people, really.'

'Come on in. There are plenty of people here for you to be terrible with. Drink?' He glanced at the beer in Alex's hands. 'Bottle opener?'

Alex followed James through the sitting room to the kitchen, which was, disorientingly, underneath his bedroom. The lights were low, the music was loud, the air was full of smoke. The other guests clustered in small groups, sitting on the sofa, at the table, on the floor by the disused fireplace, standing by the window, the stereo, the doorways. There was more light in the kitchen. Alex put his beer down on the counter, picked up a corkscrew and prised the top off one of the bottles, offering it to James.

'So how do you know Ed then?' he asked, opening one for himself, hoping to keep James from abandoning him and disappearing into the smoky crowd. 'Did you ring his doorbell on the off chance an old flame lived there too?'

James laughed politely. 'Not exactly,' he said. 'We met at a work thing, last year's Christmas party – the company I work for sponsors the charity he works at? – and ended up sharing a cab home.' The doorbell rang. 'Excuse me,' he said, and went out to answer it, leaving Alex alone to suck on his beer and wonder why James had taken it on himself to play butler.

As he was steeling himself to plunge into the miasma of the sitting room – he ought anyway to try to find Ed, to say hello – James came back with a woman who must have been the reason he'd been answering the door, and therefore his girlfriend. Which was a pity, because for the first time in a long while, Alex was experiencing a profound and powerful sexual attraction to a complete stranger. He hadn't, in fact, felt anything quite like this since Deborah Martin's party in the summer half-term of the lower sixth, when he and Deborah's cousin, who was visiting from Ireland, had locked eyes across the garden and he had known instantly, with all the force of ancient prophecy, that he would kiss her before the night was over. She had a scar across her left eyebrow, smoked Silk Cut Ultra Low and her name was Lorna. They had snogged fiercely beneath a lilac tree, their hands burrowing inexpertly below each other's waistbands, and they had never seen each other again.

'This is Alex,' James said. 'He lives in the flat upstairs.'

His girlfriend introduced herself as Charlotte.

Alex said hello.

'My sister,' James said. 'We should find Ed. See you later Alex.'

Alex said goodbye.

Other people came into the kitchen and went out again. If they asked, Alex showed them where they could find a bottle opener or cigarette lighter. Someone tried to strike up a conversation about the mayoral election. Alex was non-committal. Otherwise he leaned against the countertop, sipping his beer and trying to look nonchalant, waiting for Charlotte to come back.

Ed came in. 'Glad you made it! Can I get you anything?'

Alex raised his beer.

Ed reached into the fridge for a bottle. 'Great. What's up?'

'Not much,' Alex said. 'I was just wondering why life seems so much simpler when you're seventeen.'

'Does it?' Ed said, scooping the corkscrew off the counter next to Alex, popping the cap from his beer and taking a swig. 'That's not how I remember it. Life's much simpler now. You're just getting nostalgic in your old age. What do you think?' he asked, turning to the doorway.

'About what?' said Charlotte, coming into the kitchen.

'Alex here thinks life was simpler at seventeen.'

Charlotte frowned and shook her head.

'You see?' Ed said. 'Catch you both later.'

'Is that the same bottle of beer you were drinking when I arrived?' Charlotte asked.

Alex looked at it, as if the answer to her question were written on the label. 'Yes,' he said.

She pulled a face. 'It must be really warm and flat by now. Horrible. Let's get you another.' She opened the fridge, pulled out two bottles, swiped the tops from them and passed one to Alex.

'You used to work in a pub,' he said.

'Nice one, Sherlock,' she said. 'Still do, actually.'

'Whereabouts?'

'Most people ask why.'

'For the money, I imagine.'

'Bermondsey. Near Tower Bridge. Because I need a better dealer.'

'Dealer? As in drugs?'

'As in art.'

'You're a painter.'

84

She shook her head. 'Other media.'

'What kind of other media?'

'Found objects. Collage. You know. At the moment, it's music boxes.'

'Music boxes?'

'Are you actually interested?'

'Yes, actually I am.'

She shrugged. 'I've been collecting music boxes, all kinds, all eras, all tunes. They're all mechanical though. Found my first one at Bermondsey market a couple of years ago. And I'm setting them up in a space, and rigging them all up so they can be wound up or set going remotely, by computer control. And I'm working on various algorithms for playing them all in various combinations and sequences.'

'Wow,' Alex said. 'I can't really imagine that.'

Good,' Charlotte said. 'You'll have to come and see it some-time instead.'

'I'd like that.'

'What do you do?'

'Very boring, I'm a lawyer.'

'It needn't be boring.'

'It is though. Let's talk about something else.'

'Okay then. Tell me a secret.'

'I don't know if I have any secrets. A secret from whom?'

'Just something you've never told anyone before. Doesn't have to be a dark secret. Maybe just something you've never said because you've never thought it was worth saying.'

Alex looked round for inspiration. 'When I was about four,' he said at last, 'I used to like kneeling on the floor of the kitchen with my head in the washing machine.'

Charlotte nodded. 'Huh. Why?'

'Because it was so cool: literally. And so quiet, a weird kind of echoing quiet, and so shiny, and all-surrounding. I think I was pretending I was an astronaut. But it was more than pretending: it felt like being in outer space. Or sticking my head through a portal into another dimension. It smelled so clean. I think it made my mother worry I might be autistic.'

Charlotte put down her beer, pulled the washing machine door open, scooped Ed's damp laundry out onto the floor, kicked it aside, got down on her hands and knees and fed her head into the machine. She looked from side to side, her dark blonde curls rippling across her upper back. Then she twisted her neck slowly round to the right, the rest of her spine following it, rotating vertebra by vertebra, her right hand and leg lifting off the floor and arcing through the air, her body pivoting on her left hand and knee, till she was bending over backwards as if under a limbo pole, her head still in the washing machine. Alex tried not to look at the crotch of her jeans, stretched between her parted thighs, or the gap between the buttons of her shirt where it was stretched across her breasts. The music pulsed from the sitting room.

'What the fuck?' Ed said, coming into the kitchen, a half-smoked joint smouldering in his hand.

Charlotte pulled her head out of the washing machine. 'When Alex was small he used to sit with his head in the washing machine for hours. I was seeing what it was like.'

'Seriously?' Ed asked, taking a pull on the joint and handing it to Alex.

'It wasn't actually for hours,' Alex said. 'No, thanks.'

'What's it like?' Ed asked Charlotte, offering her the joint.

'Interesting,' she said, standing up and straightening her shirt. 'No, thanks. You should try it.'

Ed looked at the washing machine, and at the pile of his damp clothes beside it. 'Maybe another time,' he said. 'Hey listen, if this isn't your thing' – he drew a slow curve in the air with the joint, like a very tired child with a dud sparkler on bonfire night – 'there are some people doing coke in the bedroom.'

Alex shook his head. 'We have random drug tests at work.'

Charlotte looked from Alex to Ed. 'Not for me either, thanks.'

'Each to their own,' Ed said, taking another beer from the fridge.

'Do all lawyers have to take random drug tests?' Charlotte asked when Ed had gone.

'I don't know. I very much doubt it. As it happens I've never had to take one. But it's a convenient excuse.'

'You need an excuse?'

Alex shrugged. 'Sometimes people want to know why you're saying no.'

'What's wrong with that? If it's not because of the random drug tests, why are you?'

'You see? There you go asking. It's because of the random drug tests.' He drained his beer. 'If you'll excuse me . . .'

'Sorry: we can talk about something else.'

'No, it's not that.'

'Heading off for a sneaky line?'

'Ha ha. No, I'm going for a wee. You can come along and check up on me if you like.'

'Thanks, but no thanks. See you later.'

Two men – one tall and thin, the other short and stout, like an old-time comedy double act – were arguing outside the bathroom door.

'Is someone in there?' Alex asked.

The tall one looked down at him. 'Yes.'

'Are you the queue?'

The short one looked up at him. 'I am, he isn't. The point is,' he went on, 'that you'd have to be incredibly naive to think that cocaine would be illegal if it was native to the Appalachians rather than the Andes.'

A deep rumble reverberated from inside the bathroom. Alex thought of the way the sounds from in there carried up to his sitting room. He had a half-disembodied sense that some part of him was sitting in his armchair in the dark upstairs, listening.

'What's that?' Alex asked.

'Plumbing?' said the tall one. 'Who's being naive now? If the US government wanted to profiteer from the cocaine trade they wouldn't have to be a net exporter of it – or for that matter to make it legal. It suits them the way it is.'

'That's exactly what I'm saying.'

'No it isn't. What you're saying is . . .'

The toilet flushed, taps were run, the door was unlocked and opened by a wide-eyed man with a mop of dark curly hair and the beginnings of a beard, as if he were thinking of training to be a guru.

'Steve,' the tall man said to the would-be guru. 'What was that noise?'

'The acoustics in there,' Steve said, 'are mindblowing. Try singing a low B-flat: the whole room's tuned to it. The pipes pick up the harmonics and everything. Come in and listen.' He tugged the tall man's sleeve.

The short man ducked past him, pushed him out the way and firmly closed the door. Steve and the tall man wandered away.

It was a while since Alex had been at a party where almost everyone was on drugs. Hard to remember now that there'd been a time – at university and during his first years in London – when it had been routine. Alex had taken cocaine once, or rather several times over the course of one long night, at an oligarch-themed fancy-dress party at the house of friends of friends in the second year. After he'd got over the uncomfortable sensation in his nose, like a pea going the wrong way if you laughed while eating, it briefly made him feel as if he'd won the men's downhill skiing world championship and needed to tell everyone about it before doing it again, immediately.

The short man came out of the bathroom. Alex went in and locked the door. The tiles were not blue. There was no fern on the windowsill.

Coming down, alone in his narrow bed in the dark hours of the not-yet-dawn, had been an experience he never wanted to repeat, more like lying powerless at the bottom of a mountain, waiting for an avalanche. Hyper-aware of the circulation of his blood, irrationally mistrustful of his autonomic nervous system, he thought that if he stopped concentrating on it, his heart would stop beating. Behind the obvious terror of losing consciousness and thereby dying, however, lurked another fear, harder to pinpoint, which manifested itself in his mind's eye as a caricature of two Victorian prizefighters, with tiny heads and feet, bloated barrel chests, rouged cheeks and absurdly high-waisted trousers. They seemed to have been dredged from the darkest recesses of his memory, as if he'd seen them in very early childhood while something awful was happening, something he had suppressed so deeply that only this monstrous image was still accessible, and then only when his brain chemistry was under this kind of duress.

Clare had told him he shouldn't have been alone the first time, that he'd learn to deal with the comedown. He'd decided he'd rather not have to. Henry had told him it sounded as if the cocaine had been cut with a lot of dirty speed, or caffeine. He thought they were both trying to sound as if they knew more about it than they did.

He washed his hands and wiped them dry on his trousers, not liking the look of either of the towels, and opened the bathroom door to find Steve the would-be guru waiting in the hallway, without the tall man but with half a dozen newly recruited acolytes. Alex dodged out of their way and they all filed into the bathroom, the last one closing the door behind her with a suppressed giggle. A low chanting began, Steve's mantra in B-flat, gathering voices and volume before being lost in the music and shouting as Alex made his way back through the rising hilarity levels of the sitting room to the kitchen, where he was both surprised and delighted to still find Charlotte. He told her about Steve and the B-flat bathroom; she laughed and handed him a fresh bottle of beer.

The music stopped and the main light in the sitting room came on.

'What's going on?' Alex asked.

'Police raid?' Charlotte suggested.

Alex tried not to look worried.

'Or possibly musical chairs,' she said.

'All right everyone,' Ed said. 'Steve here has been rummaging in my cupboard of embarrassing secrets and dug out a Twister board. Board? Mat. Whatever. Anyway, to punish me for owning this – though even if you waterboarded me I'd insist it was left here by the previous tenants – he has proposed a knock-out Twister tournament. Anyone who doesn't want to play should leave now.'

'I think a police raid might have been preferable,' Charlotte said.

Alex looked at her, trying not to imagine what it would be like to have their straining limbs entangled on a slippery plastic mat in a room full of strangers.

'Right then,' Ed said, flicking the mat in the air like a parent with a picnic blanket and floating it down flat on the carpet in the middle of the room. 'First up, me against Steve. Who wants to spin?'

Charlotte stepped forward.

It was easy to tell who'd taken what kind of drug from the way they played. The cokeheads were humourlessly competitive, the stoners fell about giggling, the drunks just fell about. Steve, looking more like a yogi than ever, was remarkably good. As he flaunted his contortionist acrobatics, it was embarrassingly obvious why he'd wanted to bring the game out, or would have been if everyone apart from Alex hadn't been long past caring about embarrassment, their own or anyone else's. Charlotte, too, as her washing machine manoeuvres had intimated, dispatched her early opponents with little difficulty.

Alex looked on, puzzled. He had assumed that these people – younger than him, with better haircuts and more drugs – were cooler than he was. Yet here they were, playing Twister. Were they less cool than he thought, or was playing Twister cooler than he could imagine it was? Either way, he would have to recalibrate. Either way, they made him feel old. He supposed he admired them for not caring about whether or not what they were doing was cool, but simply enjoying it.

Perhaps that was the reason – besides being a divorced corporate lawyer sliding towards middle age – that he would never be as cool as they were.

Then Charlotte was pushing him forward towards the mat. The giant polka-dots, splotches of primary colour on slick plastic, glared up at him. His opponent wasn't Charlotte, which was both disappointing and a relief, but a heavy-breather with a goatee whose name appeared to be Dave. Alex wondered if they ought to shake hands, or bow, before starting, but Ed was already spinning the arrow. 'Right leg blue,' he said. The contest was underway. Alex was half-hearted about it at first, putting his left hand on a yellow spot in a gesture that he hoped fell in the right place on the wry-casual continuum. But as their limbs became more entwined, and especially once Dave started leaning on him, Alex's competitive edge was sharpened. His legs were stronger than they used to be, thanks to all the cycling, and as he became absorbed in the game, his sensory universe shrinking to the confines of the mat, Dave's bulk and breath, and Ed's voice, Alex's confidence grew until he was able to envision himself defeating not only the stertorous Dave but everyone in the room, Steve and Charlotte included – at which point he made an overambitious lunge for a red spot with his left leg, not only stronger than it used to be from all the cycling but stiffer, too, and found himself sprawling on the ground, a triumphant Dave looming victorious above him.

He stood up sheepishly, to applause and laughter and slaps on the back from people he didn't know. Charlotte was smiling at him and he smiled back. She gave him a beer.

'Cycling,' he said. 'That's the problem. Strength without flexibility.'

'You should stretch when you get home,' she said.

James interrupted them. 'I'm heading off,' he said to Charlotte. 'You want to crash at my place?'

She looked at Alex. 'No, I'll get a cab back to mine I think.'

'Okay. But if you change your mind you can wake me up.'

'Thanks.'

They looked at each other. When James didn't leave, Alex squeezed past them with a smile and a gesture towards the toilet. The Twister mat had been put away, the lights dimmed and the stereo cranked up – Alex still didn't recognise the music – and the sitting room heaved with dancing bodies. He wondered how strong the floor was.

The tall man and the short man were still arguing in the corridor.

'So Osama bin Laden's a vampire? I thought he had Marfan syndrome.'

'Only metaphorically.'

'You can have Marfan's metaphorically?'

'Shut up about Marfan's.'

'Why are you so touchy on the subject?'

'I'm not. Metaphorically he's a vampire. He's an individual.'

'Also an unkillable aristocratic foreigner who drinks virgins' blood.'

'That's not the point.'

'The point?'

'Yes, the point is that, in the Western imagination, he's essentially a vampire, because he . . .'

'Drinks virgins' blood.'

'Because he's an identifiable individual. Like Dracula.'

'Like Dracula.'

'Exactly.'

'You've already said all this.'

'You won't let me finish. Whereas the Taliban, or the insurgents in Iraq, are zombies, because they're an undifferentiated mass . . .'

'Of scary working-class foreigners who eat virgins' brains.'

'I'm ignoring you from now on. The point I'm trying to make is that they're all, from the point of view of the West, various kinds of undead: they can be killed with impunity because they're already dead. But . . .'

'Bin Laden's already dead? That's just a rumour you read on the internet.'

'Are you being deliberately obtuse?'

They were interrupted by a blast on a foghorn. The short man yanked open the bathroom door. The would-be guru grinned at them from behind a bassoon. 'That low B-flat,' he said. 'It's really something.'

'Steve?' said the tall man. 'What the fuck are you doing?'

'Playing the bassoon.'

'Where did you find a bassoon?'

'It's mine.'

'What about the neighbours?' said the short man. 'They've probably already called the police.'

'It's all right,' Alex said. 'I live upstairs.'

'And I live downstairs,' Steve said. 'I didn't just bring my bassoon on the off chance: nipped down to get it.'

'You live downstairs?' Alex said.

'Yeah. Nice to meet you.'

They shook hands.

'Isn't that a bit valuable to be bringing in here?' Alex asked.

'No, it's not one of the good ones. It's plastic,' Steve said. He put the reed to his lips and blew again.

Alex felt a hand on his shoulder. 'Time to go, I think,' Charlotte said.

'With your brother?'

'No, he left already.'

'I didn't see him. Everything all right? You want me to call you a cab?'

'I thought I might take my chances on finding somewhere to sleep upstairs here.'

'But I live upstairs.'

'Exactly.'

Alex woke while it was still dark, with a full bladder. On his way back to bed from the bathroom he took a detour to the kitchen for a glass of water, but also to savour his happiness, walking naked through his darkened flat, knowing he would soon be returning to his bed where Charlotte was lying naked and asleep. It was years since he'd felt so happy. He stopped by the sitting-room window, drew back the curtain and stood there with his glass of water, a pleasantly heavy post-coital ache in his groin, looking out at the night sky. There were no clouds and no moon, and despite the dirty sodium glow that London was blasting into space he could clearly make out Orion skipping across the rooftops. Going back to bed he paused in the bedroom doorway to look at Charlotte's sleeping form under his duvet. A trick of the light, or the angle she was lying at, made it look as though her head had mysteriously sunk into the bedside table beside his copy of *Swann's Way*.

*

The next time he woke it was light. There was a bird outside the bedroom window that sounded like a computer booting up, the rising whine of charging capacitors. Charlotte was gone, but her head, or rather hair, was still on the bedside table. The toilet flushed.

'You're out of loo paper,' Charlotte said, coming back into the bedroom. She hadn't put any clothes on, but he hardly noticed.

'Your hair,' he said.

She rubbed her bald head. 'What about it?'

'It's a wig.'

'I have several. You didn't notice last night?'

'I wasn't really paying attention. I just assumed it was your hair.'

'It's amazing how people don't notice.'

Her brother's solicitousness the night before suddenly made sense. 'It's growing back though,' he said encouragingly.

She looked blank.

'When did the, um, treatment finish?'

She burst out laughing. 'I haven't had chemotherapy,' she said, pulling on her clothes.

He turned away from her to slide out the other side of the bed into his boxer shorts and jeans, and to hide his blushes.

'I made a video a couple of years ago,' she said, 'of me delivering a monologue in a series of different wigs. I had to shave my head to make sure they sat properly. And then I was invited to a wedding and none of my dresses really worked with the shaved head so I wore one of the wigs – a ridiculous blonde, Marilyn thing – and everyone said how much they liked my hair. I sometimes wonder why everyone doesn't do it. They used to, obviously. It saves a fortune on shampoo and conditioner. What's for breakfast?'

'I normally have porridge,' Alex said, pulling a T-shirt over his head.

'Porridge is good.'

'You wouldn't rather have a fry-up? I think I've got bacon and eggs in the fridge.'

'I'm vegetarian. Porridge is good.'

There was a tiny hole in the index finger of his left washing-up glove. Water leached in as he scrubbed at the porridge pot. Charlotte was lounging on the sofa, taking CDs from the shelf and flicking through their inner sleeves. He wondered if he shouldn't feel more disappointed to have slipped so quickly into domesticity. They'd met not much more than twelve hours earlier and now here they were, much as he and Clare had been towards the end of their ten-year relationship. But it wasn't disappointing, until he felt disappointed in his lack of disappointment. And that, too, was disappointing: wasn't he old enough by now to be reconciled to his lack of a sense of adventure, to be happy to be comfortable? He finished washing up and took the gloves off. His left hand smelled like rotting apricots doused in vinegar. He threw the gloves away and washed his hands.

'Have you ever thought of getting a cleaner?' Charlotte asked.

'Not really. You think I should?'

'Yes. What are your plans for today?'

'Hadn't really thought about it. You?'

'I've thought about taking my hangover to the aquarium.'

'Feed it to the sharks?'

'If only. But at least it's dark, cool and quiet there. Or if you're not busy I thought I might hang around here for a while longer.'

'Oh great. Maybe we could go out to the aquarium together later. Or somewhere else? We should get a paper, see what's on.'

Charlotte didn't answer. She was eyeing the washing machine through the kitchen door. 'Your washing machine fetish,' she said.

'It's not a fetish.'

'It could be, though. Who would you like to be first: Ground Control or Major Tom?'

7

Chess

Charlotte had given Alex her phone number and email address before she left but when he sat down at his computer and hooked up to one of his neighbours' unsecured wireless connections to write to her, wondering what to say, he found himself googling her instead. She had an exhibition at a small gallery in Shoreditch. Finding himself with a free couple of hours one afternoon, he went to take a look. It would give him an excuse to email her, as if he needed one. More important, it would give him something to email her about.

He took out his wallet to pay the entrance fee but then realised there wasn't one. He smiled and nodded to the girl behind the reception desk (if that's what it was), who replied with a look he couldn't interpret. It wasn't pure scorn; perhaps she was trying to temper her scorn as she thought he might be there to buy something. How else to explain his suit? Or perhaps she was trying to disguise her hope that he would buy something under a patina of scorn. She looked back at her computer screen. She probably had no opinion of him one way or the other. He thought about asking her if the musical boxes were on display but said nothing and went in to the exhibition.

The first thing he saw was a red onion on a pedestal at waist height. He bent over to read the title, or description, or whatever it was. It said only: 'Please handle the exhibit'. He looked around, then picked the onion up. It was about the weight of a real onion but appeared to be made of fibreglass. He looked at it more closely. There was a hairline fracture running around its waist. It came apart. Inside the outer shell was another fibreglass onion. That came apart too. It was a matryoshka. Alex was reminded of the story about the peasant woman and the onion in *The Brothers Karamazov*. He would have to mention that in his email to Charlotte. Inside the seventh and final onion skin was a small glass phial with a red plastic lid. He took the lid off. The smell of onions hit him in the nose. Eyes smarting, he put the lid back on the phial, the phial back in the smallest onion and reassembled the matryoshka. He didn't know what to think about it but he thought that he liked it.

The only other object in the room was a red Giles Gilbert Scott phone box in the far corner. He went over to it and opened the door. The phone rang. He looked around, went inside the booth and picked up the receiver.

'Hello?' he said.

'What is your favourite colour?' a robotic female voice asked him. He wondered if it was Charlotte's voice heavily treated or pure computer software. 'What is your favourite colour?' it asked again.

'Green?' he said.

'What is your favourite animal?'

'Cat.'

'What is the first letter of your name?'

'A.'

'How old are you?'

'Thirty-two.'

'Thank you. Goodbye.'

The line went dead. He wondered why he'd told the truth, and who he'd told it to. 'Hello?' he said. Still dead. He hung up and left the booth.

In the next room were two huge silk screen prints. On one wall, a black and white photograph of a beautiful woman who looked very familiar but who he couldn't put a name to. He thought for a moment it might be Charlotte in one of her wigs, but it didn't really look like her. Whoever it was was talking on a mobile phone. He read the description. It was a composite portrait of Emily Brontë, Merle Oberon and Kate Bush, digitally merged. Its title was *Heathcliff? It's me, Cathy.* A pop-art joke, then, but also a comment on – or interrogation of, that's how he'd put it in his email – the changing forms of cultural transmission and technological development. He felt he was beginning to get the hang of this. He turned round.

On the opposite wall was a garish full-colour airbrushed photograph of a hairless vulva. Alex felt uncomfortable looking at it, as he imagined he was meant to. Relieved there was no one else in the gallery to witness his discomposure – his eyes made a furtive sweep of the corners of the ceiling for CCTV cameras – he went close enough not to be able to see the image anymore but to read about it instead. It was called *All Pornography Is Child Pornography 1*, and was another composite, this time of twelve photographs, one from every month of a year's run of *Playboy*. It wasn't exactly subtle, but subtlety clearly wasn't what it was aiming for. He took another look at the *Wuthering Heights* picture and went through into the next room.

There were two pieces, each again with a wall to itself, both video works this time. On the first screen, a small 1980s TV, Charlotte, wearing a horrible grey polyester suit, appeared to be reading from an autocue. He picked up one of the old-fashioned Bakelite telephone receivers that hung below the screen and pressed it to his ear. Charlotte was blankly reciting a series of numbers, letters, nonsense sounds and scraps of words. Alex peered at the description. The video was called *Pattern for Raglan Sleeve Boat-Neck Woman's Sweater*. Alex nodded to himself. There were some definite themes emerging here.

The second TV, a modern 32-inch flat screen, was blank, with a row of headphones beneath it. Alex put a pair on. The words 'Life Sucks' appeared on the screen. A sound like a rapid heartbeat pulsed in his ears. A breastfeeding baby appeared on the screen for a second, then a toddler with a dummy, then a small child with its thumb in its mouth, and so on and so up through older and older girls and women, sucking on drinking straws, lollipops, pencils, cigarettes, beer bottles, reefers, crack pipes, paper bags, penises, breasts, fingers, toes, clitorises, nicotine inhalers, salbutamol inhalers, hospital feeding tubes and breathing tubes, at which point the heartbeat, which had been gradually slowing throughout the video, stopped and the screen went black. It was at once one of the most infuriatingly crude things Alex had ever seen, and one of the saddest. So sad perhaps because it was so crude. And perhaps not, now that he thought about it, the way he would have chosen to begin to get to know the woman he'd slept with.

He quite wanted to leave, get some fresh air before heading back to the office, but there was only one more room with one more exhibit in it, and he saw no point in not being thorough. Also, he was still hoping to see the wigs video.

Most of one wall was taken up with a projection of a schematic representation of a chessboard, with a game in progress. On one side there was a close-up of a famous Russian chess player's face, concentrating in slow motion. On the other was a computer motherboard, presumably processing away – in slow motion? – though you couldn't tell that from looking at it. There was a running commentary in different voices, but it didn't seem to have much bearing on the game, either this one in particular or chess in general. 'Blue elephant, D27.' A black knight advanced. 'Grey squirrel, E46.' A white knight took the black knight. 'Purple platypus, G16.' The black queen took the white knight. 'Green cat, A32.' The sound of his own voice made Alex wince.

He had given up playing late-night backgammon against unreliable anonymous human opponents, and taken up playing chess against his computer instead, or rather against the piece of software that came free with his new laptop. Gratifyingly, or absurdly, it wouldn't give up and resign, even when it was reduced to its king alone against his queen and a pawn on the seventh rank. Playing as white, he was now consistently able to defeat the machine on level seven, having found a way to thwart its Sicilian Defence, but he was making slow progress against it on level eight. The computer's infinite patience, however, along with its perfect memory and its not caring about winning, meant that, even after checkmate, he could rewind the game, undoing his moves until the point at which he first went wrong. And it still amazed him, amateur as he was, how much difference it could make whether white or black went down a tempo during the opening moves, how early a game could be lost. He was also intrigued by the way the software, on lower levels at least, sometimes seemed almost to panic if its king or queen was put under pressure. Had that been programmed in, he wondered, or was it simply that making the best move possible in an impossible situation couldn't help but look like panic?

'Blue dog, H33.'

Alex recognised that voice.

'Hello, Alex,' it said in his ear. 'What are you doing here?'

'Hello, Henry,' he said turning round. 'I could ask you the same thing.'

'I'm in London for work stuff,' Henry said. 'Had a meeting in Hoxton, saw this was on, thought I'd drop in.'

'You know her work?'

'Yeah, she's really good I think. This is very clever. The match is Kasparov against Deep Blue, from 1997. The game that Kasparov accused IBM of cheating in.'

'You recognise it?' Alex wasn't sure he could handle Henry's having quite so many hidden depths. Modern art *and* chess?

Henry waved a folded sheet of paper. 'I've read the catalogue. Did you watch *Life Sucks*? I saw it last year, it's the piece that made me a fan. You know it's eighty seconds long and the heartbeat gradually slows from the average rate for a newborn to an eighty-year-old's before it flatlines at the end? It's really neat. Surprised to see you here though. Shouldn't you be at work?'

'Slow day, bunked off.'

'That happens to lawyers?'

'It has today.'

'So here we are, skiving off together. Just like old times.'

They looked each other in the eye, as if each of them knew the other had a secret and was daring him to reveal his first.

'Just like old times.'

'You got time for a drink?'

Alex bought the third round while Henry went to the toilet. Back at their table in a snug corner, he took out his phone to check for messages. He didn't have any so decided to text Charlotte. 'Just been to see your show,' he thumbed. 'Great stuff.' He needed to get a new phone, he thought, as he thought almost every time he used this one, especially if he was slightly drunk. The buttons on it were too close together, and half of them were too sensitive, the other half not sensitive enough.

'You need to get back to the office?' Henry asked.

Alex hadn't noticed him come back. He pressed send and put his phone away in his pocket. 'No, it's fine,' he said. 'You heard from Clare lately?'

Henry shook his head and took a slurp from his pint. 'Thanks for this. You?'

'We're not exactly communicating. But I've been, um, triangulating her movements – not entirely on purpose, it's just the way Facebook works – from other people's comments on her updates, or on photos she's been tagged in. She seems well. I was briefly worried last September, when she was in Bolivia for the Carancas impact event.'

'The what?'

'A meteor strike on the border with Peru. The Peruvians

thought it was a Chilean missile attack at first. People who went to look at the crater got arsenic poisoning. But Clare was fine, obviously. On the other side of the country at the time. Not that I care, obviously.'

'Of course you do.'

'Yes, of course I do. How's Vic? Jessica?'

'They're well, thanks. Listen, I still don't quite understand what you were doing at the gallery. I never took you for a modern art lover.'

'I could say the same about you.'

'But you'd be wrong.' Henry's eyes lit up. 'Was it meant to be a date? And she stood you up?'

Alex smiled. 'No. But you're on the right track.'

'You want to tell me about it?'

He both did – it wasn't often that Alex got the chance to score points off Henry, sexually speaking – and didn't: his relationship with Charlotte was none of Henry's business.

'You know what that chess game reminded me of?' Alex said. 'I was given my grandfather's old chess set for my birthday when I was seven, maybe eight. It was beautiful. I loved it: the smooth shiny wood, the look of the grain, the feel of the polish, the smell when you took the lid off. But I didn't have anyone to play against a lot of the time. My dad might give me a game on a Sunday afternoon, but otherwise I'd spend hours playing with it by myself. I invented this game, that the white king was leading all the other pieces through a labyrinth to escape some unseen pursuers. So the white king stepped onto the board, on a corner square, then moved one space forwards, and the black king stepped on behind him, then I moved the white king forward one, then the black king, then the white queen came onto the board, and so on, up and down

106

the files like an airport security queue. The last pawn to move from one file to the next shut the door behind him.'

'You big freak,' Henry said, before draining his pint. 'Another drink?'

'Don't you have to get back to Kent?'

'At some point, but not urgently. You're the busy one.'

'Give me a second.'

Henry went to the bar while Alex phoned his secretary.

He woke up on his sofa, mostly sober, some time after midnight. His suit was crumpled and stank of stale booze. He'd have to take it to the cleaners. He brushed his teeth, drank a pint of water, took his clothes off and fell into bed. The pillows were soft and cool. Before drifting off to sleep he checked his mobile to see if Charlotte had replied to his text yet. She hadn't. He checked his outbox to make sure his message had been sent. It had. He reread the message. He wondered what he'd been thinking when he told her to get stuffed.

8

Ping

Often, in the first weeks of Jessica's life, Vic, half-asleep, had imagined she was holding another baby in her arms. She could feel the weight of it. On a deeper level, she knew that Jessica was hiccupping, honking, mewing, sighing, snorting, snuffling, whimpering, whinnying and yawping in the cot beside her. She knew that she could drop the dream baby without consequences. But on an even deeper level she couldn't let go. She tried, irrational in her semi-conscious state, to rationalise this: perhaps she was wrong. Perhaps she could be wrong in future. What if she were one night to mistake Jessica for the dream baby? She had to protect the dream baby to be sure of protecting Jessica. She had to protect them both. One morning she tried to tell Henry about the dream baby. He said that if it would help then Jessica's cot could go on his side of the bed for a few nights. She said it was okay and didn't mention it again. They didn't move the cot.

She hadn't held the dream baby for months now. But the

memory of it came back when she woke in the early hours of the morning on Jessica's first birthday. The house was quiet. Henry was breathing into his pillow. Jessica slept in her own room these days, just across the landing from Henry and Vic, and, most of the time, she slept through the night. Vic slipped out of bed, crept to Jessica's door and pushed it open. If she held her own breath she could hear her daughter breathing.

Easter had been difficult, at Henry's parents' house, with Jessica waking every forty-five minutes through the night for three nights in a row, and Henry and Vic exhausted, anxious and baffled as to what the matter could be, until finally at three o'clock in the morning on Easter Sunday she had dropped off for a solid six hours. Henry and Vic slept through Henry's father's tempestuous breakfast preparations, the clash of saucepans resounding fruitlessly through the house. When Jessica finally stirred there were two drops of blood on her pillow; the cusps of her first molar had erupted through her gum.

And now here she was, a year old, almost to the hour, almost to the minute, with nine teeth, able to stumble about unaided, and with a precocious vocabulary of perhaps half a dozen words, and tufty blonde hair that made her look like a duckling. The ghost baby was as remote as the howling red monkey who, in its first moments of life, laid there by the midwife, had done a press-up on Vic's shoulder, Jessica's formidable first act as an airbound, breathing creature. She rolled her head against the mattress, snuffled and sighed. Vic crept away to the bathroom, peed, headed back to bed. It was silly to be awake and up in the night if she didn't need to be. But she stopped again by the landing window, lifted the curtain, looked out at the clouds scudding through the moonlight, remembering the yoghurty stink of a newborn's dirty nappies.

She wrapped her dressing gown tighter round her, surprised, as she still occasionally was, by the thickness of her upper arms, which had bulked out like a butcher's daughter's from carrying Jess. She tried to be philosophical about the way her body had changed in pregnancy and motherhood, but sometimes couldn't help regretting it, feeling some mornings as if she'd woken up in her mother's skin.

Jessica's grandfather spent the morning of her first birthday inflating balloons in the playroom. 'Give your father something to do so he doesn't get in the way trying to help,' Vic's mother had said. So Vic had given him a pack of balloons and asked him to blow them up. Jessica sat on the floor at his feet and watched him. Vic leaned in the doorway and watched them, the child enrapt by the man's slow, methodical movements. He took a green balloon from the packet and stretched it between his hands. Holding the nozzle between the thumb and finger of his left hand, he pressed it to his lips and blew, cupping the swelling balloon in the palm of his right hand which he moved steadily away from his face, as if playing a mime trombone. It almost looked like he was inflating the balloon not with his breath but with his hand. He took the nozzle away from his mouth, stretched it, wrapped it around the index and middle fingers of his left hand and fed the end through the loop between his fingers, pushing it with his left thumb then taking it between the finger and thumb of his right hand to pull it tight. He let go; the knotted nozzle sprang back into place with a light thud.

'Balloon,' Vic's father said, and held it out to Jessica.

'Boon!' Jessica said, trying to grab it, knocking it away and gurgling with laughter. She lunged after it and fell sideways. Her eyes widened and her lips quivered as she thought about crying. But her grandfather picked her up and gave her the balloon and she forgot about falling over. The balloon floated out of her hands. She clapped them, still such a recently learned, endearingly effortful gesture. Watching Jessica grow was a constant reminder to Vic of how many of the things that her own body could do she took for granted (as well as how much was beyond her: imagine having the flexibility of a toddler). And she thought, not for the first time, about what it would be like when her parents started to lose the abilities that Jessica was only now learning. When her father would no longer be able to blow up and tie knots in balloons. One morning, a few years before he died, her grandfather had suddenly found himself at breakfast unable to solve a single clue in the crossword he had completed every day for sixty years.

'I thought you wanted to have a shower,' Vic's mother said, bustling out of the kitchen.

Vic went upstairs.

'Everything okay?' she called downstairs when she came out of the bathroom. No reply: she assumed everything was fine. She went to the bedroom to dry her hair and get dressed. She didn't dry her hair very often these days, partly because it was so hard to find the time; and partly because it was such an effort, physically. The hairdryer her mother had given her to take to university had burned out shortly before Jessica was born. Henry had bought her a replacement as a gift. The enormous box was waiting for her on the kitchen table when

they got home from hospital. Henry must have read somewhere that it was important to give new mothers presents for
themselves, reminders that they were adult women, human
beings as well as milk machines. He must have gone for the
most expensive hairdryer he could find. It had more settings
and attachments than anyone could ever need. And it was
huge – so huge that it would have been obvious to anyone
apart from Henry that it was designed for hairdressers to use
on other people. Drying your own hair with it was as unwieldy
as eating with a caterer's soup ladle, or shooting yourself in
the head with a sniper rifle. Hair dry, arm aching, Vic got
dressed and went downstairs.

The playroom was awash with balloons, dozens of them.
Vic's father was still on the sofa, blowing up another one,
Jessica still at his feet.

'That'll probably be enough now, Dad,' Vic said.

'Oh, okay, love. You know me, once I get into a rhythm.'

Henry came home with the cake. He'd gone into Tunbridge
Wells to get it from a patisserie recommended, he said, by one
of his clients. Vic's mother had offered to make one but Henry
had said she was doing enough already. He put the elaborately
wrapped cake in the fridge, went through to the playroom
and picked Jessica up. 'Dannad boons,' she said.

'So I see,' Henry said. 'Nice work, Trevor. She put you up
to this?'

'No, Vicky did. I think with her mother's encouragement.
Something to keep me busy.'

Henry put Jessica down and picked up a balloon. Holding
the knot between the index finger and thumb of his right hand,

he closed the index finger and thumb of his left hand in a ring around it. Then he pulled the knot as far back as it would go, stretching the neck tight like the elastic on a catapult, the body of the balloon braced against his left hand, and released it. The balloon shot into the air, hit the ceiling and drifted to the floor. Jessica was delighted. Henry tried to get her to fire the next one herself, but their hands and fingers got all tangled up. So he manoeuvred a small Windsor chair – Vic's old teddy bear usually sat on it, but had been taken to their bedroom for safekeeping until after the party – into the middle of the room and showed Jessica how to pull the knot of a balloon between two of the bars and shoot it that way. She staggered backwards into Henry's arms and shrieked with laughter.

'Ping!' Trevor said.

'Pim!' said Jessica.

'Lunchtime,' Vic's mother said from the doorway.

They ate pasta with tomato sauce. The penne were overdone. Vic pushed hers around the plate with her fork. Jessica threw hers on the floor. Trevor ate his in silence. Henry said: 'That was absolutely delicious, Linda. Thank you. Is there any more?'

Jessica started crying.

'You can finish mine,' Vic said. 'Come on, you.' She lifted Jessica bawling out of her high chair. 'Time for your nap.'

Drying up, Trevor said: 'You know what? I think I could do with a nap too.'

'Coffee?' Henry suggested.

'I'd love one,' Linda said, shaking the suds from the washing-up gloves before peeling them from her fingers.

*

At three o'clock, the doorbell rang. 'Shit,' Vic said. 'I'm sure the invitations said four o'clock. Maybe it's a delivery?'

It wasn't.

'Laura! Marcus! Hi!' Vic said to the mother and child on the doorstep. 'Come in! Jessica still hasn't woken up from her nap I'm afraid. But come on in.'

'We're early, aren't we,' Laura said. She was clutching an oversized, garishly wrapped parcel.

'No! Bang on time. Everyone else is just running late. Us included.'

Marcus was older than Jessica: nearly two. Unless he was already two and Vic had missed his birthday. But surely you weren't expected to remember your neighbours' children's birthdays if they didn't invite your child to their parties. Vic had invited all the children in the village under three whose parents she chatted with at the playground. Jenny, Jamie's mother, she counted as a friend. The others she barely knew, though like many of the people in the village, she knew plenty about them, or about their reputations: the planning disputes, the rumours of adultery, alcoholism, drug use, debt, domestic violence.

The man who was said to hit his wife was Andrew, Laura's husband, Marcus's father. Vic had thought about going to the police when Jenny had told her, but Henry had pointed out she didn't have any actual evidence. She'd once called the police out to a loud domestic dispute going on in the tower block opposite her flat in London. It was a hot summer afternoon and everyone had their windows open. After a while a patrol car turned up, siren blaring. The fighting couple fell silent. The police rang Vic. 'Did you call us out to a domestic disturbance?'

'Yes.'

'Well, we're here and everything seems quiet.'

'They stopped when they heard your siren.'

Peering out the bedroom window, hoping no one could see her, she told the police which flat she thought it was and watched them go into the building. After a while they came out and drove away. The shouting started up again. 'Getting the fucking old bill on me now are you, you fucking bitch?'

So that had been a waste of time. And she hadn't reported Laura's husband to the police, not even after the time she noticed bruises on Laura's neck. But Henry had given up going to the pub with Andrew, and started taking more interest in Marcus than in Jessica's other colleagues, as they called the toddlers she spent her mornings with; 'friends' seemed too strong a word.

Vic wondered what the neighbours said about her and Henry behind their backs. She wouldn't like to be known as the village snitch, but could cope with being thought of as a stuck-up Londoner, if only because she knew she wasn't one, not really. She was secretly looking forward to introducing her neighbours to her parents, who had made the journey that morning not from West Hampstead but from East Grinstead. And it had seemed simpler in so many ways not to invite any of their friends from London. Especially not Henry's.

Vic's father, like Jessica, was still asleep, but her mother had put the kettle on to boil as soon as the doorbell rang. On her first holiday home from university, Vic, irritated by her parents' shuffling old familiar ways, had sneered that her mother was the 'high priestess of suburban sacraments'; she still regretted saying it. Linda poured Laura a cup of tea in the kitchen. Henry and Marcus were in the playroom, mafficking among the balloons.

'I'm teaching Marcus the principles of ping,' Henry said.

Marcus fired a balloon from the Windsor chair.

'He seems to have got it.'

The baby monitor squawked. Vic turned it off and went upstairs to get Jessica out of bed.

By half past four the playroom was swarming with children. A head count appeared to show that there were only six of them, but with all the adults, too, and the folk-rock nursery rhymes pounding out of the stereo (a present from somebody; Vic couldn't remember who), it felt like a lot more. The melee seemed ready at any moment to spiral into total chaos, with injuries. Vic caught Henry's eye, with evident panic in hers.

'It's brightening up,' he said. 'Why don't we all go out in the garden?'

The pandemonium continued outside, but it was more widely dispersed; there were fewer sharp corners at infant eye-level, and the shrieks of the children, instead of bouncing off the low ceiling and ricocheting around the room, were carried off into the air and diluted with birdsong. One of the older boys was peeing in the hedge. Henry was lumbering across the lawn after Jessica, who was scurrying and laughing ahead of him. She fell over and burst into tears. He scooped her up and smothered her with kisses. Jenny came over, towing Jamie by the hand. 'It's World War Three out there,' she said. 'And a weapon of mass destruction has backfired in this one's nappy. May I?'

Vic smiled. 'Of course. We've set up a changing station in the downstairs toilet. There's everything in there: mat, wipes, bidet, towels, clean nappies, bum cream. Whatever you need.'

Jenny raised her eyebrows. 'I'd forgotten about the bidet. If you're not careful we'll be round here every time he shits himself. Come on, you.' She tugged her son stumbling into the house.

Vic tuned into the conversation of two of the mothers she didn't know so well, wondering if she could join them, but they were talking about last Sunday's church service. Vic wondered if Jessica was the only unbaptised child at the party. Henry's father sometimes referred to her as 'the little heathen'. Henry insisted that this was affectionate of him, but Vic wasn't so sure. Henry's parents had, thankfully, declined the invitation to Jessica's birthday: it was too far to come from Gloucestershire without staying a couple of nights and they had some unavoidable lunch the next day. They'd sent a card. 'Have a wonderful day darling,' Henry's mother had written. 'Present to follow!'

Henry's father had signed off, as he always did, with the words 'optimus quisque'. The first time Vic had got a card from them she'd had to ask Henry what it meant. 'It's Latin for "all the best",' he said. 'But not in that sense.'

The churchgoers' sons, officially best friends, were clubbing each other round the head with plastic lorries, tears of rage streaming down their cheeks. 'Should I?' Vic asked their mothers.

'Oh Christ.' They leapt up together and hurried over to intervene.

Vic's mother came out. 'Cake time?' she asked.

'Probably a good idea.' They surveyed the garden together. 'What did you do for my first birthday, Mum?'

'I made a cake, chocolate sponge I think, your father came home from work early, we sang happy birthday, and when you were in bed I expect he opened a bottle of something.'

'Great idea,' Henry said, joining them. 'Why don't I uncork some champagne?'

'Where is Dad?' Vic asked.

Years earlier, when her grandfather had died, as soon as the phone rang, even before she woke, she had known that it was her father calling to tell her he was dead. She had reached out from beneath the covers and pressed the button to reject the call. Then she got up, went through to the living room and called him back. It was cold out of bed. Outside, the sky was thick with one of those dark and foggy London winter pre-dawns. A thin frost rimed the barren pots on the roof terrace. Her father answered the phone quickly, apologised for waking her. When he told her that her grandfather had died, she couldn't think of anything to say except: 'I know.' Why else would he be ringing her at that time in the morning? But she had known even before he rang. It had come to her in a dream. And she knew that that was impossible, unless the sound of the phone ringing, which could only be her father calling to tell her that her grandfather had died, had sparked it in her unconscious. So she said simply 'I'm sorry,' and arranged to go home for Christmas a couple of days sooner than she'd planned. She didn't cry. An hour or two later she was in the kitchen, looking out as the cold grey December light settled over North London, waiting for the kettle to boil, her breath condensing on the glass. She remembered Auden's line about Yeats disappearing in the dead of winter. The words snuck up on her from behind her eyes. Surprised by grief, she had cried then.

No words and no tears came to her now. Her mother had

found him, unresponsive on the bed in the spare room, stretched out on top of the bedspread in his socks. His shoes, neat and unobtrusive, were side by side at the foot of the bed. One of the paramedics had stumbled over them coming into the room. Vic had called the ambulance. Henry had apologised to the guests and sent them all home with a slice of cake. Now he was with Jessica in the garden.

Vic went to the bathroom, locked the door, peed, washed her hands, dried them, looked at the frosted window pane. A time would never come when she would have to phone Jessica at six in the morning to let her know that her grandfather had died. The only grandfather Jessica would ever know would be Henry's father, who hadn't wanted to come to her first birthday party. The grandfather who had blown up all those balloons for her wouldn't be even a distant childhood memory, not even a false memory conjured by old photographs. Vic hadn't taken any pictures of the two of them playing together that morning. The sound of the shutter would have distracted Jessica, who'd have come tottering over to smear the screen with dribbly fingers. Better for them to have spent the time absorbed in each other's company, even if Vic was the only one who would remember it.

The paramedics had gone through the motions of trying to revive him, though they must have known it was hopeless.

'But his feet are still warm,' Vic's mother said.

'I'm afraid his heart stopped some time ago.'

'Are you sure? Isn't there anything you can do?'

'I'm afraid not. I'm very sorry.'

'But feel his feet. They're still warm. Can you feel them? They're still warm. He's still warm.'

The paramedics shook their heads. They asked Vic's mother

a series of questions: was he her husband, had he seen his doctor in the last two weeks, did he have any known medical conditions.

'Yes he is,' she said. 'Yes he has . . . Does it matter?'

'I'm afraid it does make a difference, yes. It makes a difference to what happens next. Did he have diabetes, high blood pressure, heart disease?'

Vic's mother looked at her. 'He didn't want to worry you,' she said.

While they were waiting for the funeral director's van to come from East Grinstead, Henry gave Jessica her bath and put her to bed. He had paused at the bottom of the stairs before carrying her up. 'Is the door closed?' he muttered to Vic. She nodded. *He didn't want to worry you.*

Her mother put the kettle on and cut them each a slice of cake. 'It won't help to go hungry,' she said. Vic forced it down for her mother's sake. Her mother didn't eat hers, or drink her tea. A meniscus formed on the surface as it cooled.

Once, when they'd been staying at her parents' when Jessica was still very small, very early in the morning, she'd taken her downstairs to feed her in the kitchen, in a chair next to the boiler. It was too cold upstairs, and Henry was snoring. Her father had joined them in his dressing gown, put the kettle on. 'Hope I'm not disturbing you, love.'

'She's more or less fallen asleep again.'

He pottered about, making himself a mug of tea. 'Can I get you one?'

'No I'm fine, thanks. I'm going back to bed in a minute.'

He sat down at the kitchen table. 'I remember,' he said, 'one morning like this, when you were no bigger than she is now, your mother feeding you in that chair by the stove. Of course, it was before we had the kitchen redone, so it was the old stove, not the gas boiler. It was cold upstairs, so she came down to feed you in the warmth. And I couldn't get back to sleep, so I came down and joined her. Joined you. Made myself a cup of tea, and her one too. And we sat here, not talking, but all together, just the roar of the stove, and a few birds maybe singing in the garden. It wasn't always easy, when you were a tiny baby. But I remember that morning, very fondly. Happy days.'

She'd wondered how her mother remembered it, if at all. If her father hadn't happened to tell her about it, no one now would know about it, or what it meant to him. She had no memory of it, obviously. She tried to think of the earliest thing she could remember about him. She took a gulp of tea, glanced at her mother's face, turned away, unable to bear how old her mother looked. She'd aged ten years today.

Vic tried to think of something to say, but found her mind skating pedantically over the surfaces of words – 'funeral director' was a mealy-mouthed expression, but then 'under-taker' had been a euphemism once – and so said nothing. She thought she ought to stop thinking such trivial thoughts, and tried to focus instead on the way she was feeling, but she couldn't access her feelings because her mind was too busy with thoughts. She thought about the way she couldn't tell what she was feeling, or if she was even feeling anything. She watched her mother clearing the table and thought she ought to do something. A draught from the open window in the playroom blew one of the balloons across the hall into the kitchen. Vic picked it up and went out into the garden.

The sun had set but it wasn't dark yet. 'Well, the nights are drawing in,' her father always said on 22 June. It wasn't pessimism; just a bad joke. He always said, 'Well, the days are getting longer,' on 22 December, too. There were still a few weeks to go till midsummer. The day's warmth lingered in the crepuscular air. She untied the knot of the balloon, careful not to pierce the fragile skin with her nails, remembering the way her father had shown her to tie them when she was a little girl, wrapping it round her index and middle fingers and pushing the end through the space between them with her thumb before pulling it tight and withdrawing her fingers. Holding the neck between her finger and thumb, she slowly released the air. It made a sound like a fart, or perhaps a death rattle, though Vic had never heard a death rattle. She had been downstairs or outside with her mother and her husband and her daughter and her daughter's friends and their parents, and her father had been alone upstairs. He'd have heard the sounds of the barely contained chaos thrumming through the ceiling, or through the open window. Perhaps he'd thought about calling out, to let them know he was in pain, but didn't want to disturb them. Or perhaps he did call out and they didn't hear. Or perhaps it happened too quickly for him to have time to call out, or to realise what was happening. Who wouldn't fail to recognise that unimaginable moment? She was holding the neck of the balloon too tight for the last of the air to escape. She relaxed her grip. Her father's breath rushed out with a sigh.

A memory came to her then, of sitting on the child seat on the back of his bike, whizzing down a country lane in sunshine, but it must have recently rained because the tarmac was slick with water. She saw sunlight dancing off the surface of the shallow ephemeral stream, heard the zip of the water spraying up off the tyres and onto her legs. She had held on tight but felt no fear, only pure excitement, enveloped in a sense of safety as pervasive and imperceptible as the air.

9

Tennis

Clare turned right at the bottom of Camberwell Grove and stopped at the pedestrian crossing. Waiting for the lights to change she watched the cars and buses creep along Camberwell Church Street. She was sure there hadn't been so many road-coloured cars before she'd gone away. But now that she was back in London every other vehicle seemed to be a German-made banker's wagon camouflaged to blend in with the tarmac. It didn't seem safe, for anyone: for pedestrians or cyclists or other drivers or the drivers of the road-coloured cars themselves. Whose idea had it been? And why had it spread so widely and rapidly? There were even more road-coloured cars than there were bendy buses. She had disliked the bendy buses when they'd been introduced, and travelling in the back half made her feel sick, but since the new mayor had vowed to abolish them she'd found her opinion swinging, like the back half of a bendy bus, back the other way, in favour of them. The lights changed. The pedestrian crossing was blocked not by a sixty-foot bendy bus but by a road-coloured car. Clare walked in front of it and scowled into the windscreen, resisting the urge to thump the bonnet. Its high-performance engine – wasted on these streets, in this traffic, yearning for the mythical freedom of the open road – growled at her.

She'd been back in England a fortnight. She'd rung her parents from Heathrow to ask if she could stay with them for a week or two, just while she sorted herself out and looked for somewhere to live in London. 'Don't be silly, of course you can,' her mother had said. 'If you'd let us know when you were landing we'd have met you at the airport.'

'I know,' Clare said.

'Well you really didn't need to worry about putting us out. It wouldn't have been any trouble.'

'I know. Sorry. I'll see you in a couple of hours I should think.'

'Well what time does your train get into Guildford? We can meet you at the station.'

Clare hung up.

She lasted less than a week at her parents' house. The problem was partly her parents themselves, hovering warily around her as if she were a convalescing invalid, their disappointment in her failure to make a decent adult life for herself ineffectively disguised as concern for her well-being. Her mother couldn't help observing how thin she was and offering her more to eat, or feigning interest in her 'round-the-world adventures' without waiting for an answer, or asking how the job hunt was going and had she got round to ringing Jacqueline yet? Her mother seemed to think it was merely a question of phoning up her former boss and asking for her old job back, but things wouldn't have been that simple even if she'd wanted it, which she didn't. Her father would frown and nod and smile sympathetically and say to his wife: 'Let's not bother her about it, dear' – a feeble tactic to ingratiate himself with his daughter, which if anything she found even more irritating than her mother's fussing. In response to both, Clare slouched and grunted and fumed, and resented her parents for making her act – and feel – like a fourteen-year-old.

But that may have been been less their fault than the fault of her childhood bedroom, where she was sleeping, or rather lying awake at night and dozing fitfully through the morning, the heat of the sunlight beaming in through the thin curtains baking her brain on the hot, lumpy pillow, a crow clattering outside her window like a football rattle. Her brother's room had been refurbished as a guest bedroom, with a double bed and neutral furnishings, and that's where she and Alex had slept at either Christmas or Easter, the alternation rigidly observed, for ten years. But now that she was single again her mother had put her back in her old single bed. The room had changed in some ways – Clare's posters and photographs had all come down from the walls and been replaced by gloomy prints salvaged from her grandparents' houses – but not in others: same old bed, same old bedding, same old curtains, same old carpet, same old wardrobe, same old chest of drawers. And either way it was all horribly familiar and all awful. A feeling she hadn't had since she was a teenager – of undirected frustration strong enough to make her cry, a free-floating urge to create something but she had no idea what – descended on her every time she went into the room and closed the door, and nothing could dispel it. The limited distractions available – crying, reading, writing, masturbating – all only made it worse. She'd once gone downstairs to play the piano, which

126

her parents had paid to have moved back into their house after Clare and Alex had sold up, but her mother had been so pleased and so patronising that she hadn't touched it since. So she lay on the floor with her headphones in, listening to the Cure and fantasising about putting her fist through the window pane.

After three nights like that she rang Jacqueline, not to ask for her old job back but to see about somewhere to stay in London. Two days later she woke up from her best night's sleep in months, in a small bedroom on the top floor of a tall house on Camberwell Grove, to the sounds of blackbirds, traffic and children going to school that jostled in through the gaps around the badly fitting sash window.

But beyond the borders of Camberwell, London was far from reassuring. The first sign that something was wrong had been the cute new cartoons on the Tube announcing that alcohol was banned and asking passengers to be considerate of each other. On the face of it, the notices were entirely reasonable, but there was something offensively gratuitous about both their mere existence and their appeal to a conservative suburban sense of decency. Most people who travelled by Tube or bus most of the time were both considerate and tolerant of their fellow passengers, unlike the hordes who elbowed you out of the way as they ploughed towards the bar at the Barbican or the Opera House. And it was their man who was now mayor.

The city seemed to have half shut down while she was away. The Tube was plastered with the usual adverts for film, theatre, dance and art, and with nothing else to do Clare scoured the listings magazines that were strewn about Jacqueline's kitchen, but couldn't find anything she'd have liked to go and see even if she could have afforded it. The shops in and around Covent Garden were filled with an incoherent mix of crusty-revival maxi skirts and porno heels; most of the window shoppers were white women in leggings and floaty floral tunics, which would have looked fine if they'd all been eight years old rather than thirty-eight. They almost made Clare's retreat into adolescence feel relatively mature. The latest series of shockingly popular vampire novels leered out from a bookshop window display. She turned up the Nirvana on her mp3-player and walked on.

What she was feeling, she told herself, was perfectly natural, the culture shock of coming home after a long absence: it would eventually pass, and London would begin to feel normal again. But she wasn't sure she wanted it to feel normal, and much as she disliked feeling the way she did, she also feared losing the insight that all was not well with the city.

She didn't stray north of the river again, apart from a visit to her old hairdresser in Camden Town, but restricted her wanderings to a narrow rectangle of Southwark, from Peckham Rye in the east to Ruskin Park in the west, Dulwich Park in the south and Burgess Park in the north.

The playground in Brunswick Park was heaving with children. She'd forgotten it was Saturday. She sat on a bench not too close to the swings and watched them running and screaming and shoving and snatching, learning how to live among people who didn't love them and would happily hurt them to get their own way. Clare didn't want children, never had.

Actually, that wasn't quite true: walking down Guildford High Street one Saturday afternoon when she was eighteen, a few weeks before taking her A-levels, she'd seen one of the girls who'd left school after GCSEs sitting at a window table in a cafe, breastfeeding. Clare had stopped and stared from the far side of the road. The girl, intent on her baby, hadn't noticed her. The envy jabbed Clare in the gut, like being winded. She hugged her arms around herself, around the absent baby she wasn't holding because it didn't exist, or because it was at its mother's breast behind the window in the cafe on the far side of the road. Clare didn't just want a baby, she wanted that baby. She wanted to be that girl she'd hardly ever thought about when they were at school together and never since, but who appeared to have found complete happiness by doing the one thing that Clare had been repeatedly, reliably told would ruin her life. Clare knew about the sleeplessness, and the expense, and the impossibility of finding time to do anything else. And being a sensible girl, she knew she could wait to have children till she'd gone to university, and started a career, and settled down with a suitable man, and had enough money. So she did all those things, and the right time to have children arrived, only for her to discover that the urge that had been so overwhelming on that Saturday afternoon in 1994 had completely disappeared.

Not that anyone believed her when she told them. She never volunteered the information, but people would ask – at least, when she'd still been together with Alex they would – and when she gave her stock response, that if it happened it happened but she really wasn't fussed if it didn't, they'd smile and nod sympathetically, as if to say they understood that what she really meant was that she was desperate for a baby but having no luck conceiving. It was exasperating. Most of the time, people were only too willing to assume Clare meant exactly what she said, especially if they were able to take offence at it. But not when it came to babies. Her more in-sensitive friends – insensitive whichever way you looked at it – asked her to be godmother to their children. Having refused the first of them, she had to refuse them all. She told them she didn't believe in God, but they couldn't see why that should matter and assumed she was being tactful, which she was, but not in the way they imagined. It wasn't that being godmother to someone else's child would only make her own childlessness harder to bear: it was that if she didn't want to be burdened with children of her own, she certainly didn't want to be burdened with any responsibility, however token, for anyone else's. But obviously there was no way to tell the solicitous parents that.

The first girls at school to have sex had made sure to tell the virgins that they couldn't imagine what they were missing, that life only really began with virginity's end. Now they were at it again. But while silencing their goading had seemed as good a reason as any for Clare to have sex with her fifth-form boyfriend, having children really did look as if it actually was life-changing, and not in a way that she either wanted or was ready for. Not anymore.

A child was causing a hold-up at the top of the slide. The child behind him gave him a shove. The pusher fell backwards and slithered headfirst down the ladder, landing in a crumpled, wailing heap on the ground. His minder rushed over to him. The pushee slid calmly down the slide and slunk off towards the swings. Clare turned away and looked towards the tennis courts.

Immediately after leaving Alex, she had seen him every-where, like a dead person: glimpses of his fringe through the window of a bus or of his shoulders stooped over a shopping trolley disappearing round the end of an aisle at the supermarket. His ghost had followed her across the Atlantic but she'd thrown it off her trail somewhere between Nashville and Mexico City. Evidently it had withdrawn to London to ambush her on her return.

Except that man on the tennis courts wasn't simply someone who looked like Alex out of the corner of her eye but on second glance resolved into a perfect stranger: he really was Alex, playing tennis against a woman who from this distance looked weirdly like Steffi Graf. Clare felt an old familiar wave of irritation rise up in her. She'd been very careful to avoid anywhere in the city she'd have any chance of running into Alex, and yet here he was, in the last place in London she'd have expected to see him, almost as if he'd done it on purpose. She knew this was unreasonable of her, which only made it more irritating. As did the fact that he was playing tennis, with apparent equanimity. The only times she'd ever tried to play tennis with him – many years ago now, admittedly – he'd flown into a rage of frustration as soon as he started losing, which was very soon. He insisted he was angry only with himself for playing badly, but that didn't make it any less impossible to share a tennis court with him. But there were no such problems today, either for Alex or for the woman who looked rather less like Steffi Graf now that Clare had had more of a chance to take a good look at her. Perhaps she was giving Alex a lesson.

It was Charlotte's serve. They'd been playing for half an hour, mostly just knocking the ball across the net or, in Alex's case, into it. But after twenty minutes or so of that, Alex, inspired by an especially flukey forehand down the line – who could say where that topspin had come from – had suggested they play 'an actual set or two'. Charlotte, who said she had played at school but not much since, was the more consistent player, sending the ball reliably over the net and into the back half of the court, but never too fast and always within reach of Alex's racket. Alex hit the ball out half the time, but when his shots went in they could be tough to return. So he imagined their styles would balance each other out and they could have a decent match, with him winning, say, 6-4.

Charlotte won the first game easily, but since she was serving that was as it should be. And she served well: no aces, though Alex hit three of his returns straight into the net, and barely clipped the fourth with the frame of his racket. It wasn't just that Charlotte served well, however; it was also that Alex couldn't help watching her rather than keeping his eye on the ball: the flex of her calves, the arc of her back, the tilt of her chin, her body sprung like a recurve bow in the still moment before loosing, the flick of her blonde ponytail – was there any chance her wig might fall off? – as she struck. 15-0. 30-0. 40-0. Game.

They changed ends. Occupying the space where Charlotte had stood only minutes earlier, Alex tried to fit his body into the shapes she'd made, imagining her ghostly template in the air. He fired two balls into the net.

'First double fault doesn't count,' Charlotte said. 'First serve.'

'Okay. Thanks.'

His next serve flew straight into the fence behind her. His second second serve went into the net again.

'You're trying to correct the mistakes you made on the previous serve and overcompensating,' Charlotte said. 'Forget what's gone before. Just concentrate on doing it right.'

He took another ball out of his pocket and shuffled to his left. 'Very helpful,' he said. 'Love fifteen.'

The game wasn't a total washout: he didn't win any points but at least at 0-30 he managed to get his second serve in. He was still quietly celebrating to himself when Charlotte knocked it back down the line with a solid forehand. Lunging for the ball, he clipped it with the frame of his racket and sent it spinning off into the next court. Alex had been doing his best to ignore the boys playing there. They must have been about fifteen; three black, one white. If Alex allowed himself to imagine the contempt he supposed they must feel for his inadequacy on the court, his game would go so utterly to pieces he wouldn't even be able to lift the racket. They knocked the ball back. 'There you go, mate.'

'Sorry,' Alex said.

'Thanks,' said Charlotte.

He quickly served out the game with a double fault. There was one ball left in his pocket. He tossed it high in the air and swung his racket behind his head. Without really paying attention to what he was doing, he sent the ball hard and fast into the far corner of the opposite service box. 'Ace!'

Charlotte didn't notice. She was collecting the balls strewn around the bottom of the fence, pincering each one between her racket and the outside edge of her foot then flicking it up, bouncing it once on the ground with her racket, collecting it in her other hand and putting it in her pocket. 'What's that?' she said. 'Two love?'

She won her second service game as easily as her first. That was fine. He was only a break down, and as he had demonstrated, if only to himself, he was in fact capable of delivering unreturnable serves if he didn't put his mind to it. The trick was finding a way to trick himself into believing it didn't matter. But every serve that didn't go in only made it seem to matter more, and eight wasn't enough to crack the problem. 4-0.

'If you want we can just go back to hitting the ball around,' Charlotte said. 'Or to the pub. Or home.'

'It's your serve,' Alex said. Time to lower his sights. If he could win just one game, his next service game, that would be enough to salvage his sinking pride. The new target was to lose 6-1. All he needed to do for now was keep his eye on the ball and try to get it over the net, to recover his cool and reserve his strength for his serve, in which he had suddenly regained an inexplicable confidence.

But things started to go wrong with that plan almost immediately. Charlotte's first serve went long. Her second dropped plum in the middle of the box, with no spin on it. Alex had plenty of time to attack it with caution, and sent it unanswerably back across court. She took the next point easily enough. But at 15-15 she hit a simple forehand return into the net. Her concentration seemed to have wandered from the court, drifting off somewhere past Alex's right shoulder. The game went to deuce. Alex's advantage. Double fault. 4-1.

'Get stuffed,' Charlotte said.

Alex smiled.

He'd phoned her in an apologetic panic the morning after seeing her show, his drunkenly mistyped text message at last giving him the momentum he needed to call her.

'Hello?' She sounded bleary.

'Sorry to wake you up. And sorry about my text. Great stuff. That's what it should have stuff. I mean, what it should have said. Not get stuffed, obviously. I meant, great stuff.'

'Who is this?'

It turned out she hadn't even checked her phone. And when she did, it made her laugh, and gave her an idea. 'You could have a whole installation based around predictive texting gone wrong,' she said.

Best of all, 'get stuffed' immediately became their shibboleth, a way of complimenting each other that no one else could understand, an instant token of familiarity. Alex soon gave up counting the number of times they'd been out together, the number of times they'd had sex. He spent as much time in Camberwell these days as he did in Islington, though she often stayed over at his place, too. When there was nothing else to do in the evenings they'd go to the pub with Ed, the three of them as comfortable together in their way as Alex, Clare and Henry had once been. And here they were, playing tennis, and he was even happy she was beating him.

Or possibly not. Alex was now only one break down. He was back in the game. Perhaps he could win the set. They changed ends. Preparing to serve, he looked around to see what could have put Charlotte off her game. A man and a woman in their late twenties, wearing expensive tennis shoes, were sitting on a bench beside the courts, rackets leaning against their knees, reading the weekend papers and drinking coffee from outsize cardboard cups with plastic lids. On the far side of the park, the playground was swarming with children, a colourful, indistinct blur of shrieking prepubescence. But it had been like that when they arrived. He drew his focus back into the court, glaring first at the opposite service box, then at the ball he was bouncing at his feet. 'This ball,' he told himself, 'in that court.' He threw it high above his head, watched it hang in the air at the still peak of its trajectory, momentarily weightless. As it began to drop he swung his racket towards and through the point of their intersection. The connection was true. The ball flew along its preordained vector, hit the top of the net and dribbled over.

'Let,' Charlotte said. 'First serve.'

He tried again.

She won eight points in a row.

'Six one,' she said. 'Our hour isn't up yet. You want to keep going?'

He shook his head.

'It's all yours,' she said to the couple on the bench.

'Thanks.' They folded away their newspapers, drained their coffee cups and looked around for a bin. 'You can stay on if you like,' the man said. 'Play doubles?'

'Alex?' Charlotte said. 'What do you think? Doubles? Could be fun.'

He looked at her wig, the way she'd tied it back in a big, high ponytail so she looked like a professional tennis player from the mid-nineties. He looked at the strangers' expensive tennis shoes. He looked at his watch. 'It's a nice idea,' he said, 'but I think we'd better get going.'

'Enjoy your game,' Charlotte said.

On their way out of the park, she asked him the time.

He looked at his watch.

'I thought so,' she said.

'Doubles? Hardly.'

She laughed.

'Thanks for letting me win that one game,' he said.

'Let you win? Fuck off.'

'What happened then?'

'You played well.'

136

He gave her a sceptical look.

'And there was a woman over by the playground who seemed to be watching us. And not just in a casual passer-by sort of way. More like a murderous stalker. It was slightly off-putting. But she disappeared while we were changing ends.' She shrugged. 'I don't suppose she was watching us at all, really. But you know how once you get an idea in your head?'

Alex nodded. 'Pub?' he asked.

'Shower,' she said.

When Clare got back to the house on Camberwell Grove, Jacqueline was putting make-up on in front of the mirror in the dining room. She paused with the mascara wand, as if using it to lift her eyelid, and looked at Clare's reflection. 'Natural light,' she said. 'If I do this in the bathroom I go out looking a total hag.'

Clare nodded.

'I'm going to a party. With Paula.' Jacqueline and Paula had been seeing each other for years, without ever making any public declarations of their relationship or, as far as Clare knew, even thinking of moving in together. It seemed like a very civilised arrangement. 'There's some cold stir-fry in the fridge. You're welcome to it, or anything else.'

The doorbell rang. Clare offered to answer it. Jacqueline smiled, shook her head, and went out to the hall tipping her head first to one side, then the other, as she slotted in her earrings.

'Sorry to be early,' Paula said.

'I'm glad you are. We can have a glass of wine before we go. You're not driving, are you?'

'Cabs all the way.'

'Great.'

Paula followed Jacqueline into the dining room.

'You know Clare, don't you, Paula?'

She was taller than Clare remembered, slimmer too, and had a better haircut. 'Of course,' she said. 'Nice to see you again. Jacqueline mentioned you were staying with her for a bit. How are you? How was your holiday in Cambodia?'

Clare wouldn't have figured Paula for a Dead Kennedys fan, but you never could tell. People could change a lot in twenty-five years. 'Good, thanks,' she said, with an ironic smile. 'You know: slums, soul, the whole package.'

Paula smiled approvingly.

'What about you?' she said, trying to remember which government department Paula worked at. Work and Pensions, she thought. 'Still devising new ways to kill the poor?'

Paula laughed. 'Nice to know young people today still have some sense of tradition. Were you even born when that record came out?'

'Absolutely. We played pass-the-parcel to it at my fifth birthday party.'

Jacqueline was frowning. It occurred to Clare that flirting with her host's girlfriend was perhaps a mistake. Paula didn't seem to have noticed, or if she had noticed, didn't care. 'What are your plans now you're back?' she asked. 'Writing a novel?'

'You must be joking. I spent too many years dredging through slush piles to even think about it. Anyway, I haven't got what it takes to write a novel. I mean, if I thought I could write something that I wouldn't be embarrassed to show you, Jacqueline . . .'

Jacqueline raised her eyebrows. Crude flattery wasn't going to cut it. Time to change the subject.

'What I'd really like to do,' Clare said, 'is start a magazine. A quarterly, or maybe less often, with long-form reporting – and stories – but no memoir, no poems. Each issue would have a vaguely unifying theme, based around a word with multiple meanings: "Battery", would be one, where you could have articles on mobile technology, and the war in Congo, and lithium-mining in South America, and European poultry farming.'

'And the history of siege warfare,' Paula said.

Clare smiled. '"Soap" could be another. And the magazine could be called something like 'eyebrow, with a' – she drew an apostrophe in the air with her finger.

'An eyebrow?' Paula said.

'Yes. And an apostrophe. The big problem of course is finding funding.'

'Well that's one problem,' Jacqueline said.

'Interesting,' Paula said. 'Do you have any magazine experience?'

Jacqueline looked at her phone. 'We're going to be late. Shall we?'

'Yes, absolutely,' Paula said, standing up. 'Nice to see you again, Clare. I hope everything works out, whatever you decide to do.'

Clare was woken the next morning by the sound of the front door being shut: Paula leaving. She went down to the kitchen. Jacqueline was sitting at the table in her dressing gown, eating toast and reading the paper.

'Morning,' Clare said, going to the fridge for orange juice.

'Fucking reviewers,' Jacqueline said. 'I hope you're going to eat something too. There's some fresh bread in the machine if you want toast.'

'In a minute,' Clare said. 'Thanks.'

Jacqueline put the newspaper down. 'Please don't take this the wrong way, Clare, but all that talk last night about your future got me thinking. This whole melancholy flaneuse thing is fine for now, and no doubt necessary, but it can't go on indefinitely. Barbara's going on maternity leave in three months. The job's yours if you want it: six months definitely, maybe a year. And if you do want it, I can send some freelance copyediting and proofreading your way now. So you can start earning something, and looking for somewhere more permanent to live. Coffee?'

10

Village Cricket

'Alex? Henry. I wondered if I could ask you a favour.'

'Possibly,' Alex said.

'I'm getting an eleven together for a game of cricket on Sunday.'

'Oh no, I couldn't. I haven't played since I was ten, and I was terrible then. I didn't wear my glasses in case they got broken and I couldn't see the ball before it was inches from my face. Terrifying.'

'You should have taken it up again when you started wearing contact lenses. But don't worry, I'm not asking you to play.'

'Oh. Phew.' Alex hoped he didn't sound disappointed.

'No, we need someone to keep score. Would you? It's a friendly game, we're not in a league or anything, so there's nothing riding on it. You can just copy whatever the other team's scorer writes down. They're a bit more organised than we are. And there's a free tea in it for you. Strawberries and champagne, and Vic's mother's in the kitchen baking like crazy as we speak.'

'Well in that case . . .'

'There's no need to be sarcastic. It'll be fun.'

'Okay,' Alex said. 'Why not?' As he always ended up going along with whatever Henry wanted him to do, the sooner he gave in, the sooner he could convince himself that it was what he wanted, too.

He rang Charlotte. 'What are you doing on Sunday?'

'You tell me.'

He rang Henry back. 'Okay if I bring someone on Sunday?'

'Of course. There'll be more than enough cake. Who?'

'Great,' Alex said. 'See you then.'

They met at London Bridge station on Sunday morning. Alex had been expecting to stay over at Charlotte's on Saturday night, but she said there was something in the studio she wanted to get finished and that she would be working till very late. She was waiting for him in the middle of the concourse, wearing a wig he hadn't seen before – long, red, wavy – a blue summer dress and a straw hat. 'Do I look the part?' She kissed him. 'What time's kick off?'

'Play starts at two, but we're going for lunch at Henry's first. How'd it go last night?'

'Hmm?'

'In the studio, the project you wanted to get finished.'

'Oh, yes, good, thanks for asking. Do we need to get tickets?'

He took the train tickets from his wallet and offered one to her.

'You hang onto them,' she said. 'I haven't got any pockets and if I put it in my hat band it'll clash with my hair.'

'You don't have a bag?'

'What for?'

They took a taxi to the village from Tunbridge Wells station. Henry answered the door. He took Alex's hand and gave him a hug and thanked him for coming, but barely looked at him, because he was staring at Charlotte's wig.

'This is Charlotte,' Alex said. 'Charlotte, Henry.'

'Rita Hayworth,' Henry said.

Charlotte smiled and nodded approvingly. 'Very good.'

'Come in,' Henry said. 'We're in the kitchen. End of the hall, turn left before the stairs.'

Charlotte went first.

'You sly fucker,' Henry said to Alex as he shut the door. 'So that's what you were doing at her show. Where did you two meet? When?'

'The week after we went to her exhibition. I wrote to her to tell her how much I liked her work.'

Henry raised his eyebrows.

'The week before. At a party of my downstairs neighbour. We were pretty much the only people not doing coke, so it kind of brought us together.'

Henry smiled. 'Nicely done.'

The sound of laughter rippled down the hall.

'Come on,' Henry said.

In the kitchen, Vic and Charlotte were sitting at the table, which was set for lunch. They stopped laughing when Henry and Alex came in. Vic's mother was at the counter by the sink, chopping cucumbers. Jessica was sitting on the floor by the fridge, chewing on the brim of Charlotte's straw hat.

'Take that out of your mouth,' Henry said.

'Don't bite your bus ticket,' Vic said.

Jessica took the hat out of her mouth.

'Oh, I don't mind,' Charlotte said.

Jessica sank her teeth in.

Vic stood up so Alex could kiss her cheek. Her mother put the knife down and turned round, wiping her hands on her apron.

'Alex, this is my mother,' Vic said.

'Linda,' Vic's mother said.

Alex shook her hand. 'Hello. We met briefly at Vic and Henry's wedding.'

'Of course,' Linda said, evidently not recognising him. 'Nice to see you again.'

Alex looked at the blue cats decorating her apron. 'I'm very sorry about' – he couldn't remember Vic's father's name – 'your husband.'

'Thank you,' Linda said. 'Trevor.'

'Trevor, of course. I only met him once, again at the wedding, but he was . . .' What could he say? Vic's father had been totally unmemorable. And what right did Alex have to tell the man's widow what her husband had been like? 'He seemed a very nice man,' he said. 'I remember his speech, very clearly.' It had been inaudible, but mercifully brief. 'Very well judged, I remember.'

'Thank you,' Linda said. 'Have a seat.'

Alex sat down, relieved he didn't have to say anything to Vic about her father because he'd sent her a card soon after it happened. That was one of the reasons people sent bereavement

144

cards, he now realised: to make it less awkward the next time they met.

'Gin?' Henry offered. 'Wine? Beer?'

'Anything but gin,' Charlotte said.

'Beer,' Alex said.

'So who's playing?' Charlotte asked.

'Yes,' Alex said. 'How did you manage to scrape together an eleven? I didn't even know the village had a cricket pitch.'

'It doesn't. We're playing away. It's not far: only ten minutes down the road. The other captain's a bloke I met on the train.'

'And your team?'

'Oh, you know, guys from the village. Some of the other dads. A couple of blokes who work behind the bar at the pub. The guy who runs the post office, and his sons. The policeman. A couple of teachers at the primary school. And the rector's coming as our umpire, so we have to be finished in time for him to get back for evensong.'

'Who'd have thought such a sentence would still be possible in the twenty-first century,' Alex said.

Henry's phone buzzed and chirruped on the counter. 'Jim mate, hi,' he said, putting a finger to his other ear and walking out into the hallway.

'Daddyphone,' Jessica said, getting to her feet and staggering after him. Vic intercepted her and scooped her up into her lap. Jessica pointed at Henry and stuck out her lower lip. It quivered.

'Hey, don't cry,' Vic said, jiggling her knees.

Charlotte picked her hat up off the floor, balanced it precariously on her head and leaned forwards. Jessica grabbed the brim and pulled the hat off Charlotte's head. They both laughed. Vic joined in. It made Alex more pleased than he could say to see Charlotte getting on so well with Henry's family.

'Bad news, Alex,' Henry said coming back into the kitchen. 'You're going to have to play after all. Jim from the pub has to work this afternoon.'

'But I haven't got any whites. And who's going to score if I play?'

'I will,' Charlotte said.

'You're not helping.'

'Yes she is,' Henry said. 'Don't worry. I can lend you the kit. You can bat seventh and field at cover. You won't have to do anything except stand around and look sexy in my clothes.'

'Seventh? Why not eleventh?'

'Have some dignity. No one will think you're sexy if you're batting eleventh and not bowling, however gorgeous my whites are.'

Linda put an enormous bowl of salad in the middle of the table. 'Lunchtime,' she said.

Henry, Alex and Charlotte cycled to the cricket ground. Vic, Jessica and Linda were planning to follow by car once Jessica woke from her nap. Alex was gratified to watch Henry toiling up the gentle slopes as he and Charlotte breezed along behind, even though Henry was on a gleaming new machine with at least thirty gears and full suspension and Alex was on Trevor's old three-speed butcher's bike, which was lacking a few pounds of air in its rear tyre.

As they came over the crest of the final hill and descended freewheeling towards the village, the wind billowing in their shirts and the smell of fresh cut grass in their nostrils, the banal idyll of the cricket pitch unfurled before them – faded wicket, sparkling sight screens, pavilion, white-clad Hornby figures milling about, rusting grass roller, church spire rising behind willow, poplar and oak.

Henry made the introductions. Alex smiled and said hello to everyone without paying attention to their names. Charlotte gave Alex a kiss on the cheek, told him to break a leg and headed off to the scoreboard with her opposite number, who, grinning sweatily, all too obviously couldn't believe his luck. Henry gave a brief rundown of tactics, fielding positions and batting order while one of the schoolteachers – Alex thought he might be called Phil – unloaded a modest selection of bats, gloves and pads from the boot of his ageing hatchback. 'For those who don't have their own equipment,' he said, throwing Henry a ball. Henry caught it in his left hand, flicked it across to his right and tossed it on to someone else. The players passed it among themselves with serious nonchalance, while Alex concentrated on hoping no one would throw it to him. They didn't.

The umpires summoned the captains. Henry lost the toss. Their hosts elected to bat first. Henry deployed his field. 'You're fine there,' he said to Alex, hovering uncertainly a few feet away, before turning to consult in murmurs with the teacher who may or may not have been called Phil but, what-ever his name was, was due to open the bowling. Henry stood back. The facing batsman tapped his bat against his boots and looked up expectantly. The bowler began his run-up. Alex, keeping his eye on the ball, steeled himself to try and catch it if it came his way. The bowler released the ball. The batsman stepped forward and raised his bat. The ball bounced and flew past him. The wicket keeper – Will? – stepped to one side and scooped it out of the air then tossed it to the nearest fielder, who passed it on to the next, who, as Alex watched, horrified, threw it on to him. He fumbled it, dropped it, but at least it didn't break any of his fingers. He picked it up out of the grass and chucked it to Henry, who plucked it from the air with a smile, cursorily inspected it, rubbed it on his trousers and threw it to the bowler.

It didn't take long for Alex to realise that no one expected him to do anything much, or cared about his clumsiness. After each over he traipsed dutifully across the field to take up position at the other end of the wicket. He moved forwards or backwards or left or right as Henry instructed him. He joined in the appeals for LBW, and the celebrations when the home village's umpire awarded their first wicket (Henry's rector seemed to be making an unreasonable virtue of not favouring his own team). He got comfortable with the ritual relay of returning the ball to the bowler. He made a show of running for balls that were struck past him, but someone else always raced ahead and got there first. Whenever he looked over to the scoreboard in the hope he could catch Charlotte's eye, she was always either focused on what was happening on the wicket, or scribbling in her notebook, or conferring with the other scorer, or changing the numbers on the scoreboard in a way that reminded Alex of Carol Vorderman on *Countdown* – clearly much better at the job than he would have been. The scoreboard was like a giant, erratic digital clock, with runs, overs and wickets instead of seconds, minutes and hours.

A huge shout went up. Alex looked round. Henry was charging at him. Alex scurried away backwards, tripped over his heels and fell over. Henry dived towards him. The ball dropped into Henry's outstretched hand. But as he closed his fingers around it, it popped out, like a bean being squeezed from a pod. He grabbed for it with his other hand but knocked it away towards Alex, who lifted his hands defensively to his face. The ball crashed into his solar plexus, winding him. He instinctively brought his hands down to his gut and curled up while he struggled for breath. It didn't help that he was suddenly surrounded by cheering men slapping him on the back and rubbing his head.

'Great catch,' Henry murmured in his ear.

'Couldn't have done it without you,' Alex wheezed, struggling to his feet and tossing the ball to Henry.

'Did you see that?' Linda asked.

'What?' Vic said, retying the ribbon of Jessica's hat under her chin.

'Henry and his friend made a sort of double catch. I wonder who it will be awarded to. Or do they both get it? Your father would have known.'

Vic looked up at the celebrating fielders. 'Whoever ended up with the ball,' she said. 'So probably Henry after Alex fumbled it.'

'I think it may have happened the other way round,' Linda said.

'Dolly pushchair,' Jessica demanded.

Vic opened out the toy pushchair and strapped Jessica's doll into it. Jessica seized the handles and marched off.

'Away from the cricket pitch, dear,' Linda said.

Vic hurried over to turn her round before she reached the boundary rope.

'Your father would have enjoyed this,' Linda said. 'He could have been umpire instead of the rector.'

Vic didn't say that, if her father had still been alive, he'd have been nowhere near this cricket pitch but at home in East Grinstead, as would her mother. For a few weeks after he died, Jessica had continued to talk about him, saying 'dannad boons' whenever she saw a balloon, but she didn't anymore. Vic hadn't noticed when she'd stopped. It was like the swallows going south at the end of the summer: one day you noticed they weren't there anymore, but couldn't say when they'd left.

A car door slammed. Vic looked towards the car park. Jenny appeared round the end of the hedge, pushing Jamie on his tricycle. She waved. They waved back. 'Look, Jessica,' she said. 'Jamie's coming.'

Jessica looked, then steamed off in the opposite direction, towards the scoreboard.

'I thought this would be less work than the pushchair,' Jenny said, struggling over the final few yards. 'Christ, what a nightmare. The little despot thinks he's too grand to pedal.'

'He's still a bit young, isn't he?' Linda said.

'Hello, Linda. That's just what they want us to think. Don't believe any of it. Mind if we join you? After all that I managed to leave our rug in the car. Where's Jessica?'

'Checking up on the scorekeeping,' Vic said. She and Linda shuffled about on the picnic blanket to make room for Jenny, Jamie and their M&S cooler bag. Jenny sat gratefully down. Jamie remained resolutely on his tricycle. 'PUSH!' he shouted.

'If you're not careful I'll take the handle off and throw it away. Then you'll be forced to pedal.'

'PUSH!'

'Come and have some juice and a biscuit.'

He half clambered, half fell off the tricycle. Jenny unzipped the cooler bag, stabbed a straw into a box of orange juice for Jamie and cracked open a ready-mixed gin and tonic for herself. 'Can I interest either of you in one of these marvels of modern science?'

'I'm driving,' Vic said.

Linda shook her head.

'You're driving? You should make Henry drive back. That's part of the deal with Will. He gets to come and play cricket as long as he drives us home afterwards.'

'Henry's on his bike.'

Jenny raised an eyebrow towards Linda.

'Really, I'm fine,' Vic said.

'How are we doing?'

'It's the last over,' Linda said. 'They're 183 for 6, with three balls left. Your postmaster's taken most of the wickets.'

'Yes, Will said he has a reputation as a crafty spin bowler.'

They watched his stately run-up. The ball dropped short; the batsman leaned back and pulled it for four.

'A reputation that's perhaps not entirely deserved,' Jenny said.

The postmaster bowled again. The ball bounced in the same place. The batsman repeated his swing. But the ball snuck beneath his bat and struck the middle stump.

'Crafty as hell,' Jenny said. 'I can't believe they're shutting the post office.'

A new batsman walked out to face the last ball of the innings, and then it was tea. Henry and Will joined their families. 'Well played,' Jenny said.

'When did you get here?' Will asked, sitting down next to her.

'About five minutes ago.'

He laughed and kissed her cheek. Jamie squeezed his box of juice, squirting a thin spray of orange onto his father's white trousers. Will took the box away, grabbed his son by the ribs and tickled him into a frenzy.

'Where's Jessica?' Henry asked.

Vic pointed. Jessica and Charlotte were walking towards them hand in hand; Alex was trailing behind, carrying the pushchair with the doll still strapped into it.

'She likes you,' Vic said as they reached the blanket.

'We have an understanding,' Charlotte said, releasing Jessica's hand.

'Come and sit with Granny,' Linda said.

'No.' Jessica went over to Henry and clung tightly to his leg.

Linda unpacked the hamper and coolbox: vast tupperware boxes crammed with cold strawberries, a 12-inch chocolate cake, three litres of homemade lemonade and a stack of plastic cups.

'What a spread,' Henry said. 'Shall I open the champagne?'

Linda unsheathed a knife, cut a slice of cake, put it on a cardboard plate with a paper napkin and plastic fork, and passed it to Charlotte. 'Here you go, dear. Will Jessica and Jamie have a slice of their own or will they share their mothers'?'

'I'm not sharing mine,' Jenny said. 'There won't be any left for me. That's lovely. Thank you.'

'Shall I open the champagne?'

'We didn't bring it,' Vic said. 'Lemonade?'

'Does he want it cutting into smaller pieces?'

'I'll do it. That's perfect, thanks.'

'What do you mean you didn't bring it?'

'There wasn't room in the coolbox. It's fine. We'll have it when we get home.'

'Now who still hasn't got cake?'

'Not for me thanks, I'll stick to strawberries.'

'I dragged Alex down here with the promise of champagne.'

'It really doesn't matter.'

'Delicious lemonade, Linda. So refreshing.'

'Ready-mixed gin and tonic?'

'Lemonade's perfect.'

'No it isn't.'

'I didn't bring the champagne, Henry, because I know from long and unhappy experience what happens when men start drinking in the afternoon. You have a cricket match to finish – I daren't say "win" – and you'll need your wits about you. Lemonade?'

'Fine, yes, lovely, Linda. Thank you.'

Jenny put the gin and tonic back in her cooler.

'Dad didn't drink in the afternoon,' Vic said. 'I mean, not like that. You said, on Jessica's birthday, about my first birthday . . . What are you talking about, "long and unhappy experience"? Mum?'

Linda pursed her lips, quickly shook her head, and prised the lid off one of the strawberry boxes.

'Great catch you two,' Will said.

'Thanks,' Henry said. 'I don't know what I'd have done if Alex hadn't been there.'

'Caught it cleanly by yourself I should think,' Alex said.

'Now now, this is no time for modesty.'

'How many catches did you make, Will? Three, was it? Or four?'

'Three.'

'He had those bloody great gloves to help him though,' Jenny said.

The rector approached with the remains of a cucumber sandwich in his hand. 'If you're ready, Henry, I think we'd better get on.'

Alex drained his lemonade.

Alex watched the opening overs of their innings dutifully from the benches outside the pavilion, but after the first wicket fell and Henry went in to bat, his restlessness got the better of him – or his social awkwardness; he was once again not feeling part of the team, especially since everyone else, beneath their dismay at the fallen wicket, was failing to conceal their hope of getting a go with the bat, which was the last thing Alex wanted – and he took off for a stroll along the boundary. He hadn't gone far beyond the scoreboard when he almost tripped over a small brown dog snapping at something it had dragged out of the hedge, which looked like some kind of tiny albino rodent, dead and bloodied. He peered closer. 'Oh Christ,' he said, looking round in a panic for the dog's owner. 'That could kill you,' he said to the dog. The dog took no notice. 'Excuse me,' he shouted to the field. 'Whose dog is this?' He tried to grab its collar but it ducked away. 'Come on, spit that out.'

'What's going on?' Charlotte appeared at his elbow.

He gestured helplessly at the dog. She knelt down, took its lower jaw in her left hand, looked into its eyes, murmured soothingly and tugged gently at the string coming out of its mouth. The dog released its prize with a whinny of devotion. 'Where's the nearest bin?' Charlotte asked. 'The pavilion?'

154

'I think so. Thanks.'

They set off towards the pavilion with the dog at their heels.

'Who throws a tampon away in a hedge?' Alex asked.

As if in answer, the dog scampered back to its hunting grounds and reappeared shortly with a bloody condom dangling from its mouth. 'Oh, fuck. Hold that,' Charlotte said.

Alex took the end of the tampon string between his fingertips and held it at arm's length.

'It's only a tampon,' Charlotte said.

'Yes, but whose?'

Charlotte rolled her eyes. 'Do you have a tissue?'

'Good idea.' Alex dug one out of his pocket and was about to wrap the tampon in it when Charlotte took it from him and extricated the condom from the dog's teeth.

'A condom needs a tissue but a tampon doesn't?'

'Twice the fluids and no string. So yes.'

They carried the gory relics to the pavilion and dropped them into a bin.

'Apart from the littering,' she said, 'they're quite cheering signs really.'

'What do you mean?'

'Well, whoever they were, they used a condom and weren't put off by a bit of menstrual blood. Good for them. You know what Jenny said to me earlier? That she couldn't believe how much time she'd wasted not having sex before she had children. She's funny.'

'She is.'

She gave him a look he couldn't quite read. 'I should get back to work really. The arcana of cricket scoring are completely fascinating.'

Alex watched her go. When she sat down he lifted his eyes

to the scoreboard. The fourth wicket had just fallen; Will was making his way out to join Henry at the crease.

'Alex! There you are,' said the teacher whose name was probably Phil. 'You need to pad up.'

'On my way,' he said. 'Though you never know, maybe that's a winning partnership out there.'

'Unlikely,' Phil said.

Sure enough, on the last ball of the twentieth over, Will was caught in the slips. They were 94 for 5. Alex walked out to a thin round of applause. He hadn't felt so exposed since the school concert in 1991 when he'd botched his clarinet solo. The unfamiliar box pressed uncomfortably between his legs. Will, coming the other way, raised his hand. Alex tried to high five him. 'Well played,' he said.

'Not really, but thanks. Good luck. Here, you'll need some gloves.' He handed them over. 'And look out for that outswinger.'

Henry was waiting for him in the middle of the wicket. 'Ready?' he asked.

'Not really, but as I'll ever be.'

'You're not facing, so there's nothing to worry about. Just be ready to run. We're out of batsmen now, so the main thing is not to concede another wicket. We're unlikely to win but at least we can avoid a lower-order collapse. Especially since they've exhausted their best two bowlers. Only run on my signal. And unless it's the last ball of an over we're only going to run if we can get two. And we'll go for a single at the end of each over, so I'm always facing. Understand?'

'Sounds perfect.'

And, for a while, the plan worked very well. They made thirty runs off four overs, the most successful partnership of the innings. Alex, though still on zero, couldn't help but feel he was contributing as he ran dutifully up and down the wicket on Henry's command after each lusty blow over the infield. Henry made a half-century. As he raised his bat in celebration, acknowledging the quiet applause, the bowler had a quiet word with his captain, who made a few slight adjustments to his field. The next delivery, the last of the over, was unexpectedly slow. Henry's mistimed leg-side drive was stopped at mid-on. The batsmen were nearly halfway down the wicket.

'Go back!' Henry shouted.

Alex stopped and turned. The fielder was poised to throw the ball at his stumps. He would never make it in time. Better, though, for him to be run out than Henry. And perhaps he would make it. Perhaps the fielder would miss. He ran, raising his eyes to the wicket as he touched his bat to the crease. The bails were intact. He turned to smile at Henry. But Henry was walking to the pavilion, his stumps in disarray, the wicket keeper mobbed by jubilant fielders. The rector at square leg had his finger raised in a mockery of benediction. Over.

The postmaster was approaching. Alex went to greet him mid-wicket.

'Have you faced a ball yet?'

'Actually, no.'

'You'll be fine. You've been out here long enough. Defend your stumps. Otherwise let it go past unless you're sure you can clobber it. I'm not much of a runner.'

Alex watched the bowler thundering towards him. He flinched. The ball flew past him. He managed somehow to block the second delivery and, beginning to get his eye in, struck the third through mid-wicket for four. His confidence swelled. He tapped the bat against his feet, fixed his gaze steadily along the wicket to the ball in the bowler's hand. Time for another four, just like the last one. The ball was short and wide outside off stump. Alex went for it, but the ball clipped the top edge of the bat and was caught by the wicket keeper. Walking back to the pavilion, he glanced over to the scoreboard. Henry was bending over with his hands on the table, leaning in close to Charlotte's chair, sharing a joke: they were both laughing. The other scorer was frowning over his paperwork.

'A catch and four runs,' Henry called, straightening up. 'You're better than you say you are.'

'On paper,' he said.

'Get stuffed,' Charlotte smiled.

Alex shrugged. 'I should get these pads off.'

They lasted five more overs, putting on another 37 runs, mostly thanks to the postmaster, who hit six fours and a six before he was caught on the boundary. But it wasn't enough. The visitors were all out for 161. 'Very respectable,' was the general verdict on their performance, as the players shook hands and slapped each other on the back.

'Well played everyone,' the rector said. 'Must dash.' The way he didn't expect any of them to join him was almost admirable.

'Coming for a pint?' the home captain asked, magnanimous in victory.

'Jessica needs to get home,' Vic said. 'And there's that champagne in the fridge.'

'Next time, I'd love to,' Henry said. 'Thanks, mate. Come on, Jess. Let's get you in the car with mummy and I'll race you home.'

*

After dinner Henry and Alex went outside for a cigarette and what was left of the second bottle of champagne.

'You want one?' Henry offered.

Something about the summer evening, or having spent the afternoon playing cricket, even though he'd never played as a teenager, took Alex back to being fifteen, and summer evenings of surreptitious smoking. 'Fuck it,' he said. 'Why not.'

They sparked up.

The old familiar but long-forgotten headrush took Alex by surprise. He blinked, looked at the tip of his cigarette to steady himself. 'When did you take up smoking again?' he asked.

'Shortly after Vic's mother moved in.'

'Must have been a difficult time.'

'Yes, it was. Terrible for both of them.'

'It must be difficult for you too, though. I mean, if you want to be selfish about it for a moment, that's fine with me.'

'It hasn't been easy. I mean, of course I liked Trevor. We got on well, and I suppose I loved him in a way, because he was Vic's dad. But it obviously doesn't compare.'

'And how are you coping with having Linda in the house?'

Henry shrugged. 'I don't mind. We get on quite well, to be honest. It's tough on Vic though. You'd think it would be helpful having her mother around, but she doesn't like it. What?'

Alex was giving him a puzzled look. 'I seem to remember you found it very difficult when Vic's mother came to stay with you when Jessica was born.'

'Did I? Maybe. It's fine now though. Amazing how much difference getting enough sleep can make. Jessica goes through the night now, most nights. Some days I almost feel young again. What time's your train?'

'The last one's at 10.15.'

'We should get moving then. I like her, by the way. Charlotte, I mean. Thanks for bringing her to meet us. It means a lot.'

Charlotte was unusually quiet on the train back to London. Alex asked if anything was wrong. She shook her head. He tried to cheer her up with self-deprecating stories about his lack of prowess on the cricket pitch.

'It's annoying, isn't it,' she said at last, looking out the window, arms folded.

'What? Being no good at cricket? Not really.'

'No. My not laughing at your jokes.'

'That's okay. I suppose they're not very funny.'

'They're funny enough. Just as funny as usual.'

That stung. 'Fine. I'll be quiet. Just let me know when you're ready to tell me what's wrong.'

She looked at him. 'I can't believe I never noticed before today. But you're the only person I know who never laughs at my jokes.'

'I think you're very funny.'

'You think that because I laugh at your jokes.'

'I laugh at your jokes too.'

'No you don't.'

He didn't know what to say. He laughed.

11

Pool

The first time Henry had run away from his marriage – the dry run, the dress rehearsal – back when Jessica was just over a month old, he went to see the (soon to be ex) husband of the last woman he'd slept with apart from his wife, though that wasn't how he usually thought of Alex. He told Vic he was going to London for work and would be staying overnight, packed his essentials in an overnight bag – wallet, passport, phone, USB memory stick, sunglasses, change of clothes – kissed his wife and daughter goodbye, and walked out.

Alex didn't answer the doorbell. Henry shouted through the letter box, peered through the front window (there was a faint rectangle on the far wall where the piano used to be), looked at his watch, thought about phoning, thought better of it and sat down on the doorstep to wait. A dark grey cat passed by, paused at the gate, gave him an affronted look as if to ask what he was doing there, and went on its way.

*

In those first weeks and months after Clare had left Alex, when he was still living in the house they had shared, he had come home from work every day hoping to find her waiting for him on their doorstep. (He still thought of it as 'their' doorstep; she didn't. She'd left her keys on the kitchen table when she moved out.) But he couldn't immediately place the silhouette that confronted him that evening as he slouched home from the Tube station, because although familiar it was entirely unexpected. He stopped at the gate.

'Henry? I'm so sorry. I completely forgot you were coming.'

'No you didn't. You didn't know.'

'I didn't? Oh. Phew. Unless – what are you doing here? Is everything okay? Jessica? Vic?'

'They're fine,' Henry said. 'I've left them, though.'

'Just you then.'

'Looks that way.'

Alex nodded. 'In town for work?'

'In theory.'

'Need somewhere to stay?'

'If that's okay?'

'Come on in.'

'Thanks.'

Henry had never imagined that it would be so easy, that Alex would be so non-judgmental.

'Just push the door shut behind you. Beer?'

'Why not. Thanks.'

'You should have called.'

'It seemed too much to say over the phone.'

'What, "Can you put me up for the night?" Hardly.'

'No, that I'm leaving Vic.'

Alex nearly dropped his beer. 'You're what?'

'It's over. I had to go.'

'What happened? What did you do?'

'It isn't that. She hasn't thrown me out. She doesn't even know I'm not coming back yet. But I couldn't stay.'

'Sit down, drink this, and start from the beginning.'

Henry took the bottle, looked at the condensation beading on it, picked at the foil around the neck and lip.

Alex drank, waited.

'Cheers,' Henry said, without drinking.

Alex said nothing.

The first night home from the hospital after Jessica was born, Henry and Vic agreed that he would be on baby duty, sleeping on a camp bed in Jessica's room, bringing her to Vic if she needed feeding, and soothing her back to sleep. In the last month of the pregnancy they'd both read, twice, a manual that had been recommended to them by two-thirds of their friends and relations with children under five, which said that babies needed to learn to go to sleep by themselves in their own beds: that parents who relied on feeding, rocking or bed-sharing were only, in the breezy cliché of the former midwife who'd written the book, making a rod for their own backs. Despite her repeated assurances that parenting wasn't easy, her cheerful tone and forthright advice implied otherwise, and Henry, diligent, intelligent and accustomed to doing well at whatever he did – he'd got straight As in his GCSEs (including art), passed his driving test first time, captained the second XI at both football and cricket, reached grade seven (with merit) on both piano and saxophone, reliably gave women orgasms when he slept with them; and had been brought up to believe that these accomplishments counted for something – was quietly confident that he wouldn't find parenting as hard as everyone else appeared to. Sitting on the camp bed at five o'clock in the morning, after four days without a proper night's sleep, two hours without any sleep at all, and a screaming two-day-old infant in his arms, singing to her, hushing her, but not – still going by the book – rocking her, he finally understood what it felt like to be truly, truly terrible at something that actually mattered, and which he had no choice but to persist with anyway. Vic's mother appeared in the doorway. 'Let me take her.'

'I'm fine.'

'You need to sleep. Vicky needs to sleep. Jessica needs to sleep. Let me take her.'

'No really, we need to be able to do this.'

'You will. But not now. Not tonight.' Linda took the baby.

'Don't rock her,' Henry said, collapsing back onto the bed.

When he woke it was light, and late, the sun coming in high through the window, and quiet. He went downstairs. They were in the kitchen, the three generations, two mothers, two daughters. Vic was feeding Jessica; Linda was brewing tea. Henry stood in the hallway.

'Morning,' Vic said, looking up.

'Sleep well?' Linda asked, offering him a mug.

'Yes, thank you.'

'This one did too, once she calmed down and drifted off.'

Jessica pulled away from Vic's breast. All three of them smirked at him. He put his mug down and went up to the bathroom to urinate, thunderously. Since then he hadn't been able to look at his wife or daughter without seeing his mother-in-law's features lurking in their faces.

'And the crying at night,' Henry said to Alex. 'You can't imagine. It's like when you've drunk too much and are up all night vomiting and every time you hope it's the last time, then half an hour later you're up again, retching your guts out over the toilet bowl.'

He sounded like Clare, Alex thought. Not for what he was saying, but for the inadequacy of it, for how utterly his attempt at an explanation failed to explain his behaviour.

'Everyone says it gets easier,' Alex said.

'Maybe. But when? Tomorrow? Next week? Next year? When she starts school? Leaves home? I have to sleep. I'm not cut out for this. I'm a terrible father. Vic's mother can't wait to step in and take over. When she looks at me it's like she's gloating at what a bad parent I am.'

'That's paranoid. She doesn't want you out the way.'

'You don't know that.'

'No, but I strongly suspect it. You're her granddaughter's father, for fuck's sake.'

'You don't understand. You can't.'

Alex drained his beer. Time for a new line of questioning. 'Where were you planning to go?'

'Honestly? I thought you might be looking for a lodger.'

'The house is on the market. I'm moving out.'

'You wouldn't have to if I moved in.'

'I can't stay here.'

'We could find somewhere together.'

'Let's go to the pub.'

'That's not what I meant.'

'It'll do for now. And I need a bigger drink.'

*

Alex plugged two pound coins into the slot in the pool table and pushed in the lever, savouring the heft of it, the thunk and rumble of the mechanism discharging the balls. As he racked them up, it occurred to him that this was possibly the aspect of the game he relished the most; it was certainly the part he was best at. He and Henry hadn't played often, and not for years, largely because they were so mismatched. But playing pool would give them something to do other than talk, and would make the pauses in their conversation easier. Besides, Henry needed a boost to his confidence.

'Play for break?' Alex asked, chalking a cue.

'You go ahead,' Henry said.

Alex struck the cue ball carelessly towards the red at the apex of the triangle. It made contact slightly off-centre. The momentum was distributed through the pack, balls rolling and skidding unpredictably every which way. A red dropped into each of the far corner pockets. 'That was lucky,' Alex said, trying not to smile.

'Have you been practising?' Henry asked.

'No.' The luck couldn't last. Alex lined up on a tricky red at the far end of the table. He didn't want to win – that wasn't the plan – but even worse would be for Henry to suspect he was trying to lose to make him feel better. The red spun slowly against the cushion and tumbled into the pocket.

'Nice,' Henry said, sitting down and taking a heavy draught from his pint.

Alex potted five reds before managing to sink the white too. It was his best performance ever at a pool table, just when he needed it least. He went to pick up his drink, trying to disguise his relief as disappointment. In order to win, it seemed, he had to want not to win. Henry had once said to him over the pool table at college, twelve years before, that he had 'the technique but not the temperament', throwing his game off even worse than it already was. He tried to foment the memory into a desire to defeat Henry now: if he started wanting to win, he was bound to lose. The trick was to forget that the reason to want to win was that he really wanted to lose. But did he really want to lose? Maybe losing to Alex was just the reality check that Henry needed, proof that leaving his wife and daughter was wrong. Alex didn't, when it came down to it, much care if Henry chose to ruin his own life. But it was the principle of the thing. It was a moral question.

Mid-eighties Springsteen belted out from the pub's sound system. As they listened to the interminable fade-out at the end of 'No Surrender' – Henry in the meantime had pocketed four yellow balls – Alex said: 'Being single again, the whole freedom thing, trying to recover the unrecoverable past and all that, it's kind of overrated.'

'So's parenthood,' Henry said, miscueing.

Alex drained his pint. 'Another one?' he asked. Perhaps getting drunk would interfere helpfully with his game.

'I'll get them,' Henry said.

Alex waited for Henry to come back with the drinks and took a long draught before lining up his shot.

Less than two minutes later the black rolled across the baize, dropped into the corner pocket, rumbled through the mysterious passageways of the table's digestive tract and clicked into place beside the last two reds.

'I've never played that well before,' Alex said. 'I wonder if I ever will again.' He dug two more pound coins out of his pocket and gestured towards the slot. 'Shall I?'

Henry leaned on his cue, staring at the three yellow balls

left on the table. 'The thought once crossed my mind,' he said, 'that if she died in her cot at least I'd get a few hours' sleep before we realised what had happened. How can I call myself her father, how can I stay after thinking that?'

'Because you have to,' Alex said, knocking the remaining yellows and the white into a pocket and replacing his cue in the rack. 'But not tonight. Tonight you can sleep. Come on. One more pint and then back to mine.'

Jessica was sleeping when Henry got home at lunchtime the next day. Vic kissed him. 'How'd it go?' she asked.

'Fine,' he said. 'Everything okay here?'

'Everything's fine,' she said.

When Henry ran away from his marriage for good, four months before Jessica turned two, he went to see the last other woman he'd slept with. Charlotte didn't seem surprised when she answered the door of her studio. She was bareheaded. He realised he was shaking as she put her arms round him and kissed him wordlessly on the mouth. It was only the third time they'd met. A few weeks after she'd kept score for them during his first and only foray into captaining a village cricket team, he'd sought her out in Camberwell. She'd broken up with Alex in the meantime, so they had no reason to feel guilty on that front, at least, as they fucked drunkenly against a wall in her studio, most of their clothes and her Rita Hayworth wig still on, both taking care not to knock down any of the musical boxes hanging above and to either side of them, or to get tangled in the web of electrical wiring that connected them all. This time it seemed for a moment as if they wouldn't even get as far the wall, as they slowly collapsed together in the doorway, Henry's knees buckling and his weight pulling Charlotte down after him. But this time they didn't have sex straightaway. She put her mouth to his ear. 'Hungry?' she asked.

He supposed he was. She got to her feet, picked up his bag, took it inside, told him to sit on the futon, brought him a beer from the fridge, turned the electric fire on, made a phone call and went out, pulling on a green woolly hat, saying she'd be back in ten minutes. He drank the beer, huddled by the electric fire and stared at the musical boxes. She must have reconfigured them: there was no space anywhere among them for anyone to press up against the wall.

Charlotte returned with the takeaway. 'Rice, cabbage, medium plate chicken,' she said, unpacking it.

'Chinese?' Henry asked.

'Uighur,' she said.

'God I've missed London.'

'Another beer?'

'Thanks. I suppose you're wondering what I'm doing here.'

'I thought you'd come to see me.'

'I have.'

'Well then.'

'But it's more than that.'

'Let's eat.'

They ate.

Henry tried to concentrate on his food, but every now and then looked up to catch Charlotte smiling at him. A couple of times she went to get more beers from the fridge. It was weeks, months – years – since he'd felt so relaxed, so unoppressed by obligations, so safe. The relief of being in a place where nothing was expected of him. It was like staying with his grandmother as a teenager, but with the promise of sex.

He had been dreading having to explain himself. Especially since he didn't think the truth would endear him to Charlotte. He wasn't running away from his life with Vic and Jessica; he loved them both and loved being with them, though he no longer felt the all-consuming passion for either that he once had. Falling for Vic had been a more intense version (though it always seemed more intense, every time) of the way he'd felt about a series of girls and women since the age of eleven. With Jessica it had been more surprising, and disturbing: he'd found himself violently besotted with her, ready and willing to kill anyone who might hurt her, however slightly or unwittingly. There was nothing like having children, it seemed, to strip all moral sense out of you. His feelings had since mellowed, for both his wife and daughter, and family life suited him, even made him happy.

The problem was what he did, or didn't do, when they weren't around: the hours spent holed up in the shed they called his office, pretending to work when he hadn't had any work for months. In London he had worked for six years for the web-design company that had hired him a year after he graduated. It had been a small place when he started, and he'd been given some fun projects to work on, but as the company grew, building bigger and bigger websites for bigger and bigger clients, his expertise became more specialised, and by the time he cashed in his share options and left to go freelance he was working pretty much exclusively on dropdown menus. When he and Vic moved out to Kent he imagined he was leaving the production line behind: instead he would offer a bespoke service to smaller clients. A few of his parents' friends had taken him up on it, and every so often his former employer called on him to build a set of dropdown menus. But after a while even that dried up and nothing took its place. He'd applied for a few jobs but hadn't had interviews for any of them. Vic was doing the odd bit of freelance work, and had the rent from her flat in London. Henry's contribution to the family finances was a combination of credit card debt and the allowance his mother had started giving him 'just while he was getting himself set up on his own' and never stopped, which Vic didn't know about. She thought he was working.

He played poker on Facebook and scoured porn sites for images of women who vaguely resembled his ex-girlfriends taking part in office orgies. One afternoon someone with his father's name joined a poker table where he was playing: 'hey look henry its your brother', a stranger had joked. His father wasn't on Facebook but even so he closed the browser, reopened it, logged back into the site and removed the poker app from his account. *This can't go on*, he thought. He might even have said it out loud.

What finally drove him to leave was the terrible business with the cat. It was Friday evening. Vic's friend Amy was coming to stay for the weekend. Vic's mother was away visiting her sister in Weston-super-Mare. Amy rang from London Bridge to say she'd escaped from work sooner than expected and was catching an earlier train. Vic had been planning to drive to Tunbridge Wells to pick Amy up from the station, but she was nowhere near finished getting the spare room ready – they still called it the spare room, even though Linda had been sleeping there for months, in the bed her husband had died on, which Henry found a bit macabre though he kept the thought to himself – so Henry offered to go and meet Amy instead.

'I guess that makes sense,' Vic said.

'I would offer to make her bed up and get her towels out and stuff but I'd be more likely to fuck that up. But driving I can do.'

'That would be great. Thanks.'

As he left the village, accelerating out of the thirty zone, he opened his window and fished a cigarette from his shirt pocket. His phone rang. He reached across to turn the stereo down. A pair of pinpoint lights, like reflected stars, blinked from the verge a short distance ahead. He moved his foot to the brake as the animal raced out in front of him. The bump as it disappeared between his wheels was negligible. Perhaps he hadn't hit it at all. His foot was still poised over the brake. A set of headlights approaching fast behind flooded the car. If he stopped now there was a good chance he'd be rear-ended. If the cat was dead, there was nothing to be done. If the cat was alive and well, there was nothing to be done. If the cat was injured, he'd have to take it to a vet. He couldn't afford vet's bills just now. And it was more than likely, if the cat had been injured or killed, that the lunatic behind – now in fact pulling out to overtake – was the one responsible. The other car overtook and disappeared round the bend. It would be safe now to stop, turn round, go back. But would he even be able to find the spot? He'd left it too late. There was nothing for it now but to go on.

Fifteen years earlier, on the last day of the school holidays, he had found the corpse of the family cat splayed beside the road half a mile from the house. He'd wrapped it in his sweater and carried it home, weeping, wondering what kind of hit-and-run arsehole could have done such a thing. Well, now he knew.

He got to the station just as Amy's train was pulling in. The passengers surged through the ticket barriers. No sign of Amy. He took out his phone. There was a missed call from home. And a voicemail message. He rang Vic.

'Did you get my message?'

'No, not yet. Saw you'd rung. I'm at the station, no sign of Amy.'

'I know. That's why I phoned you. She called not long after you left. She had to get off at Sevenoaks and head back to town, summoned by work. The cunts. She says she'll come tomorrow morning instead but somehow I doubt it.'

'I'm sorry.'

'Yeah, me too. As you're there why don't you pick up a takeaway? We can slum it in front of the TV.'

Driving carefully home, pointlessly alert to stray movements in the undergrowth in his headlights' penumbra, he tried not to think that if he'd pulled over to answer his phone when Vic rang, the cat would have safely crossed the road, and he wouldn't have had to spend however much he'd spent on petrol and Vic's consolation takeaway.

The phone rang at nine the next morning. Vic answered it. 'Hey, how are you? . . . Oh, I'm sorry . . . I'm so sorry . . . The bastards . . . If there's anything I can do . . . Okay . . . Let me know . . . Take care.'

'Amy?' Henry asked. 'Stuck in London?'

'No. Well yes, she's not coming. She texted me ten minutes ago. But that was Jenny. Jamie's distraught. Well, they all are. Ernie didn't come home last night and Will's just found him dead by the side of the road.'

'Ernie?'

'Their cat. Hit and run. Some bastard going too fast through the village. Didn't even stop. Just killed him and carried on. Can you imagine?'

'Can you stay?' Charlotte asked as she cleared away the foil and cardboard detritus.

'Yes,' Henry said, trying to help.

She took the greasy cardboard lid from his hand and threw everything into a black bin bag in the corner. 'Good,' she said. 'Then wash your hands and let's go to bed. Everything okay?'

'Everything's fine,' he said.

12

Snap

Alex was prospecting in his right ear with a cotton bud when the phone rang.

'Alex? Henry. I wonder if I could possibly ask you a favour?'

'Possibly,' Alex said. He gouged out a nugget of wax, dark brown and foul smelling. That couldn't be good.

'It's Jessica's birthday next month, and Vic's asked me to spend the day with them. It'll be the first time we've spent any protracted time together since I left and I think I may need a little moral support.'

'Moral?'

'You know what I mean.'

'Charlotte's not going with you, I take it.'

'No.'

'When?'

'You are her godfather, remember.'

'I said when.'

He wondered if there was something wrong with his ear,

and if he should make an appointment with the doctor. Instead he decided to look it up on the internet.

'Alex? Henry. Listen, something's come up.'

'Oh yes?'

'Charlotte . . .'

A voice in the background: 'Don't try to involve me in this.'

'You're not coming.'

'What?'

'You're not coming to Jessica's birthday party.'

'Er, no. I can't.'

'What could be more important?'

'Nothing. It's not that. I can't go. All day in that house, with Vic and her mother? It wouldn't be fair on Jessica. The atmosphere would be totally poisonous, spoil her birthday. I'll make it up to her next weekend.'

'Are you sure that's the right decision?'

'Yes.'

'Okay. But I was sort of looking forward to it. I'm already at London Bridge. I've got her a present and everything.'

'Well, you still have to go. Christ. That's why I'm calling.'

'Yeah of course. Well good. But, Henry, listen. For someone who thinks exclusively with his balls, you really need to grow a pair.'

'Thanks, Alex.'

'You're welcome.'

'Oh, hi, Alex.' Vic looked over his shoulder, Jessica clinging to her leg. 'It's just you?'

'Yes, just me. Was I supposed to bring a child? I could go and see if I can find one unattended in the playground if you like.' As often seemed to happen with Vic, Alex worried that what had been intended as charm instead came across as aggression. 'That was meant to be a joke.'

She smiled. 'Very funny. No, I mean I thought you were coming with Henry. Didn't you catch the same train?'

A car pulled up at the gate.

'Ah.' Alex shifted the heavy Hamleys bag from one hand to the other. 'He didn't tell you?'

'Tell me what?'

The car door opened.

'Jenny? Jesus, I can't believe you drove. It's less than half a mile.'

'Half a mile is a hell of a long way,' Jenny said, clambering out of the driver's seat, obviously pregnant, one hand supporting her bump. She opened the rear door, released Jamie from his seat and helped him climb to the ground. 'If we'd tried walking we'd still be at the corner of our lane. Just you wait.'

'I don't think . . .'

'You don't think Henry's the only man who'll ever get you pregnant? Self-esteem, woman, self-esteem. Hello, Alex. You must be the human shield.'

'Hello, Jenny. Congratulations.'

'Commiserations more like. Congratulate me when I've squeezed him out.'

'Actually Henry's not coming,' Vic said.

'You had second thoughts? Told him he was NFI? Good for you. Don't worry, Alex, you're not alone among the women and children. Will – you've met him, haven't you? – should be along at some point. Come on, Jamie. Let's give Jessica her present and get stuck into the juice and crisps. And before you leap to judgment, Alex, I'll have you know he eats very healthily at home. If only I could say the same about me. Happy birthday, Jessica, my love. Are you going to lead the way?'

In the kitchen, Jessica asked: 'Where's Daddy?'

Everyone looked at Vic. 'Daddy's not coming, sweetheart,' she said. 'He's a bit poorly today so he's had to stay at home.'

'Home?'

'His new home, in London.' She looked at Alex's Hamleys bag. 'He's sent you a present, though, hasn't he, Alex.'

Everyone looked at Alex. 'Yes,' he said. 'Absolutely. And he says he'll come and see you and take you out for a special treat next weekend, when he's feeling better.'

'Present?' Jessica said to her mother.

Alex offered Jessica the bag: 'Your daddy asked me to give you this.'

She clung to her mother's leg. Alex gave the bag to Vic and watched as they unwrapped together the wooden Noah's Ark – handcrafted, handpainted, exquisitely tasteful and priced accordingly – that he'd bought the previous weekend. Jenny said it was beautiful. Jessica seemed unimpressed.

'Typical Henry,' Vic said.

Alex felt himself blush. 'And this is from me,' he said quickly, proffering the alphabet snap cards he'd picked up on impulse from the newsagent at London Bridge, along with the pack of sugar-free gum and copy of *Private Eye* for his unexpectedly solitary journey.

'Cake,' Jamie said.

178

'Not yet,' Jenny said. 'You have to earn your cake. Go and play with Jessica while Mummy has a sit down.'

'I'll put the kettle on,' Linda said.

Watching Alex trying to teach the rudiments of snap to Jessica and Jamie, despite Jenny's protestations ('Really, Alex, they're two, there's no point'), Vic fell into counting up, not for the first time, the profit and loss of her separation from Henry. In the credit column today, the things she didn't miss: the way he thought that using half a bottle of washing-up liquid was a substitute for actually scrubbing the grease off the pans; the slow, silent, passive-aggressive battles over how to stack the dishwasher, which he probably didn't even realise they were fighting; his body hairs in the bath, which she had to rinse out before running the water for Jessica. She'd taken a savage pleasure in throwing his half-eaten, overpriced, unpasteurised cheeses out of the fridge. And she'd bought herself a new, cheap, small hairdryer. Debits: the half hour in bed after Jessica woke up every morning now that Henry wasn't around to get her out of her cot; sex, in general, if not with Henry in particular, though sex had meant sex with Henry for so long now that it was hard to imagine, let alone remember, how it might be different with someone else. Without Henry in bed with her, she could always have a quick, easy orgasm last thing at night, but the novelty of that soon wore off and these days she tended to stay up too late, quietly enjoying her sole possession of the house after her daughter and mother had gone to bed, and would fall asleep as she was pulling the duvet up over her shoulder.

Linda gave her a cup of tea. She was finding her mother

less annoying since Henry had left, and was more sympathetic to Linda's view of Trevor, though that didn't, paradoxically or not, alter her own feelings about her father. Neither did learning the details of his drinking problem, which according to her mother had started soon after he took early retirement: beer at lunchtime continued through the afternoon, which led to whisky through the evening, which led never to violence, at least, but to vomiting and weeping through the night. It was all deeply humiliating for everyone. Vic wished her mother hadn't told her. And it didn't change the fact that she missed her father every day. She wondered if she'd feel similarly about Henry if he'd died rather than having merely fucked off with another woman. Because despite occasionally finding certain aspects of her husband's absence inconvenient, she didn't actually miss Henry – his essential self, whatever that might be – at all. Their relationship had, apparently, been founded on sexual attraction, followed by a combination of sexual attraction and habit – which is perhaps all anyone ever really meant when they talked about being in love – and then habit alone. In her reckoning of loss over the past year, Henry's departure did not rank so very highly. She occasionally wondered how Henry explained his actions to himself, if he ever tried to justify them by blaming her grief at her father's death for pushing him away.

Jessica laughed; Vic wasn't sure what at. Henry's leaving her was one thing; leaving his daughter something else entirely. She could understand the impulse to flee – she felt it too sometimes – but not following through on it. He had said he felt like an inadequate parent. Who didn't? *How could he?* she thought whenever Jessica mentioned him. And then: *How dare he?* So when people asked her how she was doing, she usually said: 'Angrily.' And that was usually enough.

Jenny was coming to the end of a story. 'So I ended up wasting most of the morning trying to rinse out the tabasco bottle – it's impossible with that ridiculously tiny hole, like a nun's arse, sorry, Linda – before putting it in the recycling. And for what?'

'Planet not saved?' Vic asked.

'Planet definitely not saved,' Jenny said.

They'd started using the slogan when Jessica and Jamie were babies to defend themselves against the washable nappy brigade, but soon found its applications were endless.

'Top up, Alex?' Linda loomed with the teapot.

'Yes please, that would be lovely. My cup's up there, out of reach of the children.'

Linda looked at the cards strewn about the floor. 'What's that one there, beginning with Y?' she asked. 'It looks like an orange or a tomato. Some sort of exotic fruit I've never heard of?'

'I think that's a yo-yo,' Alex said.

'Yo-yo!' Jessica said. She and Jamie fell about laughing.

'Exactly,' Alex said to them. 'So if you both turn over a yo-yo card at the same time, whoever says "snap" first takes both cards.' He turned the cards over and back again.

'Yo-yo!' Jessica said.

'Yo-yo!' Jamie said.

They collapsed in laughter.

'Snap,' Alex said. 'You see?'

'Snap!' Jamie said.

'I really wouldn't bother, love,' Linda said. 'Drink your tea.'

'What's that?' Jessica asked, pointing at one of the cards.

'A windmill,' Alex said. 'W for windmill.'

'Wheelwheel!' Jessica threw the card across the room, grabbed a sheaf of others and hurled them after it.

Jamie burst into tears.

'Cake?' Vic asked.

She couldn't find the candles. 'I can't find the candles,' she said to her mother, who was hovering in the doorway, drawn to the kitchen by the sound of slamming drawers and cupboard doors.

'Never mind, love,' Linda said. 'The children won't notice. They'll be too excited about the cake.'

'It's a birthday cake. It has to have candles. I thought you of all people would insist on that.'

'Not if we don't have any candles.'

'We do have candles. We bought a stupid giant box of them last year, enough to last us till she's eighteen, and never even opened it.' Grief ballooned in her chest. She gripped the kitchen counter, fought for breath.

'Are you all right, love?'

'I'm fine. Alex?' she called, going through to the playroom. The children were watching transfixed as Alex stalked slowly towards them, clapping his hands in front of his face, one above the other, joined at the heel like a hinge or jaw. 'Could there be a crocodile hiding in the swamp?' he chanted. 'Is it going to eat us up? Snap, snap, chomp. Yes, there is a crocodile hiding in the swamp. Here it comes to eat us up, snap snap chomp. I AM the crocodile hiding in the swamp!

Here I come to eat you up, snap snap CHOMP!' The children fled screaming to their mothers.

'I thought you weren't hiring an entertainer,' Jenny said from the sofa.

'Oh, we're not paying him,' Vic said. 'It's all part of his community service. Alex, could you?' She gestured with her head towards the hallway.

'What is it?' he asked.

'It's about the candles for the birthday cake.'

'They need lighting?'

'I'm old enough to play with matches. They need finding.'

'I don't know where they are.'

'I didn't suppose you did.' She handed him the phone.

'Henry? Alex . . . No, everything's fine . . . Yes, of course, a little bit at first, but she's fine now, very happy, playing . . . Yes, just about to have the cake . . . I don't know, I expect Linda made it . . . Did you? I don't think they've done that this year. But listen, about the cake. We can't find the candles . . . Where? . . . In what? . . . How? . . . Okay . . . Yes, got it, thanks. I'll ring you again if I can't find them . . . Bye. And, er, get well soon.'

Vic raised her eyebrows.

'They're with the Christmas decorations in a box in the attic. Shall I?'

Roofspaces had always held a special fascination for Alex. As a child he'd been forbidden from following his father up the stepladder into the attic, to see what lay concealed beyond the tantalising glimpse of exposed brickwork, rafters and foam insulation, never mind going up there to explore by himself. Had he been a different sort of boy he'd have done it anyway, taking the opportunity on one of the rare occasions when his parents and sister went out, leaving him alone. But those sorts of boys, in his experience, didn't have the sorts of parents who'd make such a fuss of banning them from the attic. He still didn't know the reason that had held him back: whether obedience or fear, and, if fear, whether fear of falling between the rafters and through the ceiling below, his father's official reason for keeping him out; or fear of being found out; or fear that his father had an ulterior motive, that there was something hidden up there that he didn't want Alex to see. When he'd finally been allowed through the trap door he was predictably disappointed. A much smaller space than he'd imagined – was this really the entire area of each floor of their house, or were there further concealed spaces behind the end walls or around the chimney? – was filled with cardboard boxes and black bin bags of old clothes, toys, books, video cassettes, a record player, an 8mm film camera, a sledge, a tricycle, a pram: all the detritus of their lives that seemed, to his father at least, in too good nick to chuck out but not good enough to give away.

When he and Clare had bought their house in Tufnell Park, possibly the most exciting thing about it was having an attic of his own. When they got the keys, while Clare wandered around downstairs wondering yet again where to put the piano, he hauled himself up into the roof and sat down with his back to the chimney, imagining all the uses the space could be put to, all the hobbies it could be devoted to, if only he had had any hobbies. Mostly what came to mind was the model railway he'd never had as a child. Still, it would be a good place to work when he had to bring work home, to keep Clare from complaining about his filling the house with law. He never did get round to converting it into a study, though, or into anything else, and when they sold the house, most of the junk that had accumulated there over the years – a lot of junk, in not so many years – went into the skip. Maybe it was just other people's attics that Alex liked so much.

He was surprised by the tidiness of Henry's loft – and it must have been Henry's, since Vic hadn't known where the candles were. Everything was in neatly stacked towers of cardboard boxes, their contents written on the side in block capitals and black marker pen. He dug out the candles from the box marked 'Christmas Decorations', put everything else away, then stood for a moment, his head in the apex of the roof, stretching his back and enjoying the stillness of the attic, disturbed only by a faint rasping sound, as if a ghost were cleaning its teeth. He looked around, trying to isolate the source of the scraping. It appeared to be coming from inside one of the rafters. He dug his keys out of his pocket and tapped at the apparent source of the noise. It stopped. He waited. It started up again. He prodded the wood again, harder this time. The key sank into the rafter. He pulled it out, accidentally tearing a thin strip of pine off the surface. A stream of ultrafine sawdust trickled to the ground. The revealed wood appeared to have the texture of cardboard rather than raw pine. He scraped at it with the key. It was softer than cardboard. Small clumps of compacted sawdust fell to the ground. He kept digging. The end of a piece of wire appeared. He was about to flick it with the tip of the key when it moved spontaneously. His hand flinched. Another antenna appeared, burrowing out of the sawdust.

Alex held his breath and watched as the beetle slowly emerged, like a crocodile crawling out of a swamp, or a horse struggling in quicksand, or a zombie rising from the grave. Did it want to come out, or had it been happy inside the rafter? Were those meaningful questions to ask of a beetle? He disinterred it with his key. It clung on like a drowning sailor to a life raft, blindly flailing its antennae – which were sickeningly long, maybe half an inch, almost as long as its body – against the air and the light. It lifted a front leg and rubbed its head, as if trying to clean off the sawdust that was clinging there. Except it wasn't really sawdust: it was wood that had passed through the beetle's digestive system. The creature was covered in its own shit. Alex turned the key round and pressed its flat side gently against the edge of the rafter. There was a quiet crunch. He took a tissue from his pocket and wiped his key on it. Then, not knowing what else to do with it, he put the tissue back in his pocket.

He breathed out and listened to the silence – which was disturbed only by another faint rasping sound in the rafters. He raised his key again and continued excavating. The narrow tunnel that the creature – the creatures – had bored was quite beautiful in its way, a few millimetres in diameter, the walls smooth and curved, its course meandering along the grain of the wood. A large lump of digested wood pulp plopped to the ground. Alex bent over to look at it. It quivered, stretched, yearned. He shuddered and recoiled, feeling as if he might be sick. The larva writhed at his feet: fat, white, ribbed, blind, gross. He crushed it with his toe. He looked around, stretched his leg out, and wiped his shoe on the edge of a cardboard box marked 'Curtains'.

*

Will had arrived and was reading a story to the children in the playroom. Their mothers were laughing in the kitchen. Alex paused on the stairs, not wanting to walk in at an embarrassing moment. 'Oh, don't,' Jenny was saying. 'It's like getting drunk and falling under a bus, only worse. You throw up, shit yourself, let some bloke you've only just met shove his hand up your vagina. And of course it all hurts like buggery . . .'

'Only worse,' Vic said.

'Only worse,' Jenny repeated. 'And then you recover and the memory fades and come next Friday night you find yourself doing it all over again.'

'At least I won't be.'

'Oh, stop staying that. You just need to wait for the right man to come along.'

'You're the one who needs to stop saying that.'

'What about Alex? He seems nice. And he's good with the kids.'

'Oh, don't be ridiculous.'

'Talk of the devil,' Jenny said. 'Hello, Alex. Got the candles then?'

She must have known he was there all along. He went down the last few stairs and into the kitchen, trying to hide his embarrassment.

Alex stood at the front door. 'Doddodial!' Jessica said, throwing her arms round his legs. Will, Jenny and Jamie had gone home almost immediately after the cake ceremony – 'We're getting an early night,' Jenny had said; 'remember when that used to mean something else?' – and Alex had thought it was probably time for him to be going too.

'Thanks for coming,' Vic said.

'Thanks for having me.'

'You're good with her.'

'She's good with me.'

'Where does that crocodile game come from? I've never heard it before.'

'I made it up.'

'Just now?'

'No, when I was about eight. I played it with my sister.'

'I didn't know you had a sister.'

'She lives in Alaska.'

'Alaska?'

'She's a geologist, married to another geologist, a Canadian; they met at university in Vancouver, when she was doing her PhD.'

'Do you see her often?'

'Almost never.'

'You must miss her.'

'I suppose I miss her every day.'

The sudden intimacy was awkward.

'If you wanted to come again sometime,' Vic said, 'I think she, I mean Jess, I mean we, would like that. Seriously.'

'Thank you.' He smiled at Jessica. 'Snap, snap, CHOMP.'

She ran away happily screaming down the hall.

He phoned her on Thursday evening. 'Vic? Hi, it's Alex . . . Is Henry coming down this weekend? . . . He is? Oh, good. It's just I wondered if I might take you up on your invitation, to come again sometime . . . Oh, he won't? . . . When? . . . I don't want to impose, it's fine if you, you know, but in case you meant what you said . . . Okay, great, thanks, yes, that would be, that would be great . . . Yes, and I've got something to show you . . . No, not really, just something I think you ought to see . . . No, nothing like that . . . It's hard to explain on the phone . . . See you Saturday then. Thanks . . . Bye.'

No one answered the door. He lifted his hand to knock again but changed his mind and instead wandered round to the back of the house and looked through the kitchen window. Linda was at the sink, flaying carrots. He watched her, wondering how to attract her attention without making her jump, until she looked up with a start. If she'd been using a knife rather than a vegetable peeler she could have taken a finger off. Recognising him then, she smiled and gestured for him to come in, wiping her hands on her apron and going to open the back door.

He was sitting at the kitchen table with a mug of tea when Vic and Jessica appeared. 'Oh hello,' Vic said. 'Sorry I didn't hear you knock. We've been changing the world's filthiest nappy. Time for potty training to begin in earnest this summer, I think. Procter and Gamble have bled us dry long enough.'

Alex smiled. 'Hello, Jessica.'

She buried her face in her mother's thighs.

'We're off out to the swings,' Vic said. 'Want to come?'

At the playground a group of bigger children were loitering on their bikes. Alex wondered how old they were. Eight? Ten, maybe? He was so bad at judging that kind of thing. Vic pushed Jessica on the swing. Alex stayed close, but not too close (Jessica was still being wary of him), feeling awkward, and eavesdropping.

'Ugh, you've got blood on you. There. It's disgusting.'

'No it isn't.'

'Yes it is. It's disgusting. No! Don't touch me! Now I'm going to get Aids.'

'David hates blood. I once had like one drop of blood on me and he was about two metres away and he pegged it round the whole close.'

'No I didn't.'

One of them caught Alex's eye. He looked away and studied the graffiti. Under the slide someone had drawn two crude naked figures in black marker pen. A curvaceous cartoon woman captioned 'sex education for boys' and a stick-figure man with a giant penis captioned 'sex education for girls'.

The older children clambered onto their bikes and rode away. Jessica yelled incoherently. Vic lifted her from the swing and she ran over to the steps of the slide. 'Be careful there,' Vic called.

With Jessica out of conversational earshot, Alex asked: 'So Henry's coming down tomorrow, is he?'

'He hasn't cancelled yet.'

'By himself?'

'Do you mind very much about Charlotte?'

'Not really. It was over between us before they, you know?'

'Yes, I know. You should come down here during the week. Saturdays there's nothing but dads – we're a bit early for them yet – but on weekdays you'd meet no end of eligible nannies.'

'Thanks, but really, I'm fine. I don't want to cramp your style when the dads turn up, though.'

'Trust me, dads are not my favourite people right now.'

They watched Jessica come smiling down the slide. 'Well done!' Alex called.

'So what was it you wanted to show me?' Vic asked.

Alex took a matchbox out of his pocket, opened it, took out a folded tissue and unwrapped it. 'I found this in one of your rafters last weekend when I went up into the attic to get the candles.'

'Eurgh. What is it?'

'*Hylotrupes bajulus*. Old-house borer. Though it's more likely to be found in new houses, apparently.'

'And you're showing it to me because?'

'Well, strictly speaking you're required to report it to the Building Research Establishment's Timber and Protection Division. And you should probably call in pest control too. And you might' – it seemed better to give all the bad news at once, before his nerve failed him – 'need to get a roofer in to replace the infested rafters, because burning them might be the only way to eradicate the beetles. And, more to the point, their larvae.'

'You're joking.'

'I'm really sorry.'

'We're hardly getting by as it is. I can't pay for the roof to be redone.'

'Henry would have to pay for it of course.'

Vic snorted. 'Henry? He's got even less money than I have.'

'What do you mean?'

'Turns out he hasn't earned anything for years. He confessed all when he told me he'd left us. Said he couldn't bear to go on lying to me any longer. Self-righteous dickhead. I know he's your friend and everything, but really. He'd been living off his credit cards and a bank loan, and an allowance from his mother, can you believe it. Once his credit was exhausted he walked out.'

'I'm sorry to hear that.'

'Not as sorry as I was.'

'But you still have work?'

'Some, sure, but not as much as I did. People are cutting their marketing budgets, and farming out less copywriting to freelancers. And there are more freelancers than there used to be, competing for less work, because so many in-house copywriters have been laid off.'

'You've got the flat in London,' Alex said.

'The rent doesn't do much more than cover the mortgage. I've thought about selling it – sorry.'

'You really don't need to worry about me.'

'I don't. I just haven't found the time to put it on the market.'

'What about your mother? Doesn't she contribute?'

'Turns out my father put all their savings into bank shares in 2006. There was some fuck-up with his pension, too, so my mother hardly sees anything from that. The state pension is next to nothing, obviously. Now that Henry's gone she's asked if she can move in permanently – as if she hadn't already – and is trying to sell the house but no one's shown any interest. Maybe we'll all have to move in there if we need to get our roof done. Why did you have to tell me about that?'

'I'm sorry. I thought you should know.'

'How much will it cost?'

'I've no idea. But – I could help with it. I sort of feel like it's my fault.'

'Don't be stupid.' She looked at the crushed beetle perched in his hand. 'Put that thing away, would you? I don't want to think about it now.' She looked up. 'Be careful, Jessica love, don't go up on there. Not on there. NOT ON THERE. Good girl.' She turned back to Alex. 'What were we talking about?'

'Your mother's house. Couldn't she rent it out?'

'Not without rewiring it first, and we can't afford that.'

'What if Henry wants to come back?'

She folded her arms and raised an eyebrow.

'I see,' Alex said.

'In some ways I wish he had left sooner, before Jessica was born, or when she was too young to miss him. Having had him in her life, and then abandon her, must be worse than never having known him.'

'He hasn't abandoned her.'

'Even if she could understand that, she'd still feel as if he had.'

And Alex had been so sure he'd been doing the right thing when he had made Henry go home the first time he had tried to leave Vic, when Jessica had been only a few weeks old.

'And then there's the cost of the divorce,' Vic said. 'Who'd have thought it could cost so much to divide up so little?'

'If you need a new lawyer . . .'

'You do divorces?'

'No, but I know people who do.'

'Pro bono?'

'I'm afraid not.'

'Then I think I'll stick with who I've got.'

'Who's that?'

'I doubt you know her. My parents' solicitor in East Grinstead since for ever. She was very nice and efficient over Dad's will. Though there wasn't much to be disposed of there, either.'

Jessica leapt up from the bottom of the slide and ran over

to them. She stopped in front of Alex and looked up.
'Doddodial!'

'Here's the sportive infant,' he said. 'Snap snap CHOMP!'
She ran away. He turned back to Vic. 'You should put my
rent up.'

13

Swimming

Clare studied the ornamental handles carved in relief on the giant granite bathtub, wondering what the technical name for them might be. According to the breathless account in her pocket guide to Rome, the tub, along with the one in the other fountain on the other side of the square, had been taken from the Baths of Caracalla – though she was fairly certain they hadn't actually, functionally, ever been bathtubs – sometime in the sixteenth century by Pope Paul III, while he was building the French Embassy, where Tosca stabbed Scarpia with the breadknife, only not in that order.

A scooter buzzed into the square, slowed, and began a circuit of the bathtub, like a plane joining the stack over a runway. The woman riding it – sharply tailored Armani-grey summer dress, sandals, sunglasses, helmet – appeared to be looking for someone. Clare adjusted her posture and expression, pitching them, she hoped, somewhere between unhurried expectancy and idle curiosity, so she was ready to greet

Daniela, if that's who the woman on the scooter turned out to be, but wouldn't be embarrassed if it wasn't.

For as long as Clare was living with Alex, her mother had every year for her birthday paid for them to go on what she insisted on calling, following the lead of the adverts in the paper, a 'Euro city break': Barcelona, Prague, Vienna, Budapest, Paris, Berlin. Her first birthday after leaving Alex, two years ago, she had spent in a bar in Cusco, where she found herself for the first time in her life claiming to be younger than she was. Last year, not long back in England, she'd intended not to celebrate at all, but then Henry of all people, bless him, had sent her a message – 'hey birthday girl im in london wheres the party' – so they'd gone for tapas near Goodge Street and got hideously, gloriously drunk, somehow made it back to her flat, where she'd offered him the sofa with assurances that her flatmate, whom she barely knew, wouldn't mind at all, opened a bottle of whisky they'd got hold of somewhere along the way, and got even drunker, before both passing out on the sofa. There was never any chance of their ending up in bed together, which she was grateful for. He was a dad now: off limits. Waking up the next morning, she'd felt like a teenager for the half-second before the headache kicked in. And it had really put the boot in. So this year she'd accepted her mother's offer, though she'd put up a formal show of ingratitude masquerading as filial concern. 'Are you sure you can afford it?'

'Of course we can,' her father said. 'There's all the money we were saving up for the grandchildren.'

'Don't be so unkind, Frank,' her mother said, though it wasn't clear which of them she thought he was being unkind to. 'Where would you like to go?'

Alex had always said Rome was too hot in August. 'Rome,' Clare said. And so here she was. Alex, she had to admit, hadn't been wrong. Sweltering, and smoggy with it, the city had a post-apocalyptic feel, largely empty except for the hordes of tourist undead. She'd spent the afternoon sitting by a (Bernini?) fountain in the Villa Borghese gardens, wondering whether or not she dared to dip her feet in. She hadn't, in the end, remembering the blisters she'd got in Barcelona from walking around the city in wet sandals after paddling in the sea. Then she'd strolled back to the convent where she was staying (it had been Jacqueline's suggestion that she rent a cheap room from commercially minded nuns rather than going to an overpriced hotel), showered, dressed, dithered over make-up, been distracted by the knickers hanging out to dry on a line below a window across the courtyard (she couldn't tell if it was a very large pair, or a very flimsy pair casting a shadow, or possibly two pairs, one large and one small, in any case presumably not nuns' underthings but a guest's), and was now waiting to be picked up for her implausible – and possibly illusory – date with a woman she barely knew.

She'd got an email from Facebook on her birthday, telling her that her godmother had posted on her wall: 'Happy birthday, darling! Your mother tells me you're going to Rome – have a lovely time! *Buono vaggio!*' There were many reasons she didn't much like Facebook, but one of them was the problem of not knowing how to use it properly. Since nobody seemed to know how to use it properly, she suspected there wasn't a proper way to use it, and had found that the best way to get round the problem was not to use it at all. But she wasn't able simply to delete her account, because of the gnawing sense that she might then unwittingly miss out on something.

It made no difference that she'd never seen anything on Facebook that she would have minded missing out on. Late nights lurking on the site reminded her of evenings in the bar at college, staying till closing time, out of range of the rugby team, waiting for something unspecified to happen that was clearly never going to. Worried less by what her godmother might write than what she might read, Clare had ignored her request to be friends for several weeks, until her mother brought it up on the phone one Sunday morning and she had to use the one-time-only excuse she'd been keeping in reserve, that she hadn't known because she never looked at Facebook.

But she needn't have worried about her godmother's being shocked by anything that Clare's other 'friends' might post. Because if you were to plot Facebook users' activity on a graph, with writing on the X-axis and reading on the Y, Clare's godmother would be found way off in the lower right corner, deep among the compulsive oversharers, who informed their friends, and their friends' friends, and their friends' friends' friends, of their every movement, their every blog post, their every badly framed snap of their every child, not to mention their unborn children (as if sharing their wives' or girlfriends' private medical records with the world were an entirely normal thing to do), confirming Clare's sense that pregnant women were too often treated – even, or especially, by overly proud fathers-to-be – as mere baby-vessels, drained of all subjectivity, their agency siphoned off and replaced by amniotic fluid.

But still she wouldn't delete her account. And, finally, the obscure something that she'd been afraid of missing out on appeared to materialise. Shortly after her godmother wished her happy birthday, she got another email from Facebook saying that someone called Daniela had posted on her wall, suggesting that as she was coming to Rome, they should meet up. She assumed at first it was spam, but then she saw they had five mutual friends, and seeing their names she remembered, of course, who Daniela was – last glimpsed heading across the Bolivia–Chile border towards the Atacama Desert, never, according to the old ways of the world, to be seen again. And yet, now, here she was. Clare felt momentarily relieved she wasn't going to Brisbane. She replied to Daniela to say that would be great, and after a couple more messages each way, that casual friendliness had phased into an apparently definite arrangement.

She pushed her sweat-slicked sunglasses back up her nose and took a surreptitious closer look at the woman on the scooter. It was impossible to say whether or not she resembled the woman Clare had met in Bolivia, but she could certainly be the woman in the photographs on Daniela's Facebook page. Initially unfussed as to whether or not the arrangement came to anything, Clare now wanted very much not to have to spend the evening alone. The feeling was unexpected – she'd been all the way round the world by herself, and most of that time more than happy with it – but her circumstances in Rome were sufficiently different from that, and sufficiently similar to the holidays she had used to take with Alex, for her to find herself missing him, after all, rather a lot. So she would be glad to have company. The scooter slowed then came to a stop, engine puttering. The rider took off her helmet – hair tightly plaited – and said *ciao*. Clare walked over, glad she'd made the effort with her make-up. '*Ciao*, Daniela.'

They air-kissed, both cheeks, Daniela produced a helmet from nowhere and handed it to her, Clare pulled it over her head, buffetted by the smell of old hairspray, fumbled with the straps, regretted her choice of skirt, hitched it up, and clambered onto the scooter behind Daniela. She hadn't ridden pillion since she and Alex had spent a fortnight on an Aegean island the summer before they were married, and had hired a scooter one day to explore up into the mountains. The hairpin bends had taken a bit of getting used to, but with her arms round Alex's waist it was simple enough for them to shift their weight together, leaning in on the corners as a single body. But she didn't feel she could hold onto Daniela, so instead reached down behind her back to hold onto the grab bar. It felt wrong, like offering herself up to be handcuffed.

'*Sei pronta?* Are you ready?' Daniela asked.

Clare found the footrests, adjusted her posture, nodded. '*Sì.*'

Daniela opened the throttle and the scooter lurched away. Every muscle in Clare's body, from her pelvic floor to her fingertips and toes, clenched reflexively. She couldn't have let go of the grab bar even if she'd wanted to. She wondered where she'd get cramp first, and wished she felt more like Audrey Hepburn. Until, that is, she allowed herself to trust Daniela's driving, and was able to relax into the ride, and got used to the grab bar, and suddenly they were zipping round the Colosseum, and it was all such a cliché that she found herself wishing, on the contrary, that she felt rather less like Audrey Hepburn. And then she got over that too, and focused on simply enjoying the ride: the air rushing past, the empty roads (there was something to be said for going to Rome in August, after all), the view over Daniela's shoulder, out through the Aurelian Walls (was that the Porta Maggiore?), the buildings taller here, newer, grimier, over a railway, and then running along beside the tracks. She wondered where they were going.

Actually, fuck, where *were* they going? Daniela had invited her for an *aperitivo*, but this seemed a long way to go to get to a bar, and in the wrong direction. Clare had been blithely taking *Roman Holiday* as her frame of reference, but what was happening to her could just as easily have been filed under 'Roman Abduction'. She had no idea where she was, or who she was with: a woman she'd spent three days with in Bolivia a year earlier, who'd contacted her on Facebook, who'd picked her up by the roadside twenty minutes ago. Perhaps she wasn't the woman she'd met in Bolivia. Perhaps she wasn't even the woman who'd contacted her on Facebook. She considered jumping off and running away the next time the scooter slowed for a corner. But she wouldn't have known where to run to, and anyway Daniela (if that was even her name) would catch her up in no time, and that's if she even managed to run anywhere at all, rather than collapsing in the street with a broken leg, or worse.

They were now in smaller, quieter streets, residential, tree-lined, down-at-heel, graffiti everywhere, peeling stucco, peeling advertisements, peeling paintwork on shutters, grilles across groundfloor windows and doors, spiked railings along the tops of crumbling walls. You could be strapped to a rusting bedframe in the basement of one of these houses for days – years – and no one would ever find you.

The scooter slowed, came to a stop outside some gates on a corner. Clare dropped her eyes to the pavement, looking where to plant her feet so she could take off running without tripping over the curb. There was a bike rack. Which was weird. New and shiny, too. She looked up. Inside the gates was a courtyard, with tables, and drinkers at them. A bar. Unsteady with relief as she climbed down from the scooter, she almost fell over. Daniela had to help with the helmet strap. Following her through the gates, Clare felt about three years old.

One of the tables shuddered into activity as they approached. There were seven or eight people sitting at it. Half of them stood up, all turned their heads to greet Daniela with smiles, kisses, words. Daniela introduced Clare: smiles, handshakes, names instantly forgotten, kisses from Marco. There was an empty chair. She sat down.

'What will you drink?' her neighbour – Alessandro? Lorenzo? Luca? – asked.

'A beer, please.'

'Small? Medium?'

'Medium.'

'Blonde beer is okay?'

'Perfect, thank you.'

He summoned a waiter, gave the order, turned his attention away to one of his friends.

'Everything is okay?' Daniela asked.

'Yes,' Clare said. 'Lovely. Where are we?'

'Pigneto.'

Clare nodded.

'You have seen *Accattone*?' Marco asked, leaning across from the other side of the table. 'The Pasolini film?'

She shook her head.

'Okay. Well it is not really like that here anymore.'

The attention ebbed and flowed around the table, for the most part bypassing Clare, though she was more than happy with that, half-listening to the rapid incomprehensible voices, the laughter, enjoying the beer and the heat of the evening, the sense of being in Rome among Romans, who would take turns occasionally to break into English to ask her a friendly question – was this her first time in Rome? how long was she staying? where did she live? how was the weather in London? – and listen politely to her answer before being reabsorbed into the native conversation. She let her attention drift to the starlings in the trees, the traffic in the street, the people at the other tables. She let someone order her another beer. And then by general consent, implied or explicit, it was time to go for dinner.

'You will join us,' Marco asked, or announced. 'Unless you have other plans?'

'No,' Clare said. 'No other plans. That would be lovely. Thank you.'

As they were leaving the bar, Clare wondered how she could ever have thought the area's crumbling charm seemed threatening. She pointed to some graffiti on the corner: '*Insurrezione è amore.*'

'Insurrection and love?' she asked.

'Almost,' Marco said, swinging his leg over his scooter. 'Insurrection *is* love.'

Clare took her helmet from Daniela, popped it on her head and hopped onto the Vespa as if it were something she'd been doing all her life.

When they got to the restaurant some of their party had already arrived, and their numbers had swelled yet further. A waiter was drawing yet another table up alongside the three already pushed together.

'What are we celebrating?' Clare asked Daniela.

'Eh?'

'Is it someone's birthday?'

'No, no.'

The waiter looked at them. '*Anche voi?*' He threw his arms up in apparent despair.

'Should we go somewhere else?' Clare asked.

'No, no. Don't worry. He is joking,' Daniela said. 'This is a typical Roman restaurant. Everything is fine. You will see.'

Clare didn't see, but was glad everything was fine. 'What's with the ties?' she asked. The walls were festooned with snipped-in-half neckties.

'They are forbidden,' Daniela said. 'If a man comes in wearing a tie, they cut it off. Of course, now people come wearing ties on purpose. Sometimes then they do not cut it off. Come.'

Somehow there were now enough chairs round a large enough table for everyone to sit down. The waiter brought jugs of wine, bottles of water, baskets of bread, then pulled up a chair at the corner of the table beside Clare and sat down.

'You are joining us?' she asked.

He looked at her blankly. '*Allora*,' he said, producing a notepad and pencil.

A long, heated, general and incomprehensible discussion broke out. Eventually everyone fell more or less silent. '*Va bene*,' the waiter said, turning to Clare. '*E tu?*'

'Is there a menu?'

He opened his hands expansively, shrugged his shoulders, raised his eyebrows, and reeled off what she presumed must be a list of dishes. The only word she was sure she could make out was 'carbonara'.

'Carbonara,' she said.

'*La carbonara?*'

'Spaghetti carbonara.'

He seemed disappointed. '*Sicura?*'

She looked him in the eye. He made a very small adjustment to the notes on his pad. '*Quindi sette carbonara.*'

When he'd gone, Clare turned to Daniela. 'Everyone is having carbonara?'

'Maybe half of us, I would think. It is very good here.'

'So what was all the discussion in aid of?'

'I don't understand. What discussion?'

'With the waiter, just now. All of you.'

Daniela frowned. Her eyebrows were quite something, perfect for semaphoring punctuation across crowded rooms. 'You mean when we were making the order?'

'I suppose so.'

'Well we were making the order. You are having carbonara too? I hope he didn't persuade you to order tripe. Unless you like tripe?'

'If he did, I didn't follow him. And no, I don't like tripe.'

'Okay. But if you do, the tripe here is very good.'

Clare filled her wine glass, grabbed a piece of bread. The bread was very good. The wine had alcohol in it.

And the pasta, when it arrived, was quite the best pasta Clare had ever eaten. Not the carbonara so much, though it was excellent, but the pasta itself, the texture of it. Who knew plain old spaghetti could taste so good?

'This is amazing,' she said.

'*Buono?*' the man opposite her asked, the one who'd ordered her first drink at the bar. Alessandro? Lorenzo? Luca?

'*Buonissimo?*' she ventured.

He laughed, the edges of his eyes crinkling into the crow's feet of someone who laughed a lot.

The meal went on for a long time, though they didn't eat all that much: pasta, pudding, coffee – not the seventeen courses of stereotype or legend. But it was well after eleven by the time they settled up. Clare added her twenty euros to the cash on the table and no one asked her for any more. The waiter smiled and shook her hand at the door. She thanked him and he thanked her and the night outside where the scooters were parked under the trees was warm and thick with the rasp of cicadas, and really she couldn't remember the last time she'd had such a good meal.

'I hope it's not too far out of your way to drop me back at the convent,' she said to Daniela.

'You are tired? We are going to a *centro sociale* now.'

'Social centre?'

'Yes. But you also have another word for it.'

'Squat,' Marco said.

Weren't they all a bit old to be going to a squat party? Or maybe that was only her. She realised she had no idea how old any of them were.

'The convent has a curfew at midnight,' she said.

Marco shrugged. 'They will let you in at six tomorrow morning.'

'I think I should be getting back. I don't want the nuns to send out a search party.'

The man with the laughter lines joined them. Clare gazed at the moon while the Italians talked.

'Lorenzo will give you a lift,' Daniela said at last. 'He has a car.'

'Okay, *Cenerentola*,' Lorenzo said. 'You come with me.'

Clare was too tired – she'd got up at five to catch her flight – to wonder for more than a moment whether this was all part of an elaborate pick-up ritual. 'Okay,' she said.

He had a red Mini, one of the properly tiny original ones from the 1960s, with old 'Roma' plates, and he drove it as if he had delusions of being Jason Bourne. She'd felt a lot safer on the back of Daniela's scooter, even taking into account her absurd fears of being kidnapped. She glanced across at Lorenzo's face, lit by the flicker of passing streetlamps and flaring headlights coming the other way. The streets were still relatively deserted. His laughter lines were creased in mild concentration. If he was showing off, he was doing a good job of hiding it. Maybe this was simply the way he drove. And they hadn't crashed yet. She didn't want to talk for fear of distracting him, and he seemed comfortable with the silence. The corner of his mouth twitched. She looked away, out through the windscreen, and tried smiling too.

'You will need me to drive you tomorrow?' Lorenzo asked as he pulled up outside the convent.

'Tomorrow?'

'I am driving you to the countryside?'

Fuck it, she thought. *Why not.* 'That would be great, thank you. And thank you for the lift this evening. I don't think I can ask you in for coffee. The nuns wouldn't like it.'

He smiled so she couldn't tell if he'd understood or not. 'See you tomorrow,' he said.

Before getting into bed Clare paused by the window. Across the garden of the convent was another window, open, lights on, curtains not drawn, where the knickers had been hanging out to dry in the morning. A half-naked androgynous figure – short hair, skinny frame – was moving through the room. The person bent over, breasts dropping into view, intent on something, oblivious to how visible she was, or simply not caring. What was she doing? Stretching? Unpacking? Giving a handjob to someone invisible below the window frame? Or even, now, her head disappearing from view, performing oral sex? A terrible verb, that, the one favoured by po-faced, prurient, pseudo-scandalised newspapers, and terrible in part perhaps because of the way in which it was so horribly accurate: the performance required of both parties, either of subservience and skill or, reciprocally and even worse, of grateful ecstasy. The woman raised her head, looked out the window, seemed to meet Clare's eye. The light went out.

Clare got into bed and must have fallen asleep, because when the alarm clock buzzed to wake her up, Grace Kelly had just brought in a new pair of pyjamas for her in a very small suitcase. Her serene highness must have brought the alarm clock, too, because Clare didn't have one. She turned the light on, looked for the source. There it was, thudding against the mirror over the sink. An insect of some kind. Fly? Beetle? Wasp? Hornet. It was huge. Once upon a time Alex would have chased it out the window or annihilated it with a rolled-up copy of the *Economist*. Clare approached with caution. Abandoning its vain battery for a moment, it dropped to the narrow shelf below the mirror, took a few steps, raised an inquiring antenna in Clare's direction, compound-eyeballed her. She grabbed the glass from the other end of the shelf and turned it upside down over the hornet like a belljar. She peered at it. It wasn't as big as it had seemed in flight, but still much bigger than a normal wasp, and darker, too, more orange than yellow, like a regular wasp grown overripe. It buzzed against the glass. She thought about leaving it like that, but worried she'd forget it was there in the morning, lift the glass, get stung, or someone else would, the woman who came to clean the room. She lifted the edge of the glass a few millimetres. The creature crawled forwards, poked its head out. She snapped the edge of the glass down, ground it against the shelf, severed abdomen from thorax. A serious weakness, this, that a wasp's means of propulsion and weaponry should be so easily separated. Though the flexibility it provided, or something, must have more than made up for it. That's how they'd evolved, and they weren't in any danger of extinction. She swept the two halves – legs and antennae still waving, sting impotently thrusting – into the bin. She turned out the light, looked out the window – wondered what her antics would have looked like to someone watching from across the courtyard – and climbed back into bed, pulling the sheet up over her head. She turned the light out, pulled her arm in under the sheet and closed her eyes. Again, the buzzing. Another hornet? She pulled the sheet down, listened. Silence. The buzzing only in her ears.

Clare lay back on the sun lounger beside the pool in the shade of a stone pine and watched the swarms of linden seeds, their desiccated bracts spinning high on the thermals that gusted up the hillside, against a backdrop of blue skies and jagged mountains softened by heat haze.

Marco's parents' villa was somewhere up in the Sabine Hills – Lorenzo's Mini had barrelled off the motorway at the exit for Magliano Sabina – which made her think of the upward spiral of Giambologna's *Rape of the Sabine Women* in the Loggia dei Lanzi in Florence. She'd felt increasingly nervous as the car wound its way up the narrow unmarked roads. They weren't expecting her, hadn't invited her. But when they reached the villa everyone was friendly rather than surprised, greeting her and Lorenzo alike with, '*O, ciao!*' and kisses on both cheeks. Perhaps he'd mentioned he was bringing her. Perhaps everyone had assumed he would. Perhaps no one cared either way.

'Nice house,' she said to Marco.

'It was my grandfather's. He was a farmer. Now it's my father's. He is an architect.'

'You have a bathing costume?' Daniela asked.

'No,' Clare said. 'I wasn't planning to do an Anita Ekberg, so . . .'

'Anita Ekberg?' Marco asked.

'Yes, in the Trevi Fountain, though I know she wears a dress, so . . .'

'You like Fellini?'

'Sure.'

'Here,' Daniela said, passing her a handful of orange lycra. 'I will show you where you can change.'

She looked at herself in the bathroom mirror. 'Bathing costume' wasn't the first expression that sprang to mind. The bikini couldn't have been a worse colour on her. She didn't much care for all the bits of string dangling from it either. But at least it fit all right. And perhaps the startling orange would look slightly less terrible in daylight. She tied her shirt round her waist as a makeshift sarong, took a few breaths, went outside.

'The English are famous for their bad skin,' one of the deeply tanned women said to her. 'But yours is *traslucente.*'

'Translucent?'

'Yes. You used to be a model, perhaps?'

210

She shook her head. Was she being complimented? Or was there a subtle barb in the choice of tense? Why did she have to overthink everything that everyone said to her?

'Does anyone have any suncream?' she asked. Someone handed her a bottle. She looked at the label: factor four. That would stop her burning for about thirty seconds. A hat in the shade it was then.

It was hot even in the shade. The Italians were stretched out in the sun around the pool. No one was in the water. Clare sat up, took off her hat and sunglasses, untied her shirt from around her waist, stood, took half a dozen steps to the edge of the pool, raised her arms to shoulder height, bent her knees, lifted her heels, pushed off with her toes, dived in. She sliced cleanly into the water, barely feeling the impact, only the transition from heat and noise to cool silence. She glided as far as the momentum of the dive took her, opened her eyes, checked quickly that the strings of her bikini hadn't come unravelled, pulled her arms back in a single breast stroke and kicked her legs in a gentle crawl to reach the shallow end, surfacing as her fingertips touched the edge. The sunlight and cicadas broke back in on her senses.

She smoothed her hair back – she'd have enjoyed swimming more as a teenager if she hadn't had hair nearly down to her waist – looked around – no one was paying her any attention – and pushed off into a front crawl, counting her strokes, measuring out the pool. After four lengths she began to feel the burn in her muscles, but knew she just had to swim on through it. And then she'd lost count of the number of lengths she'd swum, and long since given up counting the strokes, knowing through some pre-numerical sense of rhythm when she was reaching the end, when to turn, jack-knifing into a somersault and pushing off from the wall in one continuous motion, smooth as a violin bow sustaining a note while changing stroke.

At the end of the last length, though it only became the last length in that moment, instead of tucking her head down into a turn she stretched out her fingertips to the edge and surfaced, face first, to sweep her hair back out of her eyes. She placed her palms on the hot tiles, pushed off the bottom of the pool with her toes, brought her right foot up onto the tiles between her hands, walked towards the towel draped over her sun lounger, still in one continuous fluid series of movements.

'You swim well.'

She took the towel away from her face, looked up. Lorenzo was offering her a beer. She took it, swigged, said 'Thank you', happy to leave it ambiguous whether she was grateful for the beer or the compliment.

'*Salute.*' He looked her in the eye, took a sip.

'Cheers.'

'Where are you from?'

That was disappointing. One of the many things she'd liked about Lorenzo was that he'd avoided asking her that question. It seemed to be the Italian equivalent of London's 'What do you do?' Though neither of them was as awful as being asked at Oxford where she'd gone to school or, even worse, 'which school' she had gone to, the question as much as the answer identifying the class origins of the speaker.

'London,' she said.

'You were born there?'

'Near enough.'

'You were not born at the sea.'

'Like Venus you mean? No. I learned to swim at the municipal pool in Guildford. I used to have the badges to prove it sewn onto my swimming costume.'

The corners of Lorenzo's eyes creased up. 'On Monday we are all going to l'Isola d'Elba. Maybe you would like to come too?'

'I'd love to but I'm flying back to London tomorrow.'

'So you change your flight.'

He almost made it sound possible.

'You're all going?'

He looked around the pool. 'I think so, yes.'

'How do you all know each other?'

The corners of his mouth shrugged. 'We have always known each other, more or less.'

'That must be nice,' she said. Though she wondered if it was, really. This movement of friends en masse, not only in the short term from bar to restaurant to party to country house to holiday island, but in the long term, too, from the labour ward to the bench in the piazza, was something she both envied and dreaded, the exchange it demanded of one kind of freedom for another. Did it happen among similar groups of people in England, too? She supposed it did, though with more moments of rupture. She had moved through nursery, primary and secondary schools with the same group of friends – though there had been times when she had hated one or some or all of them, and she was in no doubt that they had returned the sentiment – but then she had peeled off alone to Oxford, and formed, or joined, or been absorbed into different groups. For others the rupture happened earlier, like Henry being sent to boarding school when he was seven, but then progressing in a cohort to public school, Oxford, beyond. She'd been amazed, the first year at university, how many people Henry seemed to know already, how many schoolfriends he had in other colleges. It had made it so much easier for him in many ways, though it had also denied him the opportunity to be unknown, to cast a new first impression, start over. But that was perhaps an illusory, and certainly a short-lived, freedom.

They ate dinner as the sun was setting, around the table on the terrace on the west side of the house: vats of perfectly cooked spaghetti with raw ripe tomatoes and basil leaves; focaccia fresh from the bread oven; meat grilled over glowing embers (somehow 'barbecue' didn't seem the right word for it); red wine from unlabelled bottles. It seemed as if everyone and at the same time no one was responsible for preparing it all. Afterwards there was coffee and grappa and marijuana. Maybe she would go to Elba with them after all. It wouldn't be hard to change her flight, call in sick at work, or even tell the truth, take a week off. Jacqueline wouldn't mind. And then everything came suddenly to an end.

'Did you enjoy the food?' Daniela asked, passing her a joint.

'It was excellent, thank you.' Toke. Exhale. 'And the swimming made me hungry.' Headrush. She passed the joint to Lorenzo. 'Shit. Is that really strong or am I just getting old?'

'It is grown in Abruzzo,' Daniela said, 'by a collective. It is a small operation, no long supply chains, no gangs. The cannabis is very clean.'

Her choice of words reminded Clare of something. 'Like that coke you bought in Bolivia.'

'I don't understand?'

'The cocaine, in Bolivia, that you passed on to Axel, who gave it to Ollie, who shared it with me. It was amazing. Really strong. Pure. And clean, Ollie said, like this weed.'

There was an awkward silence.

'You didn't eat much in Bolivia,' Daniela said. 'In fact I seem to remember you ate absolutely nothing. I was a little bit worried about you.'

'I'd been ill,' Clare said. 'And the food wasn't great. Not like here.'

'Not like here,' Daniela repeated.

'There is a joke in Italy,' Marco said, 'which isn't really a joke, that everything is either of the left or of the right. Parma ham is of the right, mortadella is of the left. Cannabis is of the left, cocaine is of the right. You understand?'

'That's funny,' Clare said.

'It is and it is not,' Marco said.

'Are you coming with us to l'Isola d'Elba too?' Daniela asked.

There was no mistaking the thrust of the invitation now. Clare wondered how long her presence had been unwelcome. Since she mentioned the cocaine? Or earlier? Perhaps everything had been fine until two minutes ago, but the faux pas made her retrospectively unwelcome since the pick-up in the Piazza Farnese on Friday. 'I'd love to,' she said, 'thank you, but I'm flying back to London tomorrow.'

'What a shame. Lorenzo is driving back to Rome tonight. He can give you a lift.'

Lorenzo was putting the joint to his lips. He paused, looked at Daniela, looked at Clare, looked at Daniela again, passed the joint on across the table. 'Sure,' he said. 'No problem.'

*

They bombed back towards Rome down the A1 in silence. Or at least without saying much. The Mini howled through the night. Music filtered weakly through the stereo speakers. Eventually she asked him about it. He turned the volume up. Spanish guitar, jazzy horns, and cascading over them a man's voice, rich and light and smoky and clear and fast and unhurried and soulful and effortless.

'Who is this?' she asked.

'Fabrizio De André.'

'I like it.'

'You don't know him?'

'Not till now.'

'No? He is very famous in Italy.'

'Is this new?'

'No, it is quite old. He is dead, ten years ago.'

They listened without speaking any more until they were back in Rome, engine idling beside the giant granite bathtub.

'Daniela,' Lorenzo said, 'has a problem with cocaine.'

'I'm sorry,' Clare said.

His crow's feet creased without smiling. He put the handbrake on.

'Thank you,' Clare said. 'For the lift.'

'You're welcome. See you soon.'

Somehow she doubted it. But it was nice of him to say so.

The chatter of English voices at the departure gate the next morning was both nuisance and relief. They flew past Elba. Fog banks hovered in the valleys of the Alps like vaporised glaciers. Jets with black contrails crosshatched the sky over Lake Geneva. The North Sea bristled with arrays of wind turbines, turning slowly. Waves scuffed the surface of the water, seen from this height apparently unmoving. A lonely cloud dragged its shadow across the sea, a rainbow dangling beneath it. After they landed, there was the usual announcement about taking all their personal belongings with them. Impersonal belonging, Clare thought, wouldn't be a bad way to describe the feeling you ought to have in a public space, a park or piazza.

Back at work a couple of weeks later, idling on Facebook, wondering how the trip to Elba had gone, Clare looked to see if Daniela had posted any photographs. But they were no longer friends.

14

Hide-and-Seek

Henry was waiting for Clare on the platform at Stroud. He gave her a hug, took her suitcase, led the way out across the hot tarmac to the car park, unlocked a scalloped black BMW.

'Where did you get the Batmobile?' she asked.

'It's my mum's.'

He put her case in the boot, opened the passenger door for her. As they were driving out of town, she asked: 'What the fuck are you doing, Henry?'

He glanced at the speedometer. 'Around thirty.'

'And being evasive. You know what I mean.'

He kept his eyes on the road. 'Wait till you meet her.'

You know I never like your girlfriends. 'Sorry. I didn't mean to be rude. What I meant was: thanks for inviting me. I just want to be sure you're sure you know what you're doing. And I may not get you to myself again.'

'Because I'm getting married?'

You're already married, and that didn't stop us before. 'I meant this weekend.'

'I know you did. And it's nice to know you care.'

'I do, I do. Though fuck knows why.'

'Have you eaten?'

'Do you mean, why am I so grouchy?'

'No. My mother wanted to save you some lunch. I said you'd have eaten.'

'Oh. In that case yes. I got a sandwich at Paddington.'

'Alex is there.'

'I know.'

'Are you ready to see him?'

'Why wouldn't I be?'

As they drew up, Henry's mother appeared round the corner of the house: an ugly, asymmetrical heap of Cotswold stone, but charming enough when the sun was shining. 'Clare! Just the person I wanted to see. Henry darling, take her bag up to her room. Clare, come and help me pick the raspberries.'

'Hello, Madeleine.'

Henry's mother handed her a basket. 'You look well,' she said, linking their arms and striding down the lawn towards the fruit cage.

'I'd have thought it would be too late for raspberries,' Clare said.

'Nonsense. Never too late for raspberries. Henry said you'd have had some lunch?'

'Yes. But I don't mean the time of day. I mean, in the year. The season.'

'Oh come on, darling. It's only September. Don't be such a

pessimist.' Reaching the fruit cage, she unhitched a loop of orange binder twine and wrenched open the guano-encrusted gate. 'Fucking pigeons,' she said. 'We need more cats. Here you go' – picking a raspberry – 'try that. Pretty good, no? Never too late. There are heaps; only harvest the really dark juicy-looking buggers.'

The raspberry burst in Clare's mouth. She'd forgotten this, her friendship with Henry's mother, how well they'd always got on. Madeleine was one of those posh women who swear all the time and as the mood took her she was capable of either being unblushingly offensive or putting anyone at their ease, though she'd always been nothing but lovely to Clare.

'You know Alex is here?'

'I thought he probably would be.'

'Have you seen each other since . . . ?'

'No.'

'Awkward?'

'Shouldn't be.' She shrugged. 'We'll see. Who else is here?'

'Charlotte, obviously, her brother James, Ed – you know Ed? Henry's new best friend. Lives underneath Alex; they met on the stairs, I think, like living in a sitcom. Henry's schoolfriends, Caspar and Jasper. You must have met them before.'

'Here, a couple of times, and at Henry and Vic's wedding. Toby?'

'No.' Madeleine picked a raspberry seed out from between her teeth. 'You haven't heard? They're not speaking to each other. Well, Toby isn't speaking to Henry. Refuses to be in the house with him. He disapproves of his abandoning his daughter. As do I, of course, but I don't think not speaking to him is the answer. It would be rather hypocritical, for one thing, abandoning my son for abandoning his daughter. It's not what a mother hopes for, of course, either the bad parenting or the squabbling siblings, though I've never got on with my sister. To be honest, I don't think I've ever forgiven her for *not* leaving her husband. Still, I suppose they'll get over it eventually.'

'Henry and Toby?'

'Who else are we talking about? Of course, Toby likes to appear to be taking the moral high ground, but really I think he's just as worried about his inheritance as he is about Jessica's absent male role model. Doesn't like the idea of Henry frittering away all my money on ex-wives and alimony before he gets his hands on half of it.'

'I'm sure that isn't true.'

'Sweet of you. You don't think they're rushing into it?'

'Henry and Charlotte?'

'Who else?'

'Well, I can see some people might think he should have waited till he and Vic were divorced before getting engaged to Charlotte.'

'Henry's idea of deferred gratification is cutting the fingernails on his right hand first,' Madeleine said. 'I suppose we were always too easy on him to compensate for being too hard on Toby. Oh well,' she sighed. 'That should do it,' picking a last raspberry and popping it into her mouth. 'Mm. Heavenly. Let's get these up to the house. Seems a shame to share them with all those louts but I suppose we have to. And I've already made the meringues.' She shut the gate against the pigeons.

Henry's parents' house had always felt like a refuge to Clare, a place the nagging anxieties of everyday life had never been able to reach, left for dust on the M4 somewhere around

Bracknell, whether she'd been driving there in her mother's car during the university holidays – revision, reading, essay-writing, her non-existent future career: all forgotten for forty-eight hours – or out of London in a hire car, over the Westway towards a smoggy sunset, worries about rent and electricity bills left behind with the unread manuscripts and agents' contracts.

But that had all changed the last time she and Alex had gone there, the summer before Henry moved out of London. They'd left the M4 at Swindon and were hurtling towards Cirencester along the empty dual carriageway, Interpol thundering from the stereo (turned up high enough to drown out Alex's literal-minded altered-lyrics singalong, 'We're not going to the city, we're going to the country'), the windows down, the smell of the English summer evening rushing in, dew settling on cut grass, when Alex turned the volume down and mentioned that he'd brought some work with him to do over the weekend. Clare turned the stereo up again, fixed her eyes on the road, put her foot to the floor. The next night, after dinner, while Alex was hunched over his contracts at the desk in Henry's parents' study, the rest of them had gone outside to smoke a joint and ended up playing strip dodgeball on the lawn. It hadn't been Clare's idea: neither the dodgeball, which Henry had started by scooping a half-deflated football out of a flowerbed and chucking it at Caspar (or possibly Jasper, she could never remember which was which); nor the stripping, which had been suggested by Caspar's girlfriend, though only after Clare had in a sense initiated it by taking off her skirt because it was difficult to run in and she was worried about tearing it. She woke Alex up climbing into bed beside him in her pyjamas. He asked what they'd been doing. She told him.

222

He appeared to think she was joking and went back to sleep. No one said any more about it. That weekend was one of the many contenders for the title of Moment At Which Clare And Alex's Marriage Definitively Failed.

She licked congealing raspberry juice from her fingers. 'It's so nice to be here,' she said.

'It's lovely to have you here again,' Henry's mother said, opening the kitchen door. 'It's been far too long. Just pop the basket by the sink, would you? If you want to find the others, just follow the guffaws. Or if you want to freshen up, your bedroom's on the first floor, second door on the right.'

'With the green William Morris curtains?'

'Oh god, yes. You remember those? I've been meaning to replace them for years.'

Bladder emptied, hands washed, hair brushed, minimal make-up checked, Clare joined the others. Henry's father, sprawled in his favourite armchair, was holding court in the drawing room, his audience arrayed in a tableau: Henry at the window, hands in pockets, looking out; Alex perched on the edge of the sofa, all attention; Caspar and Jasper sprawled either side of him; a pair of rangey grey-eyed blonds on the piano stool, obviously brother and sister; and a beautiful boy lounging like an odalisque on the hearth rug. The odalisque noticed her first. 'Hi,' he said, not getting up. 'I'm Ed.'

'Hello everyone,' Clare said. 'Carry on, please, don't mind me.'

Charlotte shook Clare's hand and joined Henry at the window. Clare took Charlotte's place on the piano stool. James smiled.

223

'Hello,' Alex silently mouthed.

She smiled, nodded. It almost felt like being back in their first group tutorial at Oxford, or in a dream about it, in which most of the details were wrong – the wrong people in the wrong place at the wrong time – but the situation was unmistakeable. Everyone else had seemed to know where they were and why they were there and what they were supposed to say and where they were going next, and she had felt lost and confused and tongue-tied and bewildered. But this was nothing like that, really, except that Alex was there, looking like he was at home but secretly feeling exactly the same way she did. And didn't she, actually, feel at home here? And it was fine seeing him again, it really was. It was normal. It was good. This was the way they were supposed to be: two friends among a group of friends, not in love, not a couple, not best friends; but not resentfully out of love either, not avoiding each other, not enemies. If the atmosphere in the room was strained, it wasn't because of any residual tension between her and Alex; it was because the others were worried that there was, that she was finding it difficult to be there – or that he was. She would have liked to have been able to reassure them that everything was fine, that they had no reason to tread carefully on her account – or on Alex's either, though she couldn't speak for him anymore.

'What I was trying to say,' Henry said, 'is that we're a lost generation. There was a leap from the early seventies to the early eighties, leaving us out completely. They were all older than us, until suddenly they were all younger than us. It's really depressing when you think about it. It was all Sampras and Agassi and that lot – mainly Sampras, obviously – and then it was suddenly all Federer and Nadal.'

Alex got out his phone and thumbed through the internet. 'Kafelnikov,' he said. 'Born 1974. Kuerten, 1976. Both world number one.'

'They never won Wimbledon,' Henry said.

'Lleyton Hewitt?' Jasper suggested.

'Born 1981,' Alex said.

'You know what makes me feel old?' Charlotte said. 'Smartphones.'

'They just make me feel poor,' Ed said.

'I hate the way they can settle arguments so quickly,' James said. 'It makes conversation so much more difficult if you can't throw around competing unsubstantiated statements of fact.'

'We seem to be doing all right,' Caspar said.

'But only by having a meta-conversation. It's not the same.' He looked at Henry's father. 'I'm disappointed you live in range of a phone mast, to be honest.'

'What?' Henry's father said. 'Yes, exactly.'

'The signal's pretty crap actually,' Henry said. 'But they've got wireless broadband now. I think my father's secretly addicted to online porn. Apparently it can make you go deaf.'

'I heard that, you cheeky bugger,' his father said.

'Don't be silly, darling,' his mother said, coming into the room. 'He just plays poker on Facebook for fantasy money. It's tremendously tedious but it seems to keep him happy, doesn't it, darling? You're a virtual millionaire.'

'Tennis!' Henry's father said. 'Who's up for a game of doubles? Charlotte? Edward? Henry? Jasper? Anyone?'

Clare looked at Alex, who was looking at Charlotte. Clare looked at Charlotte too. Charlotte was already looking at Clare, as if she recognised her from somewhere. Clare realised that

Charlotte was the woman she'd seen Alex playing tennis with the previous summer, but with completely different hair. They exchanged disarming smiles.

'You three, then?' Henry's father said. 'Alexander, Charlotte and Clare?'

'Stop calling him Edward,' Henry said.

'What? Who? I didn't. I called him Alexander.'

'No, not Alex, Ed.'

'All these awful bloody diminutives. I suppose you'd like me to call you Hen and your bride-to-be Char, too.'

'Not at all. But Ed isn't short for Edward. His name's Ednan.'

'Well why didn't you bloody say so? And stop calling him "Ed"?'

'It's what he likes to go by.'

'It's not his name.'

'Dad, please.'

'It's fine, Henry,' Ed said. 'Really. He's not the first.'

'Terrific. That's me and Edward and who else? Ladies?'

'I don't think anyone wants to play, Dad. I thought I might go and split some logs. Who wants to come with?'

'Don't your parents have some Mellors-type chap who can do that for them?' Caspar asked, reclining against a tree trunk and lighting cigarettes for himself and Jasper.

'Marie Antoinette had milkmaids, but that didn't stop her,' Alex said.

'Marie Antoinette split logs?'

'Only if you believe the more scurrilous Jacobin pamphlets.' Henry wiped his face on his sleeve. 'Anyone else want a go?'

'I'll leave it to Mellors and Marie Antoinette,' Caspar said.

'This is hard work,' Alex said in a vaguely northern accent. The others gave him quizzical looks. 'Bob the Builder,' he said. 'I watch it with Jessica sometimes.'

Clare stepped forward and picked up the wedge. Henry opened his mouth to speak. 'Don't even think about telling me what to do,' she said, lifting a log onto the stump. 'I've been splitting logs since before you were out of nappies.'

Charlotte had brought her camera with her. Clare felt it on her as she raised the sledge hammer, heard the whirr of the shutter, in burst mode, as she brought the sledge down in a controlled arc, sliding her right hand along the shaft to meet the firm grip of her left hand at the base, letting the weight of the head do the work; the clang of iron on iron; the wedge ripped clean through the oak; the two halves collapsed from the stump with a sharp crack, like pool balls into corner pockets.

Caspar, cigarette clenched between his teeth, applauded. Clare proffered him the sledge hammer. He shook his head. She let it fall to the ground, smiled for the camera. 'I like your wig,' she said.

'Thank you,' Charlotte said.

When Clare came out of the bathroom Alex was hovering on the landing.

'Oh, it's you,' he said.

She looked at him, wondered if he'd known it was her and was saying that to give the impression he hadn't been waiting to see her. Or maybe he hadn't known, and just needed the toilet. Or maybe he had known, and didn't particularly want to see her but needed the toilet so waited anyway. And, anyway, why did she care what he was or wasn't thinking?

'It's me,' she said.

'How are you?'

'Okay, actually. You?'

'Good. I've been good. How's work?'

'Up and down. You?'

'Yeah, the same. Actually I'm thinking of chucking it in. I saw a job going at the Competition Commission. You know, used to be monopolies and mergers.'

'Good for you.'

'Thanks. So, where are you living now?'

'Peckham, more or less.'

'More or less Peckham or more or less living there?'

It was the kind of effortful joke he made when trying to impress strangers. 'Both,' she said. 'It's fine, apart from the Italian woman downstairs and her terrible cooking.'

'That resists a stereotype. You've been round for dinner with your neighbours? That resists a stereotype too.'

'No, but the smells come up the stairwell. Rotten garlic, bad cabbage and fetid kidneys.'

'Sounds revolting. I'm lucky enough to live upstairs from the world's best cook. Ed, I mean. You know he can tell when rice is ready by listening to it?'

James came round the corner. 'Queue?' he asked.

'Just him,' Clare said.

'Go ahead,' Alex said.

'Don't be silly,' James said. 'I'll go downstairs.'

'Go on,' Clare said to Alex. 'There's no point hogging the bathroom without even being in there.'

'Good point. I'll see you downstairs then.'

'Sure.'
'It's good to see you.'
'You too.'

'He's a man of great merit,' Henry's father said loudly at the other end of the dinner table, through badly suppressed guffaws.

'He read *War and Peace* after they moved here,' Henry explained. 'That joke's the only thing he got out of it. It means someone's a shit. I tried to explain it doesn't work in Russian, but . . .'

'Who cares?' Henry's father interrupted. 'Shit off!'

'What about the bit,' Alex said, 'where Nikolai drives the sleigh through the snow to the Christmas party and gets so cold he can't think straight anymore? It's amazing, like Tolstoy invented modernism but nobody noticed.'

'I wouldn't know, darling,' Madeleine said. 'That Shitoff business from Henry's father has rather spoiled Tolstoy for me.'

Ed leaned towards Clare. 'I'm half-expecting someone to get murdered in the library.'

'I'm not sure they have a library, specifically,' Clare said. 'There is a billiard room, though.'

'You're joking. I've got lost seventeen times already and still haven't wandered in there by mistake on my way to the toilet. How many generations of Henrys has the house been passed down through?'

'Oh, none. Don't be fooled by his father's lord-of-the-manor act. They bought the house fifteen years ago. Actually, Henry's mother bought it. His father used to work in the city but lost everything in that Lloyds thing in the eighties and now isn't allowed to own anything, not even his own pants. It all belongs to Henry's mother. She had her own PR business, set it up after he went bust, sold it for a small fortune in 2001.'

Madeleine brought in the gravy.

'I was searching for something in my email the other day,' Henry said, 'and saw I'd bought four tickets to see Bob Dylan at the London Arena in May 2002. But the weird thing is, I have absolutely no memory of going to the concert. Can any of you remember going with me? It's a bit disturbing.'

'I hate Bob Dylan,' Jasper said.

'Henry thinks he has a good memory because he can't remember what he's forgotten,' Madeleine said.

'Delicious beef, Madeleine,' Alex said. 'Thank you.'

Murmurs of assent rippled around the table.

'Oh, don't thank me,' she said. 'Thank the cow. I just put it in the oven.'

'If you look at a graph of crime rates plotted against the disappearance of leaded fuel over time, the correlation is extraordinary,' Henry's father said, wiping raspberry juice from his chin with a gravy-stained napkin. 'Lead fumes rot your brain, brain rot leads to crime. QED. There's a direct correlation between low IQ and criminality.'

'That's quite a leap, Dad.'

'Is it? The average IQ in Britain's prisons is well below the national average.'

'That just means there's a correlation between low IQ and getting caught,' Alex said.

'Or between scoring badly on IQ tests and the kinds of activity that are classified as crimes,' Charlotte said.

Clare went to the toilet. When she came back Charlotte was still talking. 'Or those thin plastic strips you find on some bin bags, that I think you're supposed to use to tie them up with, but no one possibly can because it's impossible, they're so staticky they'll stick to anything and they're so weak they'll snap under the slightest pressure. Or single sheets of toilet paper – who uses those?'

'I do,' said Henry's father. 'I find a single sheet of lavatory paper to be exactly what I need when I cut myself shaving.'

'But why are they that size? Who decided, and when, on the optimum dimensions for a sheet of toilet paper?'

'I suppose they're modular,' Alex said, as Clare squeezed past behind his chair. 'Some people tear them off in multiples of two, some in multiples of three. If they were twice as long, people who currently use three sheets at a time would have to use two new ones, the equivalent of four standard-length sheets. Just think of the waste.'

'You've thought about this way too much,' Caspar said.

Clare reached her seat and sat down. 'What's she talking about?' she asked Madeleine.

'Her next art project.'

'Sounds more like a stand-up routine. What's her art like?'

'Cumbersome. Do you dislike her more for marrying Henry or for going out with Alex?'

'It isn't that. Either of those.'

'What then? Just that you're used to being the funniest girl in the room?'

'Not when you're around.'

'Oh, I'm no girl. Haven't been a girl for years.'

'Nor have I.'

'Oh, darling, you all still look very much like children to me.'

'You don't like her either.'

'Don't be silly. I adore her.' Leaning forward, speaking up: 'Are you all right there, Alex? Need anything? Help yourself to wine. Don't wait for Henry's father to offer it to you, you'll never get anything that way.'

'I'm fine, thank you.'

'Have you seen your goddaughter recently?'

'Yes, last weekend in fact. Oh, I have to tell you. She asked me to draw a lion, so I did my best, but she just got crosser and crosser and crosser, until she was screaming at me: "No! A lion! A lion!" And I was more and more flustered, and kept saying: "But it is a lion! Look! It's yellow! There's its mane! There are its whiskers!" Eventually Vic came in and Jessica, in floods, asked her to draw a lion. So Vic picked up a pencil and drew a line. A straight line. One stroke. And Jessica looked at me full of reproach, pointed at the line and said: "A lion."'

Madeleine laughed. 'Does she make you read endless *Topsy and Tim* books? Christ, they're dull.'

'They're worse than dull,' Clare said. 'I found myself flicking through them at my parents' house recently. There's one about a paddling pool, all about how unpleasant buses are, and public parks – all the horrid other people – and Dad saves the day by coming to pick them up in the car and taking them home where he's bought them their own private paddling pool. It's Thatcherism distilled for toddlers. Christ, their mother even looks like Thatcher.'

'I can't imagine how you grew up to be so left wing,' Henry said.

'They redid them about ten years ago,' Alex said. 'I don't think the paddling pool one is available anymore.'

'Its ideological work was done,' Ed said.

'And their mother doesn't look like Thatcher now,' Alex said. 'Though come to think of it she has a passing resemblance to Samantha Cameron. There's a lot less background detail in the new drawings. But read them often enough and you start wondering things like: is their mother having an affair with the swimming teacher? Does their father have a drink problem?'

'Clare, darling, help me clear the plates, would you?'

Alex almost knocked his chair over as he stood up.

'You trained him well,' Madeleine said.

Alex, collecting plates, pretended not to hear, though his ears had flushed red.

Clare supposed she'd have to help, though there was no need to seem too willing. By the time she reached the kitchen door, a plate in each hand, Alex and Madeleine were genu-flecting at the dishwasher.

'There's a woman from the village who helps out,' Madeleine was saying. 'Her predecessor insisted on overwatering the cyclamen. I used to follow her around the house, emptying the water out of saucers. I had to let her go eventually.'

'Couldn't you have asked her not to do it?'

'Darling, I tried.'

'I hired a cleaning lady last year,' Alex said. 'Charlotte's idea, in fact.'

'Kitchen too filthy?'

'Bathroom.'

'Sorry I asked. And now?'

'Spotless. She's wonderful, actually. Can't think how I managed without her.'

'You didn't. Is she Polish by any chance?'

'Yes, actually. I don't often see her, as she comes when I'm at work. Though obviously we met the first time and I gave her a key and so on. She came with reliable references.'

Alex had a way of telling stories about the less fortunate as if he were delivering a BBC report from a third-world disaster zone.

'I saw her last week, however,' he said, 'as I had to wait in for the gasman and it was the day she came, and we got talking. She said she hoped I wouldn't mind if she didn't come in next week, as she had to go and see her mother-in-law in Hull.'

'Hull?' Madeleine said. 'I thought you said she was Polish.'

'She is, but she worked in Hull when she first came to this country. Her husband had a job at the docks. But he died in some kind of industrial accident. I didn't really follow that part of her story, and didn't want to probe her about it. Something to do with a lorry tyre bursting when he was standing next to it, I think, though now I say that out loud it doesn't sound very likely. But anyway, her mother-in-law still lives in Hull, and she's been diagnosed with cancer, so Agata . . .'

'I'm glad she has a name,' Madeleine said.

'What? Yes. Didn't I say already? Sorry. So Agata needs to go up and see her, but her main employer – she works nights, cleaning offices with some dodgy cowboy outfit – won't give her the time off so she has to go there and back in a day.'

'Dreadful,' Madeleine said. 'What about you, Clare?'

She carried the plates over to the dishwasher. 'What about me?'

Madeleine took the plates from her, scraped them, rinsed

234

and stacked them. 'Do you have a cleaner or do you do everything yourself?'

'Neither,' Clare said. 'I live in squalor.'

'Port? Brandy? Cigars have been banned, I'm afraid.'

Henry ignored his father. 'I think we should play a game,' he said.

'Bridge or charades?' his mother asked.

'How about hide-and-seek?' Charlotte said.

'Now you're talking,' said Ed. 'Who's going to count?'

'I will,' Alex said.

'To a hundred, slowly.'

Alex closed his eyes, leaned back in his chair. 'One, two.' He heard the scraping of chair legs, the drumming of feet across the floor, out of both doors, into the kitchen and the hall, up the stairs, laughter receding into silence. 'Thirteen, fourteen. Any chance of a brandy while I count?' No reply. Henry's father had left the room, too. Alex wondered if he was playing.

'Help yourself,' Madeleine called from the kitchen.

'My eyes are closed.'

'Don't be ridiculous.'

He opened his eyes, helped himself to a brandy – 'twenty-five, twenty-six' – settled into one of the armchairs in the bay window, swirled the cognac, sniffed it, sipped it, closed his eyes, swallowed, leaned back. 'Thirty-seven, thirty-eight.' It was tempting to stay in the armchair and drink brandy until he passed out, or the others got bored and gave up. They could come and find him. 'Fifty-three, fifty-four.' Wasn't there a bowl of chocolates on the sideboard? He opened his eyes. Yes there was. He went over, helped himself to something that looked nutty and not too sweet, returned to the armchair. 'Seventy, seventy-one.'

He had learned to enjoy his own company since Clare had left; he had learned many years earlier that it was something that had to be learned: not for an hour or two, while travelling, or alone in his room – that was time he'd been able to fill for as long as he'd been able to read, or to snap two plastic bricks together – but for days on end, day after night after day. The first time he'd spent a night alone, the only person in the house, had been the summer half-term when he was fifteen. His parents and sister went away – to Suffolk, or Devon, or Derbyshire, or some other distant, picturesque county – but he said he needed to stay behind to revise for his GCSEs. Before they left, the opportunities for autonomy, including but not limited to non-furtive masturbation, appeared infinite. But within ten minutes of their car pulling out of the driveway he was at a loss. No longer.

But still, he was here to join in. 'Ninety-nine, one hundred. Ready or not, here I come.' He opened his eyes. Silence. The candles were burning low. He took the snuffer from the dresser and doused them. The smoke curled waxily into his nostrils. He went through to the kitchen: empty. Madeleine had gone.

He stood in the front hall, the still centre of the house, the staircase rising above him in its jagged spiral, held his breath and listened. Clocks ticked. Beams, joists and floorboards groaned. Mice scurried behind the wainscot. Beyond the front door, an owl screeched; pheasants and wood pigeons, their dreams disturbed, flustered in the branches of the fruit trees. The first time he'd come to the house, Alex had parked in the driveway outside the front door and rung the bell. Henry had taken ages to unlock it, fetching one key after another and struggling with the bolts. 'Next time, use the tradesmen's entrance,' he'd said when at last he got it open. 'We all do.' Alex hadn't been through the front door since. One of the reasons it was so easy to get lost inside the house was that it had been enlarged several times over the centuries, and with every addition the orientation had been changed, a new set of front rooms in the latest fashion being added to a new side, relegating the old front rooms to a more modest function and aspect, as if the house were slowly spinning on an axis, or growing organically around the armature of the staircase. A muffled laugh trickled down the stairwell. He thought about chasing after it but decided instead to be methodical about this, starting on the ground floor in the room to the left of the front door, and working his way up through the house, clockwise around each storey.

The door to Henry's father's study was closed. The last time Alex and Clare had been here together she'd had a strop about his bringing some work with him. His hand on the study doorknob, he'd asked her if she would have liked him to stay behind at home to do it and she'd said: 'Yes.'

'I don't see why. It's not going to spoil your fun. You're not the one with work to do.'

'I do have work to do, and I've left it at home. But anyway, that isn't the point.'

'What is the point?'

She'd walked away and he hadn't seen her for the rest of the evening, but she'd seemed to have forgiven him by the time she came to bed.

He went into the study. Henry's father was hunkered at his

computer in the semi-darkness, a glass of port brimming beside the keyboard.

'Excuse me,' Alex said.

'Come in.'

'Are you playing?'

'Poker.'

'Not hide-and-seek.'

'I don't think they have that on Facebook.'

'Anyone else in here, under the desk?'

'That'd be the day.'

'I'll leave you to it. Good luck.'

He flicked on the light switches in the drawing room. Reflections of electric candelabra glistened in the piano's mahogany veneer. It was the first piano he'd heard Clare play, the first time they'd all come to Henry's house, in the Easter holidays of their first year at university, after he'd fallen for her but while she still seemed more interested in Henry, who was still theoretically going out with his old girlfriend, though she was in India and Alex had seen him snog half a dozen girls since Christmas. 'Oh, a piano,' Clare had said, and eased her way through a Chopin Prelude from memory. 'Sorry,' she said, lifting her hands from the keyboard and placing them in her lap after the final chord, 'I'm a bit rusty.' Later she and Henry had played duets: Mozart, Schubert, Debussy. It was funny, Alex thought, watching her fingers scurry across the keyboard, and seeing how easily she got on with Henry's mother, the way Clare chastised him for having gone to private school, when in her own way she was just as much a product of wealth and privilege as he was. Her parents hadn't paid for her schooling directly – nor had his, entirely, as he'd once pointed out to her (never again), because he'd got a scholarship – but they'd bought a house in one of the nicer parts of Guildford, which amounted to much the same thing, and they'd shelled out for piano lessons, violin lessons, ballet lessons, swimming lessons, riding lessons, skiing lessons, while his parents had paid (a proportion of) his school fees and thought that was enough. The total outlay in each case probably wasn't all that different. Henry's parents meanwhile had paid for both packages. Alex wondered if any of them thought they were getting a good return on their investment.

The shadows under the piano stirred. He crept closer. 'Hello,' he said.

James rolled over and crawled out. 'Am I the first?' he asked, getting to his feet and brushing the dust from his knees.

'Afraid so.'

'I'm not. Did I hear you mention brandy earlier?'

'You did. You want one?'

'Christ, yes. Will you join me, or do you have to get on with the seeking?'

'I think I've got time for a quick one.'

Back in the dining room, James poured two hefty glasses and closed the door with his foot on his way to one of the armchairs in the window. Alex took the other chair and a long draught of cognac.

'You've known Henry a long time,' James said.

'Nearly fifteen, fourteen years.'

'And you're his daughter's godfather, is that right?'

'Yes, Jessica. She's lovely.'

'Does Henry see much of her?'

'Yes. Well, I think so. Depends a bit what you mean by "much".'

'More than you?'

'Well I see her quite a lot. Does Charlotte talk about her? About Jessica?'

'She seems to like her. And her mum's doing okay?'

'Vic? Yes. Well, you know. It isn't easy. But yes, all things considered, she's fine. You never got back in touch with her?'

James shook his head, drained his glass. 'Do you have a sister?'

'I do,' Alex said. 'She lives in Alaska.'

'Really?'

'Really.'

'Did you have that thing, when she had a boyfriend she was really in love with for the first time, and it made you jealous because you weren't the most important boy in her life anymore?'

'Not really,' Alex said. 'But I see what you mean.'

'And then one day at last she had a boyfriend you weren't jealous of because he was actually right for her?'

'Is that how you feel about Henry?'

'Not really.'

Alex didn't ask about himself.

'You should probably get back to your seeking,' James said.

'You want to help?'

'I'm going to turn in. See you tomorrow.'

The rest of the ground floor seemed to be clear. On the back stairs Alex ran into Ed. He wondered if it was weird of him to be more jealous of Henry's newfound friendship with Ed than he was of his relationship with Charlotte. But then he reassured himself that Ed was more Charlotte's friend than Henry's, really, even if Henry didn't realise it. And Ed and Alex were still friends, and still living in the same house as each other.

'We must stop meeting like this,' Ed said.

'Call that a hiding place?'

'I got lost again on my way back from the toilet. You found everyone else already?'

'No, only James. He's gone to bed. You want to help?'

'Isn't that cheating?'

Alex looked at him.

'Sure. Happy to.'

Light, voices and the click of billiard balls spilled along a corridor.

'Is that the billiard room down there?' Ed asked.

Alex nodded.

'I wasn't sure if Clare was being serious or not.'

Caspar was lining up on the red. Smoke curled from two cigarettes in the ashtray beside the half-empty vodka bottle on the window sill.

'Found you,' Alex said.

'Gutting,' Jasper said.

Caspar jerked his elbow. The cue ball hit the red and cannoned into a pocket.

'Sorry,' Ed said.

'What are you apologising to him for?' Jasper said. 'That puts him ahead.'

'Oh. So you're not playing pool then.'

'Billiards. You want to play?'

'If you don't mind explaining the rules.'

'Vodka?'

'I'll see you later,' Alex said.

Alex reluctantly turned his attention to the bedrooms, morbidly and irrationally anxious of walking in on Henry and Charlotte having sex. He checked his own room first, certain no one would be in there. It was a small single room next to the bathroom – they'd probably once been one larger room, before being partitioned on the arrival of modern plumbing – where he'd slept the first time he came to stay, thirteen and a half years earlier.

The twin room next door, where Caspar and Jasper were sleeping, he'd once shared with a boy called Tom, whom he hadn't thought of in years, but whom he now remembered strumming a guitar in Henry's parents drawing room and singing 'Bob Dylan's Dream' while Clare absentmindedly played along on the piano, improvising an unobtrusive descant in the upper registers. The room was empty.

He paused outside Henry and Charlotte's door: silence within. It was probably safe to enter. Looking at the clothes strewn around the generically decorated double room, he wondered if Henry felt the absence of a childhood bedroom in this house which his parents had moved to when he was already almost an adult. Then again, he'd gone to boarding school when he was seven; perhaps he'd felt the absence of a childhood bedroom more strongly in the house – houses? – his parents had lived in when he was much younger. Or perhaps he didn't feel the absence of a childhood bedroom at all. Alex wondered where Henry thought about when he thought about home.

The double room across the landing was Clare's, as it had been the last time they'd been there together, four years earlier, when it had been his room too. The window was open, the smell of dew and damp foliage wafting in on the breeze with the sounds of the night, ruffling the curtains. The first time they'd shared the room they'd had sex in the garden, too, an urgent fuck against a tree near the fruit cage. Alex wondered if Clare had thought of it, as he had, while they were eating their raspberries at dinner. He coughed, inhaled, wheezed, felt an old familiar tightening in his lungs. The dust was getting to him. He went back to his own room for his inhaler. Holding his breath, giving the salbutamol time to calm the inflammation in his bronchioles, he heard someone else breathing. He looked under the bed. Henry was lying on his back, fast asleep, snoring into the bedsprings. He decided to leave him there.

He found Charlotte at last in the airing cupboard, on a high hot shelf behind several piles of towels.

'You must be roasting up there.'

'It's very cosy. I almost feel like a Mitford.'

'Do you need help getting down?'

'Don't try to be gallant, it's unbecoming.' She climbed down the shelves as if descending a ladder, hopped from the last shelf to land neatly on both feet, dusted off her jeans. 'Where's everyone else?'

'Ed, Jasper and Caspar are in the billiard room, James has gone to bed, Henry's asleep under my bed, Clare I haven't found yet.'

'So I didn't win?'

'I don't think it's that sort of game.'

She hesitated, as if thinking about kissing the tip of his nose, then smiled instead. 'I'll go and retrieve Henry. Which is your room again?'

He told her and they went their separate ways. The bedroom at the end of the corridor was Henry's mother's. Alex paused at the door. He didn't want to barge in on her getting ready for bed. There were voices inside.

'When I was a child I always thought having a sofa in your bedroom was the height of sophistication.'

'Oh, so did I. I still do. That's why it's there. You know, about Henry, I always rather hoped he might marry you. Did you ever . . . ?'

'Once, yes, actually, we did.'

'Oh, darling, I didn't mean that. Though I must say I'm quite pleased. Is that very wicked of me?'

Alex turned queasily away and headed back towards the billiard room.

Alex was in Clare's room. Or she was in his room. They were in their room. He was planning to leave her. 'Give me one good reason why I should stay,' he said. 'I'll give you two,' she said, crawling onto the bed and pulling up her nightdress. Her intent was unmistakeable – which was strange, because he'd always worried he'd misunderstood her even when she wasn't being ambiguous – and more than a little surprising. In the early days, when sexual experimentation had felt like a categorical imperative, and it had seemed important that no part of each other's body should be out of bounds, they'd dutifully tried anal sex, both ways round, his anus as well as hers, with extreme care and plenty of lubrication, but quickly agreed that

244

it wasn't for them, either way. 'Listen,' she said, looking back over her shoulder. 'I can play opera.' The room filled with music. He woke up, alone in his single bed. Clare was nowhere to be seen. But the opera was still playing. He looked at his watch: half-past seven. He pulled on his jeans and glasses and went out onto the landing. Henry's other friends were staggering bleary-eyed from their rooms like extras in a disaster movie. 'What's going on?' James asked.

'*Nessun dorma*,' Alex said.

'What?'

'Puccini. It's Henry's father's idea of a joke. But it also means he's made breakfast. See you in the kitchen.'

'Does anyone else have dreams that are structured like bad jokes?' Alex asked after his second cup of coffee.

'How do you mean?'

'Oh, you know. The cannibal king and queen are going to bed and the queen looks in the mirror and says: "God I look fat." And the king says: "Don't be too hard on yourself: you have had eight children." And the queen says: "I should go on a diet." And the king says: "Cut down to four a day?"'

'That's what you dreamt about?'

'No. That's just an example of a bad joke.'

'What did you dream about?'

'I couldn't possibly tell you.'

Henry's father burst out laughing. 'Four a day!' he said.

15

Not-Boggle

The last time Vic had taken a typing test she'd clattered out 90 words per minute. In a two-minute game of online Boggle – though not actually Boggle, as the game's Facebook page was at pains to point out, since Boggle was a registered trademark of Hasbro, with which the page was in no way affiliated – she ought, in theory, to be able to score up to 180 words. But she rarely did much better than 60, and her score didn't vary much with the number of words that were available. If anything, she found the higher-scoring boards more paralysing: too much choice. The best strategy, she had found, was to type away automatically at the obvious three-letter words – *ate*, *eat*, *eta*, *tea*, *tae*, with or without plurals – while searching for the longer, more elusive ones. Still, 30 words per minute was probably faster than she managed to write when she was working, when she had (in theory) the entire English language at her disposal. Playing not-Boggle online was a peculiarly destructive way to waste time when she was supposed to be working. If anyone had ever challenged her over it, she'd have said it was useful thinking time, but it wasn't. It crowded her mind with words stripped of meaning, bereft of syntactical relations with other words; words that related to each other only by having collections of letters in common. It made coherent sentence formation virtually impossible.

She needed to find another distraction, one that created less interference, one that was more productive, however indirectly. Jenny had recently taken up knitting, and complained about how much money she spent on yarn – rare and exquisite blends of cashmere, alpaca and silk – but at least she had something to show for it all; Amy, on the other hand, had once explained that she liked to unwind at the end of the day with a silver-plated vibrator ('naturally anti-bacterial') and 'twenty minutes max' of 'female-friendly' online pornography. When she got home that night, after her daughter and mother were both asleep, Vic had taken a few sideways glances at a free porn site, and confronted by the startling ugliness of it all – the soft-lit pseudo-romantic schlock of the more 'tasteful' videos in its dishonest way even more repugnant than the brute hydraulics of most of what was on offer; she averted her eyes from the truly rancid stuff – she watched in appalled fascination for a lot less than twenty minutes, shut down the window and went back to playing not-Boggle on Facebook.

And she was playing again now, many weeks later, on this sunny Saturday morning in September. Waiting for the next game to load, she looked up from the screen towards the view of the treetops shimmering beyond the window. Her eye snagged on the paint peeling on the window frames. A languid, late summer wasp flew down to the window and burrowed into the frame, buzzing like a dentist's drill. The game had begun. She turned back to the screen and started typing.

[01:59] AGE RAGE CAGE SIN SING RAISING
BRAISING CHAIN

'Why so glum, love?' her mother had asked her earlier that morning. 'Is it because it's Henry's engagement party today?'

'How did you know about that?'

'Alex told me.'

Jessica came charging into the kitchen carrying the plastic lid of one of her toy boxes like a police officer with a riot shield. 'Where's Alex?' she asked.

'He's at Grandma Madeleine's house.'

'Is Damma Maddy Alex mummy?'

'No, she's Daddy's mummy.'

'Yes. Damma Maddy is Daddy's mummy. Who is Alex mummy?'

'Another lady. We don't know her.'

'Does Alex know her?'

'Of course. She's his mummy.'

'Why?'

'Because he grew in her tummy. Would you be all right taking her out this morning, Mum?'

'Of course.'

'And you?' Jessica said to Vic.

'No, sweetheart. I've got lots of boring work to do. But I'll see you when you come home for lunch. Thanks, Mum. And

248

no, that's not why I'm glum,' she said, trusting that her mother wouldn't believe her, and would stop asking.

'Banana,' Jessica said.

'Banana what?' Vic said.

'Banana NOW.'

'Try again.'

'BANANA.'

'Try again.'

'Please.'

Vic took a banana from the fruit bowl and broke it into thirds both ways, latitude then longitude, gutted the pieces like shrimp and dropped the grey threads into the compost bucket by the sink. Jessica ate one of the ninths and said: 'Enough.'

Linda took Jessica out to get her coat and shoes on. Vic took the eight banana pieces on their plastic plate upstairs to her study.

[01:37] CHAIR CHAR CAR CARS BAR BARS BRA BRAS BRAIN RAIN

She paused in her typing to eat the last ninth of banana. It was six months since she'd gone into hospital for the procedure. They'd booked her in for it quickly, or it seemed quick to her, a week after the second, confirmatory scan.

'Don't forget your money,' her mother had called as she was on her way out the door, slinging over her shoulder the rucksack she normally used when taking Jessica out for the day, the wipes, nappies and rice cakes replaced by a new pair of flannel pyjamas, a full tube of expensive hand cream, a copy of *Persuasion*, an unopened book of crosswords and a biro. She pretended not to hear.

Driving out of the village she passed a huddle of church-going mothers on the corner by the post office. As recently as a few months ago she'd have worried about where they might have thought she was going, but now she was past caring.

Her father's ashes had been interred in the village church-yard in the autumn. It had been Vic's idea, and a tacit invitation to her mother to move in with them permanently. Her father wouldn't have seen the point of it, would have described cremation and burial as belt and braces, but there was nowhere obvious to scatter the ashes, and they were hardly going to keep them in a ghoulish urn on the mantelpiece, so burial seemed the tidy solution. He would at least have approved, she hoped, of how little space he took up in the churchyard, how small the grave was, beside a woman whose epitaph, the worst Vic had ever seen, was: SHE SUFFERED IN SILENCE. The next weekend she'd gone back to plant some daffodil bulbs she'd dug up from her parents' front garden. She passed three of the churchgoing mothers on the path near the lychgate, and they exchanged friendly smiles. Kneeling by the grave, trowel in hand, she heard them talking on the other side of the yew hedge.

'I heard she kicked him out for not earning enough.'

'No, he was having an affair, wasn't he? Up in London.'

'Well if he was, he must have had his reasons, that's all I can say.'

'Can't have been easy for him, having his mother-in-law move in with them like that.'

'It's a big enough house.'

'What about that man who comes down from London, Andrew or whatever his name is, too up himself to talk to any of us?'

'He is – or was – a friend of Henry's, I gather.'

'Oh really?'

'A banker, isn't he?'

'He must be earning enough then.'

'She says there's nothing going on, of course, but really, I must see him down here every other weekend.'

'What does Jenny say?'

'She says Henry's an s-h-i-t and that's all there is to it.'

'I can't believe the way she swears in front of her children.'

'I know.'

'Will must have the patience of a saint.'

Vic pressed the earth down around the bulbs, stood up and brushed the dirt from her hands. She'd always wondered how Jenny managed to be so outspoken and yet stay on such good terms with everyone: a combination, apparently, of scaring people and not giving an s-h-i-t what they thought. Hearing her neighbours gossip about her was a surprising relief; the things they actually said weren't nearly as bad as the things she feared they'd say, which would require them to be tele-pathic, or at least a lot more perceptive than they were.

They watched her drive past. She waved. They smiled and waved back. Leaving the thirty zone she put her foot down.

The hospital reminded her of an airport, though she felt more like a suitcase than a passenger, with the luggage label that had been clipped round her wrist when she checked herself in, leaving her agency at the door like an umbrella. She supposed she was mixing her metaphors, but blamed it on the medication she'd been given, or the not eating for twenty-four hours (which had been the hardest thing to deflect her mother's attention from). She'd changed into her pyjamas, washed and moisturised her hands, tried to get comfortable in the chair beside her bed – she couldn't bring herself actually to get into bed yet – and turned to the first puzzle in the crossword book (a Christmas present from her mother).

Now she was waiting, like the baby bear waiting for his kiss goodnight in that book of Jessica's – no, in fact, utterly unlike him. She wondered if she'd ever get used to the smell, the film of industrial-strength disinfectant overlaying but failing to mask the scent of bodily fluids, the pheromone signatures of confusion and dread. She'd done half a dozen crosswords straight off, filling in the solutions as fast as she could read the clues and write them, then given up because her fingers ached, and because it was boring, their being so easy. She tried to read *Persuasion* but her eyes slid off the page.

She waited. One of the reasons hospitals were like airports was that despite their ostensible purposes – travel, treatment – their main function was as spaces in which people waited. She stared at the last completed crossword puzzle, started to see it as a not-Boggle grid, tracing words between, across and around the solutions. She closed her eyes and saw not-Boggle grids seared on her retinas, the letters inconstant and ambiguous, slithering across the surface of the reason she was there, the reason that hospitals were really nothing like airports at all.

Through the course of the morning, her waiting was punctuated by an irregular series of nurses and doctors who came by to take measurements, give injections, ask oblique questions Vic was sure she'd already answered, and give evasive answers to any questions Vic had in return.

'Do you know how long it will be?' she asked.

'Not too long now,' the nurse said.

Vic told her the time the operation had been scheduled for. 'It won't be too long now.'

Vic knew that delay was inevitable, that there were emergencies that had to be fitted in, and complications that prolonged surgery, and that doctors as much as anyone else were prone to dawdle and gossip. But it would have been nice to have been given some indication of when her waiting might come to an end. She stared at Jane Austen again, thinking she'd have done better to bring Georgette Heyer.

'Hard to concentrate on things, isn't it,' said the woman in the next bed.

The conversational gambit was unexpected. Not the form but the fact of it. As with other passengers at an airport, Vic had assumed the protocol on the ward would be for the patients to politely ignore each other. She had occasionally been chatted up by men at airports when travelling alone, but they'd always begun by asking her where she was flying to, and the equivalent question in hospital – 'What are you in for?' – seemed too risky. In order to feel comfortable asking it, you'd have to be confident that your condition was so severe that the person you were asking couldn't possibly have something worse. And if you were as ill as that, you surely wouldn't feel like chatting with your neighbours, even assuming you were able to.

'Yes,' Vic said. 'It is.'

'I'm Sarah,' the woman said.

'Victoria.'

'So what are you in for, Victoria?' Sarah asked.

And then at last, just when it seemed she'd settled into permanently waiting for something that was never going to happen, it was time to go, and before she knew it she was out of her comforting flannel pyjamas, in a hospital gown (though 'gown' was hardly the word), being wheeled on a trolley towards theatre.

She didn't look as the cannula stung the back of her hand. 'Don't worry,' someone told her. Did she look worried? She supposed she must do. Did she feel worried? Hard to say. But the voice was reassuring, though she had no idea who was speaking, anaesthetist or surgeon or nurse or porter or someone else entirely. 'The anaesthetic will be very light. It's a quick operation. It's very small, what they have to take out of you.' Another voice asked her to count backwards from ten.

She came round swearing, a nurse dosing her with painkillers. 'There's no need for that sort of language, love.'

'Fuckity fuck fuck FUCK.'

Back on the ward an hour or so later (she was watching the clock now, anxious to get home to Jessica), her coprolalia long since subsided, a nurse went with her to the toilet to watch her pee. Whatever the test was, she passed it, as she managed to pee normally despite the looming nurse, and the bleeding must have been within acceptable limits, because they told her she could go home.

'Will someone be coming to pick you up?'

'No, they won't.'

'OK. There should be taxis outside then. Or if not you can call for one. We don't recommend the bus.'

'Right.'

'You didn't drive yourself here, did you? You're not allowed to drive now.'

'No, no. Of course not. I'll get a cab.'

Walking unsteadily out to the car park she felt like a jewel thief, or a convict on the run, or a dissident or asylum seeker crossing a border, expecting to be stopped at any moment and dragged back inside. But nobody stopped her, or even looked at her. She took a deep breath of fresh air. She knew you were supposed to feel nauseous after a general anaesthetic, but she didn't. She didn't feel sick at all. For the first time in weeks, in fact, she no longer felt as if she were being slowly poisoned. She drove carefully home with the windows down, the stereo off, nothing in her head but the roar of the engine and the rush of the wind, the chimney of the hospital incinerator receding in the rear-view mirror.

[01:07] GIN RARING BRING CHANGE [invalid word]
SCAR CAN SAC

During the second scan, the stony-faced radiographer – or sonographer, or whoever she was; she hadn't introduced herself, but Vic was fairly certain she wasn't a doctor; she wasn't the same person who'd done the first scan, either – rolled the cursor around the screen, clicking off measurements and angles and close-ups until she came to the end of her checklist and said simply: 'It's confirmed.' Vic thought she could at least say she was sorry, but perhaps they weren't allowed to do that because it would have been somehow admitting liability. Vic had to stop herself from automatically saying thank you.

She cried in the false privacy of her car in the hospital car park. When the sobs subsided she composed herself to drive home. The fuel light came on as she was pulling out of the hospital. She stopped at the supermarket to fill up, and decided she might as well do some shopping while she was there. Every second trolley was being pushed by a mother with two or more preschool children. In the toiletries aisle she stared at a tube of facewash that appeared to have an image of a fetus on it until it resolved into a breaking wave. She looked down into her trolley, and wondered why she'd thought she wanted or needed any of the things in it. Better to start again. She left the trolley where it was in the toiletries aisle and went out to the car park to get another, empty one. Faced with the rows of chained and interlocking trolleys she thought better of that, too, headed back to her car and drove home empty-handed.

'Do you want help bringing the shopping in?' her mother asked.

'There isn't any.' She'd forgotten the supermarket had been her alibi.

'What do you mean?'

'I left my cards at home, would you believe it.'

'You were gone a long time.'

'It was insanely busy and I didn't realise until I got to the till that I couldn't pay for anything.'

'You didn't have enough cash even for milk? Jessica's drunk three cups this morning and we're nearly out.'

'I didn't think of that.'

'Never mind. I'll go to the post office.'

'Where is Jessica?'

'She's asleep.'

'Oh.'

'It's nap time.'

'So it is.'

'Are you all right, love? You seem a bit, distracted.'

'I'm fine. I'd better get on with some work before Jess wakes up.'

She went upstairs to her study. A few minutes later her mother wordlessly brought her a mug of tea. At the creak of the door handle she switched tabs in her browser from not-Boggle to her email inbox. She had no new messages. She wasn't disturbed again till Jessica woke and called for her. She finished the game she was playing and poured the cold tea down the bathroom sink before going to get her up.

[00:43] BARN BRIMS BRIM RIMS BRING RANG BANG SANG SANE SCAN SIX ISM CHASM [invalid word] CARB CAR [word already played]

She'd thought she'd known what to expect at the first scan, most aspects of it familiar from the last time. The main difference was Henry's absence, but in any case she didn't want him there. She didn't recognise the sonographer but couldn't have sworn it wasn't the same person as before. She climbed into the chair, leaned back, unbuttoned her jeans, craned her neck round to see the screen. The gel was cold and gooey and

257

unpleasant but, again, not unexpected. The sonographer smeared it across her stomach with the transducer probe with one hand, rolled the cursor with the other, eyes fixed on the display, mouth sealed in professional neutrality. His frown deepened as he moved the probe up and down, left and right, pressing harder into her stomach.

'What is it?' she asked.

He asked her again the date of her last period. She told him. He said it was smaller than they'd expect for those dates, but one of the purposes of the scan was to date the pregnancy more accurately, based on the size of the embryo. So it was possible the pregnancy was less far advanced than they thought.

She knew it couldn't be, because she and Henry had had sex for the last time on New Year's Day. But that was more than she wanted to share with the sonographer so she went along with the fiction.

The sonographer said he was also having difficulty locating the heartbeat. She would have to come in for another scan, he said.

At the first scan when she was pregnant with Jessica, the sonographer had smiled when he said the embryo was the size of a bean. Her heart's strong flutter like a hummingbird's wings.

CARRIAGE MISC [00:00]

She closed the browser without waiting to see the results. She'd spotted the eleven-letter word a fraction of a second too late to type it. It was a horrible coincidence, or a sign that she'd played far too many games of not-Boggle. With dozens or even hundreds of words per game, and dozens or even hundreds of games, every now and then you were bound to see a word that spooked you, and it would be the last word you read before shutting down, for the same reason you always found something you'd lost in the last place you looked.

Sarah, the woman in the next bed when she went in for the D&C in March, had been about to undergo a full hysterectomy for ovarian cancer. Whatever cause you might have for sorrow, she knew, there was always someone whose sorrow was worse than yours. But that didn't make your sorrow any better, or stop it being yours.

One night, nearly a year ago, Jessica had been sick and there had been an earthquake in Pakistan. Unable to sleep, listening out for the next bout of retching, hoping there wouldn't be one, irritated by Henry's snoring, Vic had got out of bed and sat up in the glow of her computer screen, refreshing the US Geological Survey's list of earthquakes, looking out for after-shocks, hoping there wouldn't be any. Grotesque and disproportionate though she knew it was, she couldn't help the way that her daughter's vomiting and the earth's shaking were entangled, like a metaphor, in her tired mind.

Her mother watched the news every evening, before making herself a mug of hot chocolate – she always offered Vic one too; Vic always said 'no, thank you' – and going up to bed. She'd mutter adjectives ('terrible . . . awful . . . how awful . . . just terrible') as the headlines unfolded: mining accident in Poland (thirteen dead); suicide bombing in Pakistan (thirty-three dead); shooting in Mexico City underground (two dead); stabbing in Beijing (two dead); Holocaust denial from the

Iranian president; a Rwandan businessman convicted for complicity in genocide; a banker in Hong Kong convicted for insider trading. In the kitchen afterwards, the microwave bright and humming, rotating her mug of chocolate in its stately pirouette, she'd deplore the day's events to Vic, who would say she already knew, having read it all on the *Guardian* website during the afternoon. Her mother would shake her head, as if Vic's already knowing made her somehow culpable; the microwave would ping; and as if by magic the ephemeral atrocities would be banished from her mind for twenty-three hours. Of course that was how it had to be; how else would she get through the day? How else would anyone get through any day?

And Vic was getting through the day today, as if it were a day like any other, which it was, because it wasn't – though according to the online calculators it would have been – the day, the 'day of days', as one of Jessica's storybooks had it, the day of the tiny shrivelled thing, her son, and Henry's son, Jessica's brother's birthday. Foolish to think of it as a boy. Foolish to think of it as anything. But still.

She wouldn't want another baby, wouldn't want to have gone through another pregnancy, to be in labour now. Perhaps it would have brought Henry back, but she didn't want Henry back. Most of the time, she didn't think about it. But she couldn't avoid thinking about it sometimes, and now was one of those times. And though she accepted the way things were – was in many ways glad things were as they were – none of that negated her sense of grief.

She hadn't told anyone she was pregnant, and she hadn't told anyone she wasn't pregnant anymore. She hadn't told Henry, because he'd walked out before she missed her period.

She hadn't told her mother, because she would try to look on the bright side and say it was probably for the best. She hadn't told Amy, because she always made such a show of being bored by children. She hadn't told Jenny, because she'd just had her twenty-week scan, and everything was fine: 'Another bloody boy,' she'd said. Now Robbie was two months old, and undeniably a little love, but Jenny's endless, only semi-sincere complaining, which she'd found so appealing when Jamie and Jessica were babies, the way it took the pressure off her to be happy all the time, was harder to take the second time round. The only person she wanted to tell – the only person who had any right to know – was Jessica, but she was still too young to understand the cipher of her sibling who wasn't. Vic resolved to tell her when she was old enough, whenever that might be. Until then, it was nobody's business but her own.

She looked at the paint peeling on the window frames. When she was a child she had watched her father painting the windows in the springtime; rubbing them down with sandpaper, brushing away the dust, protecting the glass with masking tape, applying primer, undercoat and topcoat. It was the kind of thing he thought was important, like polishing his shoes every Sunday night. The battle against entropy.

She shut the computer down, picked up the plastic plate, sticky with banana traces, and went down to the kitchen. She put the plate in the sink and took the car keys off their hook.

The DIY shop, like everywhere else, seemed to be filled with parents herding pairs of children. She found herself in the pest control aisle. She thought about the beetle larvae in the rafters, wondered if she should buy something that might kill them. But the websites all said the infested wood needed to be taken out and burned. Trying and failing to treat the problem would only deprive her of plausible deniability – to the council, to estate agents, to Henry. It was easier not to think about it. She looked away from the pesticides. A bored sales assistant, dodging the family groups, seemed to be waiting for her to ask him for help. Fresh out of school, or still in it, he might not be bad looking in a few years, once his skin cleared up. 'Excuse me,' she said with a smile. 'I wonder if you could help me? There are a few specific things I'm looking for.'

'Of course,' he said, his face lighting up.

She let him guide her, up and down between the stacks, loading her trolley with sandpaper, paintbrushes, different kinds of paint, trying not to think about how much it would all cost. She took his advice on everything. It was easier that way, and seemed to make him happy.

'Windows, is it?' he asked.

'That's right.'

'Just moved into your own place?'

'Something like that.'

'Anything else you need help with today?'

'Not today, thank you.'

'Well, you know where we are.' He was hovering still.

'I expect I'll be back in next week.'

'See you then, then.'

'Thank you again.'

She was halfway through sanding down the sitting room windows when her daughter and her mother came back from the playground.

'Come on, Jessica,' Linda said, smiling. 'Mummy's busy. Why don't we go and make a cake for tea?'

16

Scrabble

The knee-high barriers swung open. The six of them slid forward onto the conveyor belt, shuffling into position, careful not to knock into each other. James and Ed, because they were snowboarding, had claimed the outside seats. Clare had done her best not to sit next to Alex, but didn't want to draw attention to the fact that she was trying to avoid him, so Caspar and Jasper, joined at the hip, had glided oblivious into position beside James, leaving Clare between Alex and Ed. The chair trundled round behind them, knocked them into a sitting position with a firm blow to the calves, scooped them up and accelerated away, their legs dangling heavily in the crisp Alpine air.

This time tomorrow they would be at Stansted, queuing at the UK Border – how quaint the old 'Passport Control' already seemed – or waiting for their luggage. Clare hated Stansted, the fundamental dishonesty of the architecture, the way it pretended to be a single open space when the entire purpose of airports was the division of space, the separation of people. On the flight out, Caspar and Jasper had been reminiscing about the pleasures of the snow train, the long, leisurely, drunken all-day or all-night ride through France, and she'd thought how nice that would have been, easily seduced by the romance of a long train journey, but she was glad now that they wouldn't be taking it home.

Everyone had said she was mad to be going on Henry's stag holiday. 'How on earth will you cope with the strippers and circle jerks?' Jacqueline had asked.

'I don't think it'll be like that,' Clare had said. And it hadn't been. On that score, she had no regrets about coming. But what a mistake it had been. And how could it not have been? It was always bound to be confusing, Henry's stag weekend, a retrograde step to a time when they still fancied each other but still weren't supposed to. And then there were the erotics of skiing itself, the way that, like dancing, it reminded her of muscles she'd forgotten she had, and of ways in which they could work together, ways in which she'd forgotten her body could move. And there had been moments when it had felt like dancing together, too, the pair of them synchronised in a balletic descent.

The last time she'd travelled across Europe by rail had been alone with Alex, when they were still students. They'd had inconclusive sex in a narrow top bunk, anxious about people walking in on them or the train stopping suddenly and rolling them onto the floor. They gave up in a shared giggling fit, which in its way was as good as an orgasm, though she wouldn't have admitted that at the time. It was still a happy memory for her. Though possibly not for him, since when Jasper had said, 'We should have taken the train,' Alex had said: 'Why?

It's just as uncomfortable as the plane and lasts longer. We've only got two and half days skiing as it is. Though I suppose it would have been more environmentally friendly than flying.'

'We're going skiing,' Clare said. 'It's a bit late to worry about the environmental impact. Along with the exorbitant cost, the transient high, the chances of killing yourself, all dependent on a fugitive white powder – it's no different from cocaine, really. I heard someone say the other day that when the revolution comes, it'll be easy to decide who to put against the wall: everyone who's ever been skiing.'

'I love it,' Jasper said.

Airborne at last, Alex had looked out of the window. The sky was shiny bright like a mirror, crisscrossed with the lines of vapour trails. At Geneva they had to walk along miles of travelators, past hundreds of advertisements, all of them for private banks or wristwatches. The airport toilets were the cleanest Alex had ever been in. Wealthy arrivals – and what other kind were there – could be reassured that Switzerland was exactly what they'd been expecting.

They took a minibus across the open border into France and up into the Alps, through a dismal winter landscape of low skies and soggy dun terrain. The trees by the side of the road held pompoms of mistletoe, kicking out their lower limbs like deranged cheerleaders.

Alex spent the drive worrying about the sleeping arrangements. He'd be sharing a room with James, and wasn't looking forward to reruns of the awkward conversation they'd had at Henry and Charlotte's engagement party, with more of James's probing questions about Henry's reliability or otherwise as a husband and father. But as it turned out, James was a very easy roommate: he didn't smell, he didn't snore, he was neat and tidy. He also spoke pretty good French. The first time Alex had gone skiing, on a school trip when he was fourteen, he had tried to strike up a conversation with a French girl on a chairlift, using the phrases he'd been slavishly repeating in language labs for years: '*Comment t'appelles-tu?*'

'Sorry, I don't speak English,' she'd replied in English.

Up here above the snowline, the landscape was dazzling. In the middle of the first afternoon, after the first shaky run down, they'd stopped for a beer at the top of a chairlift, on a terrace with a view of Mont Blanc. 'Skiing!' Henry exclaimed, in much the same way that his daughter would point at a dog and say *dog*. 'I love it. So good. Nothing like it.'

'Better than sex?' Jasper asked.

'I'm getting married.'

'So?'

'Skiing lasts longer,' Clare said.

'And it's available,' Alex said.

'Only for this weekend.'

'A weekend's better than never.'

'Oh, that's too sad,' Henry said. 'We'll have to take you out tonight and meet some girls.'

'Women.'

'Whatever you say.'

Less than forty-eight hours later, the chairlift was rumbling above the treetops, carrying all of them except Henry.

'I hope Henry's all right,' Alex said.

'I'm sure he's fine,' Ed said.

'Flogging the bishop, I expect,' Caspar said.

'Spanking the monkey,' Jasper said.

'Choking the chicken.'

'Beating his meat.'

'Pumping the python.'

'Slapping the clown.'

'Making the bald man cry.'

'Flagellating the one-eyed monk.'

'Giving the half-blind dog a run for his money.'

'Jesus,' James said. 'Enough already. You may have been at school together but that was a long time ago.'

'Old habits die hard.'

They collapsed in giggles.

'Why are you friends with these people?' Clare asked Ed.

'I have lots of friends,' he said.

'But you're Henry's best man.'

'Yes.'

'But he wouldn't be your best man?'

'Probably not, no.'

Henry watched the infinite succession of chairs rising from one side of his hotel room window and disappearing past the other. It was hard to make out the distant figures, swathed in their hi-tech thermal clothing. He thought he'd seen his friends go by several times already, but they couldn't all have been them. Probably none of them were. He shifted his attention to the skiers on the last few hundred metres of blue run below the chair. They came in waves, a few good skiers together – fast, smooth, stylish, controlled – then a pause, then a chaotic horde of overconfident novices, legs apart, weight back, everyone appearing in a terrible hurry to get somewhere, though they were all only heading to the lift to go up for another run down (and, yes, that was why Henry did it too). The little kids were the best to watch, fearless and flexible, like rubber kittens. Henry had been six the first time he went skiing, with his parents and brother, somewhere in Austria. They'd flown into Munich, and he'd gazed from the coach at the snow heaped up along the edge of the Autobahn. His father had taken him and Toby out onto the slopes on that first evening, as it was getting dark, and they'd trudged through the dusk up the lower reaches of the nursery slope towards a high, remote structure that looked like a rugby goal. Henry got tired long before they reached it, so they stopped, put on their skis and snowploughed down their first few shallow metres.

He thought he'd like to bring Jessica skiing in a few years' time, if Vic would let him. He assumed it was permitted by the terms of their custody agreement. He needed to spend more time with his daughter. The last weekend she'd been to stay with him in Camberwell he'd asked her what she wanted for breakfast on Sunday morning and she said 'Pancakes', so he dug out flour and eggs and mixed a batter while she was drinking her milk. She took pans, spoons and lids out of the kitchen cupboards and drawers, happily pretending to make breakfast – 'Making breakfast,' she said – while he did it for real and Charlotte slept on, childless, in the next room. Jessica watched with detached interest as he tossed the first pancake with a skill he wasn't sure he still had.

'Pancakes are ready,' he said.

She frowned.

'What do you want on it? Lemon and sugar?' Come to think of it, they didn't have any lemons. 'Honey? Jam?'

'Pancakes,' she shouted.

He slid the pancake onto a plate, dropped the frying pan on the hob, opened the fridge, grabbed a pot of jam, scooped a blob onto the pancake, put the plate on the table. Jessica scowled at it, pushed the plate away. 'Pancakes!'

'Not with jam. Okay.'

He turned the gas on, ladled batter into the pan, flipped the pancake with the spatula, nervous of not being able to toss it properly in his hurry. He put honey on this one. Jessica stared at him furiously. *'Pancakes!'*

There was an old jar of golden syrup in the cupboard. He tried that on the next one: still no good. Sugar and orange juice. Sugar alone. Unadorned pancake. Nothing was acceptable. He ate them himself, making exaggerated noises and faces of delight: 'Mmmmm! Delicious!'

Nothing worked. 'PANCAKES!' she screamed at him, tears of rage and frustration and hunger streaming down her face. 'PANCAKES!'

Charlotte came into the kitchen.

'Sorry to wake you,' he said.

She gave him a sceptical look. She had a box in her hand. She opened a cupboard, took out a bowl, opened the box, poured its contents into the bowl, put it on the table. 'There you go, my love,' she said to Jessica, who immediately stopped crying, let Charlotte dry her eyes and wipe her nose, settled into her chair and started eating the dry cereal with a large spoon.

'Cornflakes?' Henry asked, looking at the pancake detritus strewn around the kitchen.

'Cornflakes,' Charlotte said.

'Pancakes,' Jessica said, her mouth full of them.

'How did you know?'

'I phoned Alex.'

'Alex?'

'I didn't feel I could call Vic.'

'Where did you get the cornflakes from?'

'Newsagent.'

'I didn't hear you go out.'

'I'm not surprised, the noise you two were making.'

Never had he felt so inadequate.

She kissed his cheek. 'You're covered in flour,' she said. 'Thanks for making pancakes. I'd love one with jam.'

'Pancakes,' Jessica said, smiling at him.

If Vic had ever said and done what Charlotte had said and done, Henry would have felt it as competitive parenting, and it would have made him angry. Unfair, perhaps, but he couldn't help the way he felt. And he was so glad to be marrying Charlotte. He missed her a lot. He wished she was there with him in the hotel in the Alps, had been thinking about her all morning. Well, almost all morning, when his mind hadn't drifted to pondering what it was, exactly, that was so sexy about women skiing at speed. There weren't many people who looked good in salopettes, but Clare was one of them. Henry didn't like being by himself.

He blinked. Vitreous floaters skidded, hid themselves among the condensation on the window pane. The walls of the hotel, inside as well as out, were clad in wood, like a giants' sauna. With the radiators on full blast and the windows shut, it got almost as hot as a sauna, too. With the windows open, you could hear the churning roar of the piste-bashers in the middle of the night. As Ed had said, there was something bizarre about lying in bed halfway up a mountain while men and machines were toiling out there in subzero temperatures so you could slide down the slopes in ease and comfort in the morning. But then, as Clare had said, wasn't everything like that?

He peeled a shred of dried semen from the crevice between the thumb and forefinger of his right hand and rolled it absent-mindedly into a ball, then pulled himself to his feet and limped to the bathroom. He flicked the semen into the bin and washed his hands. Ed's washbag was on the shelf above the sink. He peered into it. There wasn't much in there that Henry didn't have himself: toothbrush, toothpaste, shaving foam, razor, moisturiser, nail clippers, painkillers, condoms. The secrets of Ed's superior grooming must lie elsewhere. The one thing he had that Henry didn't was a roll of dental floss. Henry had fallen asleep on Friday night to the sound of Ed's flossing, fast and expert, like light rain spattering against a window. He wondered if gay men generally had better oral hygiene.

Henry didn't floss regularly, and certainly not frequently, though he occasionally helped himself to a foot or so of Charlotte's if there was a niggling piece of gristle caught between his teeth. He had tried flossing every day, but gave up after a couple of weeks because there was no satisfaction in it; after the first excavation the floss always came out more or less clean. Whereas flossing only infrequently yielded gratifyingly visible (not to mention smellable) results. It was like hoovering, which was only worth doing in Henry's view when you could hear the grit rattle through the nozzle, and see the carpet change to a cleaner shade. Keeping his teeth clean felt like less of an achievement than cleaning them really well when they really needed it, and when the mood took him.

And the mood had taken him on Friday evening, so it was with redoubled confidence – from both an impressive afternoon's performance on the slopes and a squeaky clean mouth; the used floss had smelled terrible, Ed's mouthwash had burned like bile – that he had descended on the night life of the resort, remembering his promise to Alex to help get him laid. He hadn't been looking to pull anyone himself, obviously; he had every intention of being faithful to Charlotte. As they went down the stairs and through the door into the basement club, the noise and the heat and the smell hit them like a wave – like the hotel boot room but with dry ice – and for that first disorienting moment, Henry could have been nineteen again.

'Christ,' Clare shouted. 'It's like DTMs.'

'What?' Ed shouted back.

'Horrendous night club in Oxford.'

Henry offloaded his ski jacket onto Alex and headed for the bar, pushing his way to the front with the practised ease that had come in so useful in the chairlift queues earlier in the day. 'Seven vodka Red Bulls,' he called to the barman.

'Excuse me,' a female voice at his shoulder. 'We were next.' There were four of them, English, well-groomed, probably not much older than nineteen. Just what Alex needed.

'I'm so sorry,' Henry smiled, running his tongue between his upper lip and his exquisitely flossed incisors. 'Make that eleven vodka Red Bulls.'

He gathered up his seven glasses – amazing the skills that could come back to you, in the right circumstances; like riding a bike, or tossing a pancake, or skiing – and headed for the corner table that Ed, presumably, had managed to acquire. 'Join us?' he asked the girls.

'Who's that glaring at us? Your wife?'

'Not at all. An old friend.'

Maybe 'old' was a mistake.

'Not sure there's room for us. We're going to dance. Catch you later maybe.'

'Great. I'm Henry, by the way.'

'Thanks for the drinks.' They didn't tell him their names.

He put the drinks down on the table. The outside of the glasses was slick with condensation but he hadn't spilled a drop. He picked one up, toasted his friends and downed it.

'What was that?' James asked.

'Vodka Red Bull,' Henry said. 'I thought we needed the caffeine.'

'Not that. That.' He pointed in the direction the girls had disappeared in.

'They didn't tell me their names. I pushed in front of them at the bar and thought I'd better buy them a drink to make up for it.'

'You're marrying my sister in three months.'

'I hadn't forgotten.'

'Right,' Ed interrupted. 'Here you go everyone. Get this filth down you and I'll go and find us something decent to drink.'

Henry left the bathroom and hobbled back to his station by the window. Time or the chairlift had stopped, leaving ranks of frustrated skiers suspended helpless in the alpine air. Henry wasn't sorry to see it.

'Oh for fuck's sake,' Jasper said. The chairlift was still bouncing after its sudden stop several minutes ago. 'Shouldn't we get some sort of refund on our ski passes if this goes on much longer?'

273

'If you don't, perhaps you can claim it on your insurance,' Ed said.

'If I were James Bond,' Caspar said, 'I'd climb up onto the cable, and shimmy along to the pylon . . .'

'If you were James Bond,' Jasper said, 'we'd all be speaking Russian.'

'*Da*. How far do you think it is to jump?'

'Too far,' Alex said. 'Though if you want to join Henry . . .'

'In frot club?'

'Don't start that again,' James said.

'I met a Swedish carpenter in Bolivia who would probably jump,' Clare said. 'He took extreme skiing to new lengths. But it isn't so bad sitting here, is it? Rest your legs, take in the view.'

'My feet are killing me.'

'Mine are going numb with the cold.'

'Really? My toes are okay. Unlike my fingers. I should have bought a better pair of gloves.'

'But the hills are alive.'

'Jessica loves the songs from that movie,' Alex said.

'Who doesn't,' said Ed.

'Well . . .' Jasper began.

'She sings the last line of "Edelweiss" as "bless my snowman for ever".'

'But the thing that bothers me about it,' Ed said, 'is the strong implication that the biggest victims of the Nazis were the Austrian aristocracy.'

'I don't think that's right,' Clare said. 'I think it's much more stringent than that. Remember that the film was written and directed by Jews. Isn't the point that if Captain Von Trapp – who's basically the Nazis' ideal man – could see clearly enough that the Nazis had to be resisted, then nobody else has any excuse for not resisting them?'

'Maybe,' Ed said. 'But then again, it's a lot easier for Captain Von Trapp, given his immense sense of entitlement, not to mention how rich and powerful he in fact is, to resist the Nazis than it was for the average German shopkeeper, even if they'd wanted to.'

'You're making excuses. And the point I'm trying to make is that excuses cannot be made. Resisting Nazism is a categorical imperative.'

The chairlift hummed into life and lurched forwards.

'Thank fuck for that,' Jasper said.

Alex tucked his chin under the upturned collar of his jacket and looked down at the sunlight sparkling on the surface of the snow as it rolled steadily beneath them. His face felt as if it was burning, though he'd put plenty of suncream on before leaving the hotel. His chin had been pink in the mirror the evening before, but he couldn't tell if it was from sunburn, because his collar had rubbed off his suncream, or from rubbing against the fleece lining of his jacket collar, or both. He pulled the collar away and lifted his chin clear. Scoured by the wind and sun, he tucked it back in again.

'Here you go,' Ed said, reaching across in front of Clare, no hint of awkwardness in the gesture, a tube of sunscreen in his hand. 'Factor 50. I hope that's OK.'

'Thanks,' Alex said, taking it.

They were reaching the point on the lift where Alex had asked Henry on Saturday if he was planning to take Jessica skiing when she was older.

'I'm not sure. I hadn't really thought about it. I suppose I will, if she wants to. Why do you ask?'

'I don't know. I just think she'd be good at it.'

'Why?'

'She's fast, strong, has a good sense of balance, isn't afraid of much. The way she is at the playground, I think she'd make a good skier.'

'Takes after her dad,' Ed suggested.

'I'm sure Charlotte would be happy to take her,' James said. 'Does her mum ski?'

'Vic? No,' Henry said.

'How is Victoria?' James asked.

'Do we have to talk about my ex?' Henry asked. 'This is supposed to be my stag.'

'Seems appropriate enough to me,' Jasper said.

'She's fine,' Alex said. 'Well, some money worries, but no, she's fine.'

'Money worries?' Henry snorted. 'She owns three houses.'

'Well, not exactly,' Alex said.

'Look,' Ed said. 'Isn't that Mont Blanc coming into view?'

'I'll tell you what,' Henry said.

'What did I miss?' Caspar asked, joining them a few yards down the slope from the top of the lift. He'd travelled up alone immediately behind the rest of them, trying not to appear aggrieved at being the odd one out, lolling in one corner of the rakishly unbalanced chair, skis akimbo.

'Oh, all sorts of hilarity,' Jasper said.

'Henry and Alex are going to have a pissing contest,' Clare said.

'But the snow up here is pristine.'

'Not literally.'

At the end of the day, as the others headed back to the hotel, Alex and Henry caught the last chair up to the top of the mountain. They waited for the lift to stop and the slopes below them to clear. 'Times like this I regret giving up smoking,' Henry said.

'Take it up again,' Alex said. 'How many times have you quit now?'

Henry didn't reply.

The sun had dropped low enough for the entire piste to be in shadow. Alex was getting cold. 'Ready?' he asked.

'When you are.'

'Countdown from three?'

'Go for it.'

Alex knew that nothing about this was a good idea. They were short of sleep, physically tired, dehydrated, out of shape, and not as young as they used to be. It wasn't clear there'd be anyone to pick them up if they fell badly, so a broken leg could mean dying of exposure. There was everything to lose and nothing to gain. Coming second would make him feel angry and disappointed; coming first would make Henry angry and disappointed, which would be just as unpleasant. A draw might be all right, but Alex wasn't a good enough skier to guarantee that. But perhaps he was good enough to win, after all. His legs were stronger than the last time he'd skied, thanks to all the cycling, even if he was less flexible. He clenched his pelvic floor. 'Three two one go!' he yelled into the wind that was streaming into his face as he accelerated away down the slope, powered only by his own body weight, as if in flight or free-fall – forget for the moment the energy released from uranium atoms splitting apart, converted to heat, motion, electricity, motion, potential, the elemental force he'd gathered up inside him and was unleashing now – his centre of mass plummeting towards the centre of the earth, the mountainside pushing back against him, through the soles of his feet, his flexed muscles, his sprung joints, into his core, his hips responding to the contours of the piste as he made his turns, his shoulders square down the mountain, the tenuous grip of his skis rasping through the snow, his face cutting through the resisting air which pushed his cheeks back into a smile.

Crunching at speed into a tight turn as the piste veered away to the right he felt a sharp twinge in his left knee. His leg almost gave way beneath him. He transferred all his weight to his right foot, skidding round through 180 degrees into a sideslip and coming almost to a halt. A spray of snow skittered against his back as Henry barrelled past behind him with a whoop of triumph. Alex leaned on his poles, caught his breath, thought of the hare and the tortoise (either of them could be either animal at this point), counted slowly to ten, leaned very gradually on his left knee. It seemed to be okay. Feeling his pulse slowing towards normal, he pushed off steadily – no jarring movements – from his left foot and continued his run at a more controlled pace. No point really hurting himself. Let Henry win. It wouldn't be the first time. He allowed himself to feel magnanimous in defeat, and concentrated on enjoying the sensation of skiing not too fast, with two functioning knees. In forty-eight hours he'd be back in the office. No need to rush. The music in his head was Blondie's 'Atomic'.

Cresting the ridge before the final blue run down to the hotel, conscious that he would be visible from the bar, he concentrated on his style: smooth, tight turns, legs together, body facing down the mountain, confident that he looked good. Henry was waiting for him at the bottom, sprawled on the ground. Alex glided to a stop a metre away from him, spraying him with snow. 'Congratulations,' he said. 'Catching your breath? You can't have beaten me by much.'

'Can you help me get my skis off?' Henry said.

'Seriously?'

'Seriously. I think I've seriously fucked up my knee.'

By the time they got back to the hotel, everyone else had showered and changed and was ensconced at a table in the corner of the lounge, the glasses in front of them more than half-empty. Clare's voice was raised above the murmuring and muzak. '*The X Factor* is like the National Lottery. It's part of the "aspiration" con trick, justifying deep and worsening inequality with the promise that anyone can become one of the super-rich overnight. It's a way of encouraging us to vote not in the interest of society at large, or even in our own interest, but in the interest of the rich and famous people that we "aspire" to be.'

'As if voting makes any difference anyway,' James said.

'I think most people vote for whoever they think's going to manage the economy better,' Jasper said.

'What does that even mean?' Ed asked.

'Nothing,' Clare said. 'James isn't wrong. Voting's essentially meaningless if the things that matter to people's lives are out of the state's control. Real democracy is impossible without public ownership. There's a vicious cycle of privatisation and disenfranchisement. But that's all part of what I'm talking about.'

'Why don't you stop complaining,' Jasper said, 'and do something about it?'

'I've commissioned a book from a really smart political scientist at Cambridge.'

'That isn't doing something,' Jasper said. 'It's just outsourcing the complaining.'

'Or broadcasting it,' Ed said. 'Which is doing something.'

'I'm not sure it is, really,' Clare said.

Ed looked up at Henry and Alex, drooping in the doorway, arms around each other's shoulders. 'What the hell happened to you?'

The chairlift rumbled and shuddered past another pylon. Far below them, black against the snow, lay a lost glove and a ski pole, reminding Alex of Luke Skywalker's severed hand and a light sabre. He kept the thought to himself.

Because of Henry's reduced mobility, they all agreed to spend Saturday night in the hotel bar. Alex, feeling guilty, and at the same time feeling he had no real reason to feel guilty, and so resenting Henry for making him feel that way, got the first round of drinks in.

'Is your friend OK?' the woman behind the bar asked as she poured the lager.

'He will be, I think,' Alex said. 'Thanks for asking.'

'I saw him fall. It looked bad. He should have waited for you. Why was he in such a hurry?'

'We were having a race.'

She shook her head as she picked up a spatula and swiped off the foam bulging out of the top of a glass.

'I saw you come down too,' she said. 'You have a nice style.' She caught his eye. 'Not too fast.'

He reminded himself that flirting was part of her job.

Back at their corner table, Ed was setting up a Scrabble board. 'Found it in the games cupboard,' he said.

No one else had even known there was a games cupboard.

'Can you play with seven people?' Alex asked.

Caspar, Jasper and James said they were happy to sit it out.

Clare hadn't played since the last Christmas she'd spent at Alex's parents' house. They'd gone for family walks in the mornings, her hands freezing in the pockets of her too-thin jacket as the sun lumbered into the midwinter air like a heron taking flight, barely clearing the hilltops, and settled in around the Scrabble board in front of the fire with tea and mince pies as soon as the sun had set. He found it cosy; she found it stifling. His question about the number of players was disingenuous. He'd been a world-class Scrabble bore in his time.

'The woman behind the bar says she hopes you're OK,' Alex said to Henry. 'Are you going to be OK?'

'I'll be fine, as long as I never ski again.'

'She also said she liked my style.'

'In that shirt? She can't have meant it.'

Alex shook up the bag of Scrabble letters. 'Whoever's nearest the beginning of the alphabet starts.'

When Alex put an S on the beginning of Henry's 'kid' to go out with 'squalid' on a triple word score, the Q on a double letter – 'I think that's 136 points' – Clare suggested to Henry and Ed that the three of them cede the game.

'Don't be like that,' Alex said.

'You don't be like that,' she said.

Jasper came back from the bar with seven more beers on a tray. 'I love it that they call these *sérieux*,' he said. He looked down at the board. 'Squalid? Skid?' He laughed. 'You should be playing dirty Scrabble.'

'What's that?' Alex asked, grateful for the interruption and distraction.

'You're only allowed to use rude words,' Jasper explained, distributing the drinks. 'And you get bonuses for imagination rather than length.'

Caspar sniggered.

'You could make a case for "length" being permitted,' Jasper said. 'But it wouldn't get you any bonuses.'

All seven of them joined in. The game – more collaborative than competitive – didn't last long. It was generally agreed that new-formed compound words were allowed. The scores were arbitrary, but the highest bonuses went to Alex for 'anal-mucus' (extending Henry's 'anal') and Clare for 'bumzit' (elaborating on Henry's 'bum').

'Enough!' Caspar said as they were trying to work out how to slot in the last few remaining vowels. He folded the board in half and poured the letters back into the bag. Alex found himself trying to read the small avalanche of perversion, fragmenting and recombining as it tumbled into darkness.

'Time to embarrass the groom,' Caspar said. 'This is supposed to be a stag weekend, remember. Henry? Tell us about your first sexual experience.'

'I'll show you mine if you show me yours.'

'You first.'

'OK. Watching Cinderella in the Disney film take a shower.'

'That's cheating.'

'Why? Your turn.'

'Well if that's the way you want to play it. The opening credits of *Octopussy*.'

They seemed to be going round the circle. Clare was sitting next to Caspar. 'Prince singing "Kiss".'

Alex opened his mouth; Clare glared at him. He raised his eyebrows in self-exculpation. 'Climbing the ropes in the gym at prep school,' he said. Now it was Clare's turn to raise her eyebrows. He'd never talked to her about that, he realised. He hadn't in fact remembered it until Charlotte told him about sitting on a football, aged four, while James tried to kick it out from under her. Did James know about that, or even remember it?

It was Ed's turn. 'Holding hands with my best friend when I was three,' he said.

'You always knew you were gay?'

'Always.'

'Was it hard, coming out to your parents?'

'My dad never knew. Well, he probably did, but we never talked about it. I told my mother after he died. Not immediately, obviously. She was very cool about it, said at least it meant she'd never have to explain to my grandparents why I was marrying a white woman. My round?'

They were within sight of the last pylon, nearly at the sign telling them to raise the bar, when the chairlift shuddered to a halt for the second time. As it swung violently forward, Alex repressed the instinct to grab Clare's hand.

Unable to sleep, his head heavy with beer and the heat of the room and James's stridulous breathing, Alex pulled on jeans and sweater over his pyjamas and went out onto the balcony.

Hands in pockets, shoulders hunched against the cold but enjoying the fresh air in his face, he watched the lights of the piste-bashers traversing the slopes, like giant Laputan machines harvesting snow.

Clare had been sitting out on her balcony for a while, huddled in her ski jacket, wishing she had a cigarette, when the French windows of the next door room slid open and Alex stepped out into the night. His profile was still handsome in silhouette: the straight nose, the square chin. 'So,' she said at last. 'You couldn't sleep either.'

She'd obviously startled him. He tried to cover it up. 'Too drunk,' he said, stumbling towards her.

'How's the view?' She got up from her chair, shuffled towards him.

'Dark.' He turned to face her. 'How's your weekend going?'

'A little strangely. Yours?'

'Bumzit,' he said.

She laughed. He moved towards her.

Their mouths were millimetres apart. They closed their eyes, put a hand on the coarse wooden balcony rail to steady themselves, touching fingertips. Hearts racing against the cold, unable to catch their breath, they caught each other's instead.

Squeezing past the flimsy partition between the balconies, tumbling through the French window, falling onto the bed, mouths pressed against each other, fumbling with buttons and zips, he remembered all – all? – the places they had had sex when they were first going out, in her bed in his bed on the floor in other people's beds against the wall on her desk on his chair on her parents' sofa on the stairs in the kitchen in the shower on the sink in the bath in the mirror in the car in Henry's parents' garden against a tree on a train to Paris in a tent on the beach on the balcony in high heels in walking boots in bare feet in nothing at all. Her body felt so familiar, but at the same time so new, like a dream about a non-existent relative. She had a scar on her back he didn't recognise, kissing her spine between her shoulder blades, tiny fragments of something under her skin.

She rolled over, took a condom, its wrapper faded and crumpled, out of the make-up bag on the chest of drawers beside the bed. 'Put it on,' she said.

As she straddled him, guiding his penis into her vagina with her hand, she hoped the condom wasn't (too) out of date. He pushed his pelvis up. She wished she'd peed before they started. She pushed gently down on his stomach with one hand. He was leaner, more muscular than he used to be. He reached round to take her bottom in his hands. That was familiar though. She'd never liked it, one of the ways in which sex could stop being sex and turn instead into using someone else's genitals to masturbate with. She took his wrists, moved his hands away, leaned forward to rest her hands on his chest – bigger muscles there, too. There was still too much pressure on her bladder. She felt dizzy. She brought her head down on the pillow beside his. He turned his face to try to kiss her, but she didn't want that. Didn't want to think about what a mistake it was that they were doing this. Wanted to enjoy it for its own sake. But she felt dizzy and needed to pee. She put a hand behind his shoulder and rolled onto her back, pulling him with her. She pulled the pillows away from her head, pushed them off the bed onto the floor, closed her eyes, enjoyed the sensation of the cool sheet against the back of her head. He was fucking her too hard. And the condom possibly was too old. At the end of every thrust she felt an uncomfortable rasp against her labia. 'Hang on,' she said, pulling away from him and rolling over onto her front. That didn't solve either problem: still the discomfort, still too much pressure on her bladder. 'Wait,' she said. She thought about getting out of bed, walking naked onto the balcony, the fresh air, the dangerous sharpness of the cold, the exposure, leaning on the rail, peeing as he fucked her. Would he mind? Would he notice? Would he like it? They'd been together ten years but never really known each other. She rolled onto her side, moved away from him towards the open door, her face into the draught. She reached an arm behind her, fingertips on his hip, not to control him but to communicate. He seemed to get it, then, responding to her touch, and they were moving in concert at last, the rhythm they'd first found with each other when they were young, and, able to lose herself in it again, she felt her mind begin to fall away, slipping towards orgasm.

Alex couldn't understand why Clare kept changing position. It seemed oddly frenetic of her, though also quite kinky. But they didn't need to have sex in every position all at once; there would always be next time. He was disappointed when she settled at last on spoons. He'd always found it awkward, lying on his side, hard to move, and he never knew what to do with the arm that was underneath him. But never mind: there would always be next time. But then he realised there wouldn't be a next time, that she was fucking him every which way because she knew it was the last time, and the sadness of that thought, or the realisation that it meant he really needed to make the most of this, to savour every moment, brought him to orgasm.

His eyes felt dry. He told himself not to forget to take his contact lenses out. He hadn't worn contact lenses for ten years.

'This isn't going to happen again, is it,' he said, rolling away from her and peeling off the condom.

'No,' Clare said, reaching for her pyjamas. 'I suppose not.'

The lift jerked into motion. As they rumbled past the last pylon, Ed said: 'Everyone ready?' They slid their skis and boards from the footrests, Alex with one hand behind his left knee to help it along. Together, the six of them raised the bar, braced themselves, ready for the off. The tips of their skis touched down on the snow.

17

Croquet

May 2010

'I know it's customary to ask your oldest friend to be your best man,' Henry said. 'And it's a real pleasure to see so many of my old friends here with us today. But on this occasion, for reasons that may or may not be obvious to everyone, I've asked my newest friend. Ed: you've been a friend to me and Charlotte for as long as we've known each other, and I just wanted to say thank you, for being such a good friend to both of us.'

Alex looked at Ed across the dining room, through the flower arrangements and the guests, the few he knew and the many he didn't – who were all these people, these friends of Henry's and Charlotte's that he'd never met? – and he thought how little, for once, he would have liked to be in the best man's shoes. What was Ed going to talk about? How was he going to skirt the herd of elephants in the room? For that matter, what was Henry going to say about them? Alex glanced at Vic, sitting next to him. She was giving Jessica another breadstick from the supply in her bag.

Henry had moved on to his immediate family. 'Mum and Dad, I owe you more than I can say.' True enough, Alex thought. Maths had never been Henry's best subject. 'My brother Toby, who sadly can't be with us today.' Alex couldn't remember much about Toby's speech at Henry's first wedding, beyond the general sense that he, Alex, would have made a much better job of it. He looked at Vic again, still producing breadsticks like rabbits out of a hat. Was Henry going to say anything about her, her magnanimity in coming today? There was no way round it: this was no way to get married for the second time. It was much too awkward, verging on the grotesque, the level of erasure involved, everything that had to be left unspoken. Better just to go to a register office with a couple of witnesses and be done with it, if it had to be done at all. Alex didn't suppose anyone would be honest enough to quote Dr Johnson on the triumph of hope over experience (not necessarily a bad thing, however Johnson had intended it).

'Jessica, sweetheart, Daddy loves you very much.'

All eyes on her, Jessica shouted 'Go home!' and buried her face in her mother's flank.

Everyone laughed.

'We'll go home in a bit, love,' Vic said. 'But there's ice cream and dancing first.'

Henry was winding up with the usual platitudes about how in love he was with his new wife.

'That was a generous interpretation,' Alex murmured.

Vic shrugged. 'No point making a scene.'

*

Vic wondered how many people had been convinced by Henry's performance as a caring father. Not many, she supposed, even before Jessica's critical response to it. His walking out on them pretty much scuppered that role, surely. The last time he'd brought her home after a weekend in Camberwell he'd asked Vic, in his most serious voice, brow at full furrow, if he could 'have a word'. They went into the kitchen while Linda took Jess to the bathroom. Henry had proceeded to explain, in solemn tones, that Jessica had wandered into the bedroom while he was getting dressed, pointed at his penis and said: 'Lollipop.'

Vic burst out laughing.

'I'm not sure it's funny.'

'I'm sure it is.'

'Are you sure someone hasn't been, you know, telling her that cocks are lollipops?'

'Yes, I'm sure.'

'How?'

'Because they'd never have the opportunity.'

'Are you sure? What about, I don't know, what about Alex?'

'Seriously? Wow. No. Just, no. I promise you, the only adult penis' – never had Henry's use of the word *cock* seemed more inappropriate – 'she's ever seen is yours, and I'm pretty certain the only lollipops she's ever seen are in *The Elephant and the Bad Baby*. There isn't a problem here. Or if there is, it's entirely of your making.'

'Right then,' Linda said, bringing Jessica back to the kitchen. 'Are you going to say goodbye to Daddy?'

Henry was kissing Charlotte – who for some inexplicable reason was wearing a Disney princess wedding dress – and everyone was applauding.

*

Clare had not enjoyed her dinner. The food had been nice enough – as you'd expect at a place like this; how much had it cost to hire? And who'd paid for it all? Madeleine, she supposed – and the wine had done what it was meant to do. But she'd been trapped in conversation with the most annoying man in the world, though it wasn't really conversation, which technically required more than one person to speak. The small talk was quickly over. After introducing himself he'd asked: 'Bride or groom?'

'I was at university with Henry.'

'Oh, really? Oxford, eh? Jolly good. I was at school with him.'

'Were you.'

'Yes, well. I like your dress.'

She didn't tell him it was Alexander McQueen, picked up on the cheap – though still more than she could afford – at the not-very-secret secret sample sale in Shoreditch. And it was beautiful – a jagged kaleidoscope of shades of blue, like ice shattering, and with such sharp tailoring, as well as being very short – but this man wasn't supposed to like it; he was supposed to find it intimidating. 'Thank you,' she said.

'Good duck this, isn't it,' he said. 'What about this coalition government then? Could be interesting.'

'That's one word for it.'

'Which of them did you vote for?'

'Labour,' she said. 'I've always voted Labour.'

'Oh, really? You don't agree with Henry, that it's time to give the others a chance?'

'No.'

'What about Iraq?'

'I was opposed to the war, went on the march and all that.

But I still voted Labour in 2005, and this time. The Tories supported the war too, remember. Were you against it?'

'Not at all. But I assumed you would have been.'

He'd more or less given up asking her questions after that, and instead explained at length how he'd gone into banking for moral reasons. He'd thought about doing something directly worthwhile himself – doctor, aid worker, that kind of thing – until he'd realised that he could do more good by making as much money as possible and investing it in worthwhile projects. A little probing on Clare's part revealed that these included pharmaceuticals – she agreed that medicines save lives – and oil companies: 'They're doing most of the good research into clean energy you know.' He was also opposed to inheritance tax, because it was more ethical to pass his wealth onto his children, so they could make the world a better place by their investments.

'You sleep soundly at night then.'

'I certainly do. Are you, er, staying here at the hotel?'

'B&B in Winchester. Though I might try and catch the last train back to London.'

He took out his Blackberry. 'Let me look up the times for you.'

The night before they had all voted for the first time, in 1997, Clare, Henry and Alex had gone to the May Day party in Port Meadow. They had made a pact to stay clean; it had seemed important not to be under the influence of anything in the polling booth. Henry succumbed to temptation the moment someone offered him a pill, but Clare and Alex kept to the agreement. Walking back into town, having decided not to go and watch the idiots jumping off Magdalen Bridge, they passed a house where someone was playing 'Come Together' by Primal Scream. She stopped beneath the window to listen. The sample of Jesse Jackson speaking at Wattstax – though she hadn't known that's who it was back then, or known enough about the world to be bothered by the appropriation of it – filled her with joy. It was like singing 'Morning Has Broken' at primary school. She was nearly twenty-one. It was a new day. Eighteen years of Tory government were coming to an end as she reached adulthood. She voted and went to bed, confident that all the complacent right-wing bastards who'd been at school with Henry were about to lose their access to power. And now thirteen years later they'd got it back, without ever having really lost it. At least Obama was the US president.

'May I?' Alex asked, pointing to the empty chair on the other of Clare.

'Of course,' she said. They hadn't seen or spoken to each other since Henry's stag. He seemed ready to pretend they hadn't had sex the last time they were together, and she was happy to go along with that. It wouldn't happen again, however drunk they both were. She felt relieved, sure that their marriage was truly, finally over. Perhaps they could be friends after all.

'Scary dress,' he said.

'Thank you,' she smiled.

'How's work?' he asked, pouring her another glass of wine before helping himself.

'Good, actually,' Clare said. 'My first acquisition since I went back is about to come out: *The Discovery of Chance: Pascal's*

Wager and the Creation of the Modern World, by a mathematician who can write.'

'What's his name?'

'Why do you assume it's a he?'

'Isn't it?'

'It is. But that isn't the point.' She told him the name.

'You're joking. I think I went to school with him. Rumour had it he shagged the German assistant in the upper sixth.'

'Amazingly, he neglected to mention either of those bits of information in his proposal.'

'Oh. Yes. Sorry. Great title. Not sure about the subtitle though. Isn't it getting two completely different things confused?'

'At least two. But you couldn't have a book about Pascal and probability that didn't have "Pascal's wager" in its title.'

'Maybe "Pascal's other wager" would be more like it?'

'You're such a lawyer. No. That sucks the catch right out of it.'

'You two at the same table?' Madeleine leaned in between them. 'Oh, that is civilised. Hello, darling,' she said to Clare. 'I hope next time you'll be sitting at the top table with us.'

'Next time?'

'Well this one isn't going to last either, is it. I mean, Charlotte's a lovely girl but I do wish she wasn't marrying Henry. I'd much rather he was marrying Ed, even: Ed's a lovely boy. Why's she doing it? Charlotte, I mean. I sometimes wonder if it isn't some sort of performance art thingy.'

Clare looked across the room at Charlotte, her baffling meringue of a dress. Could that be the reason?

'And I'm not comfortable at the thought of being the artist's mother-in-law lurking in the background. It isn't as if she's Velásquez.'

294

'Madeleine!' Alex said. 'That's a terrible thing to say. It's their wedding day. She loves him.'

'I suppose you're right. About the first two, anyway. What are you talking about?'

'Work,' Clare said.

'Oh no.'

'Well it's that or politics.'

'That's even worse,' Madeleine said.

'No it isn't. How did you vote? Conservative like the rest of your family?'

'Oh, darling, how naive do you think I am?'

'You think it's naive to vote Conservative?'

'I think it's naive to vote.'

'Well I think it's quite heartening that the Tories couldn't win an outright majority after thirteen years in opposition,' Alex chipped in.

'You voted Lib Dem, I suppose, Alex?'

'Like in 1997?' Clare said.

'It was tactical.'

'That's so missing the point.'

'Actually, I didn't vote this time at all.'

Madeleine raised her glass. 'Another realist, and still so young.'

'He probably intended to vote Lib Dem but didn't leave work in time to get to the polling station before it shut,' Clare said.

'Oh, don't be so horrible. No wonder he left you.'

'She left me,' Alex said.

Madeleine smiled.

'The Tories clearly need to hire a better PR firm,' Alex said.

'Darling, the modern Conservative Party *is* a PR firm,'

Madeleine said. 'They just don't do their own PR. They're too busy working for all the companies they'll sit on the boards of the moment they escape the House of Commons. I tried to explain that to Henry's father, but he still went out and voted for them. He meant to vote UKIP, he said, but once he was in the booth couldn't help himself.'

'Involuntary muscle memory,' Alex said.

'If you say so, darling. Anyway, lovely to see you both again. No chance of you two getting back together?'

Clare and Alex exchanged glances.

'Jolly good,' Madeleine said, and swept away.

'Why are they getting married, do you suppose?' Alex asked.

'There are only two reasons people get married: love and money.'

'If she were marrying for money she'd have been better off marrying me.'

'I wasn't going to say it. But yes, she would. So it must be love.'

'Why did we get married?'

'Don't ask me that.'

'Do you know why she broke up with me?'

'We all have our reasons.'

'She said I never laughed at her jokes. Does that make me sexist?'

'I don't think so. You always laughed at my jokes. I think it just means she isn't very funny.'

'I love you.'

'Don't say that.'

*

'Why?' Jessica asked her grandmother.

'I don't know,' Madeleine said.

'Guess. Get it wrong.'

'They should give you a job on *Newsnight*.'

'Why?'

'That's why. Where's your mother?'

'So how did you vote?' Vic asked James.

'Spoiled my ballot paper. You?'

'Lib Dem. Never again. They were the best chance of defeating the Tories where I live. What a joke.' She didn't want to talk politics with him, regretted bringing the election up. But what else was there to talk about? She straightened the hem of her dress. It hadn't been easy finding something to wear. She couldn't buy anything new, so the grim choice was either to wear one of her old dresses that were now hideously tight, or to borrow something from her mother. Ten years ago she and Amy had been the same size and wore each other's clothes all the time, but no longer. In the end she'd taken one of her mother's dresses from the eighties – a frumpy cotton floral number – and made a few adjustments: cut off the sleeves, tore out the shoulder pads, lowered the neckline, raised the hem. It actually looked quite good, though perhaps she shouldn't have raised the hem quite so much. The only person in the room with a shorter skirt was Clare. Vic had had to splash out on a new pair of shoes, though: all her old party shoes were too tight.

'I've spent most of the evening talking to your former mother-in-law,' James said. 'It's funny, I always imagined people who worked in PR had more tact.'

'She's retired.'

'Good point. Has some serious making up to do I suppose. It's nice to see you again. A – very – pleasant surprise. Isn't it a bit, I don't know, bad luck or something for the ex-wife to come to the wedding?'

'That wouldn't stop me. Seriously, though, Henry wanted Jessica to come, and he is, despite everything, still her father, and I wouldn't want her not to be here. But I sure as hell wasn't going to let her come unchaperoned. Also' – she looked him straight in his grey eyes – 'I thought there might be a chance of running into you.'

James smiled. 'I'm sorry it's taken me this long to catch up with you. Brother-of-the-bride duties and all that.'

'Of course. I suppose you have to get back to those.'

'No: I've danced with my sister's mother-in-law. My duties are done. Are you staying overnight?'

'Driving home. It should only take an hour and a half in the middle of the night. Jessica will sleep in the car.' And she wasn't expecting to sleep much herself, even once she got home, though there was no need to tell him that. Going to bed meant lying awake thinking about the beetle larvae in the roof, chewing through the rafters, maturing and mating and laying eggs in the beams. Better to spend the night driving, Jessica asleep where she could see her in the rear-view mirror.

'Pity.'

'No, that's a good thing. The thought of having a child who didn't sleep in the car . . .'

'I didn't mean that.'

'I know you didn't. You?'

'I try not to fall asleep when I'm driving.'

'Glad to hear it. You staying here tonight?'

'I am.'

'Well – I can't believe I'm actually saying this,' she laughed. 'But we went back to my place last time. So . . . ?'

He smiled. 'Would you like to see my room? The plaster moulding on the ceiling is very fine. Sorry. That sounded even sleazier than I meant it too.'

'Give me five seconds,' she said. 'Alex? Could you watch Jessica for twenty minutes?'

'Only twenty minutes?' James said on their way upstairs.

'I'm a single parent, I can be quick. Oh god. Sorry. That came out wrong. Enough talk.' She took his hand. 'One more thing. I promise not to throw your phone number away this time.'

'No need to make any promises.' He unlocked his door.

The DJ played 'Yellow Submarine'. Groups of nondescript men, fast approaching middle age, hair receding, guts straining at the waists of their suit trousers, threw their arms around one another's shoulders and sang along in close disharmony.

Clare had once found the song comforting, with its cheerful sense of a group of friends cocooned against the world, but at some point – maybe just now in fact – it had been turned inside out. She turned her gaze across the room. 'Look at these people.'

Ed looked at the scene reflected in the giant mirror behind them. 'Us?'

'Yes, us. I mean, fuck. People talk about global conspiracies and secret cabals secretly running the world. And look: here we fucking are, in their yellow submarine.'

'We are?'

'We are.'

Ed shrugged. 'If you say so.'

'You know why nothing ever gets better? Because we – the people in this room, the people like us all over the world – are all so bloody comfortable. The global economy's fucked, but here we are. And we're not listening to the band play on on the *Titanic*. Because we're not going down with the ship. We're in the lifeboats, we've always been in the lifeboats, and very comfortable fucking lifeboats they are too. Okay, so we're not in the submarines, or the helicopters, and we may complain about the people in the helicopters, but actually we're quite happy for them to be in their helicopters because they've given us these lifeboats. And all the poor fucks drowning around us, well we can blame their problems on the fuckers in the helicopters – which is who everyone's looking at; no one's looking at us – but meanwhile here we are and can you pour me another drink?'

'Are we still in the metaphor here?'

'No. Yes. But I want another drink. Come on.'

Turning from the bar, alone for a moment, Henry saw Vic and James come back into the room together, rumpled and sheepish but unable to suppress their smiles. He felt an unexpected and unwelcome jolt of longing for her. It was less than seven years since he and Vic had got married. They'd been so happy. He closed his eyes, counted four heartbeats, waited for the spasm of nostalgia to subside. He opened them again, looked round the room: so many people he could call his friends, with so much money. Time to get back to business. Here came one of them to the bar beside him now.

'George! How have you been? Thanks so much for coming.'

'I wouldn't have missed it for the world. Thanks for inviting me. It's been too long.'

'It certainly has. How have you been? Still dispensing financial advice?'

'I certainly am. Why? Do you need some?'

'Who doesn't? But not this evening.'

'No, of course. I just meant . . . What about you? Software, isn't it?'

'No, not anymore, actually. My first love as you know was always art. And, well, I'm working with Charlotte now.'

'Painting?'

'I wish . . . No, not painting. Selling.'

'Vic and James?' Ed said. 'Doesn't that almost count as incest? Sleeping with your sister's husband's ex-wife?'

'Or your ex-husband's wife's brother,' Alex said. 'No, not really. Anyway, they knew each other before Henry and Charlotte got together. Actually they knew each other before Vic and Henry were married. I guess in one sense they're the reason Henry and Charlotte got together.' If James hadn't come to his flat looking for Vic, they wouldn't have met at Ed's party, so Alex would never have met Charlotte, so Henry wouldn't have done either. 'It's funny how things work out,' Alex said.

'Charlotte, congratulations,' Alex said. 'Great dress. Great wig, too. Shirley MacLaine?'

'Thanks, Alex. And thank you for coming. But actually this

isn't a wig. It's my hair. I'm glad you like it though. Are you managing to enjoy yourself?'

'I've been talking to your uncle.'

'Oh, fuck, I'm sorry.'

'Don't be silly. He's very nice.'

'You're too nice. He's clinically boring.'

Alex shrugged.

'No, seriously, he's been diagnosed. They've tried all kinds of drugs but nothing helps.'

Alex laughed.

In the toilets there were two women Clare didn't recognise – Charlotte's friends, she supposed, or Henry's friends' wives. She smiled and nodded and went into a cubicle. They waited for her to lock the door before continuing their conversation.

'I'd heard that having children was supposed to make it not so painful, but within days of weaning it was back with a vengeance. I'm almost tempted to get pregnant again.'

'At least you had a year off. Mine came back exactly twenty-eight days after Rory was born. I rushed to the doctor, thought something was seriously wrong. Smug bastard told me there was nothing wrong but I should make sure my husband wore a condom.'

Flushing the toilet, Clare realised she hadn't had her period since, when, January? Nothing so very unusual about that. Not necessarily. She decided not to think about it.

Alex ambushed Clare on the way to the bar. 'So you've given up on the magazine idea?' he said. 'Now you're back in books?'

'Not necessarily,' she said, sitting down at the nearest table. 'I mean, I have the time. I'm only working two and a half days a week. And I'd still like to do it. But the problem, as ever, is finding funding.'

'How much do you need?' He pulled up the chair next to her.

She told him.

It wasn't much more than his last Christmas bonus. 'And that's for each issue?'

'No, that's for four over two years.'

'Seriously? Why didn't you say so before? It's yours.'

'What do you mean?'

'If you'd hired a decent divorce lawyer you'd have it already. We'll do it properly, set up a trust and so on: I'll give you half the money, the other half can be an investment by me.'

'If I'm going to do this, I don't want your help.'

'If you can find a venture capital firm to put up the money, fine, I'll walk away. But if the only thing that's stopping you is a lack of funding, why not let me help? I won't interfere in anything editorially, obviously, or anything at all to do with running it. It's just somewhere for me to put the money. Better than leaving it to lose value in a so-called savings account or be eroded by the stock market. I'm serious. Let's do this.'

'Wouldn't you rather, I don't know, put it in a trust for your goddaughter?'

'Her grandmother paid for this wedding. She'll be fine.'

'Or you might need the money yourself.'

'I'm fine too. If I haven't been laid off yet, I'm not going to be. Actually, I'm probably going to be made a partner in the autumn.'

'Really? Congratulations. But whatever happened to your

plans to go and work for the Monopolies and Mergers Commission?'

Alex watched Henry and Charlotte dancing. 'The Competition Commission, it's called now. Yes, I rather gave up on that idea. It isn't as if it would have made any difference.'

'To you?'

'To the world.'

'Do you mind, very much?'

'That I'm not going to change the world? Not really, no.'

'No, I mean about Henry marrying Charlotte.'

'Not in the slightest. Honestly. They're much more suited to each other. They're both good at sport.'

She laughed.

He looked at her, then he looked away. If ever there was a moment to say what he was thinking of saying next, the last unsaid thing between them, then this had to be it. 'The only time I minded,' he said, 'was when it was you.'

Clare watched as Jessica and Vic – her hair and clothes (had she made that dress herself?) a little dishevelled – joined the flow of wedding guests towards the dance floor, where Henry and Charlotte were swaying to the strains of David Bowie's 'Cat People', the disappointing version on *Let's Dance*. James was leaning in the doorway, looking on and smiling.

'So what do you think?' Alex asked. 'About my funding the magazine?'

'I'll have to think about it.'

'Guys!' Ed blew in through the French windows on a gust of cannabis fumes. He put his hands on their shoulders. 'Guys. You're never going to believe this, but there's a fucking croquet lawn all set up out there. Do you know how to play?'

'Sort of,' Alex said.

'Fantastic. You can teach me. What a laugh. Fucking *croquet*.'

'Sorry, Ed, you'll have to count me out. I'm drunk and I'm no good even when I'm sober.'

'All the more reason to play drunk.'

'No, seriously. I couldn't. Sorry.'

'Oh well. If you're sure. Clare?'

The man who'd sat next to her at dinner was making his way towards her, with the look on his face of someone who was planning to ask her to dance. His legs were shorter than hers and his heels were higher. There might be pleasure in turning him down, but he clearly wasn't used to taking no for an answer. Better simply to escape before he reached her.

'Croquet?' she said. 'Seriously? Oh fuck it. Why not.'

Ed helped her to her feet.

'I have to tell you I don't really know how to play properly,' she said. 'I've only ever played at Henry's house, so I only know how to play by his rules.'

'Don't we all,' Ed said.

She looked at him sideways. 'And then when we're done we can use the mallets to smash in the windows and burn this place to the ground.'

'Sounds like a plan.'

'Right then.' She took his hand. 'Which way do we go?'